WILDBLOOD

ALSO BY
LAUREN BLACKWOOD

Within These Wicked Walls

WILD

BLOOD

A NOVEL

LAUREN BLACKWOOD

WEDNESDAY BOOKS

NEW YORK

Published in the United States by Wednesday Books, an imprint of St. Martin's Publishing Group

Designed by Devan Norman
Endpaper illustration © Shutterstock.com
Case stamp based off cover illustration by Colin Verdi

www.wednesdaybooks.com

The Library of Congress Cataloging-in-Publication Data is available upon request.

ISBN 978-1-250-78713-2 (hardcover)
ISBN 978-1-250-78714-9 (ebook)

Our books may be purchased in bulk for promotional, educational, or business use. Please contact your local bookseller or the Macmillan Corporate and Premium Sales Department at 1-800-221-7945, extension 5442, or by email at MacmillanSpecialMarkets@macmillan.com.

First Edition: 2023

10 9 8 7 6 5 4 3 2 1

For anyone who needs this book
as much as I needed to write it

Some of the thematic material in *Wildblood* contains depictions of blood, gore, physical/sexual assault, sexual trauma, and death. For more information, please visit the author's website.

WILDBLOOD

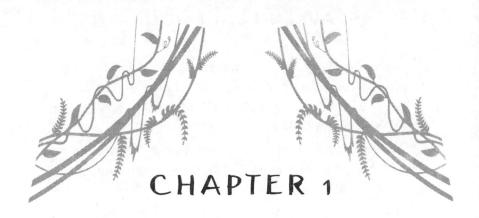

CHAPTER 1

Bunny is getting strong for fourteen. It takes my whole weight to hold him down tonight, hands and chest on his back, knees braced against the dirt floor. My muscles shake from the effort.

"You are loved," I whisper, even though I can't quite reach his ear like I could a year ago. "Come back, my little Bunny."

Maybe he can't hear me—enough rain to drown the island pours from the sky, splashing through our glassless window as it slides off the tin roof, and he screams loud enough to wake the whole jungle, even a mile off.

His wild blood flashes near my face—a small, bright yellow crackle like lightning—but his blood science has never burned very hot, so I ignore it. I focus on keeping him pinned, even with his kicking and cries. I stay on the side of his good eye, so when he wakes he knows me.

Huddled on their floor mats, our ten hut-mates sleep through it, or at least they try. It's the second time this month Bunny has raged. No one asks why anymore. A Wildblood's science flares out of control with overuse, and everyone just waves it off as Bunny being a reckless kid. But I don't think recklessness has anything to do with it.

"I'm getting my promotion tomorrow, Bun," I whisper, my voice harboring an edge of panic. "To team leader. Remember? Everything will be okay now."

Even mindless, Bunny knows I'm a bad liar. Everything won't be okay. Not if he keeps overusing his science and making his blood go wild. Not if he rages and I can't bring him back . . .

His screams shut off like a faucet. My ears ring in their absence, but I don't let up on my pressure. Not until his muscles soften, until he whines my name to make me stop. And then I lie there on his back to catch my breath, relieved to feel him breathe evenly, even if I can't.

He fishes for my hand in the dark, and his body only relaxes once he's found it. I squeeze tight, shifting to lie beside him.

"You scare me, Bunny," I say, and pat his back with a force between a soothe and a smack. "You can't keep raging like this."

"I have to rage, Victoria," he murmurs, closing his one beautiful dark brown eye. "Rage is all I have left."

Rage is all I have left . . .

I should be so lucky.

Ad in the *Wilmington Gazette,*
4 June 1893

THE EXOTIC LANDS TOURING COMPANY
Providing the greatest adventure of your life since 1872

The jungle, with its monstrous inhabitants, has long been something to fear and considered nigh uncrossable . . . **BUT NO MORE.** Whether you need to cross the island for business or pleasure, our skilled tour guides will provide a safe and pleasant experience you'll remember for years to come. The **QUICKEST WAY** to the other side is through!

Enjoy our Rare Beauties and experience the jungle in a way never before possible with the Exotic Lands Touring Company.

A COMPANY YOU CAN TRUST TO KEEP YOU SAFE

CHAPTER 2

*V*ictoria.

I wake to a whisper.

The jungle always whispers, when the rain isn't there to block it out.

The storm cleared out sometime before dawn and the sounds of gulls and breeze through the branches find their way in the open window.

Bunny makes it a point to sleep in on our days off, but he needs it more than ever after last night. I, on the other hand, have a list of things to get done, even if the only work-related one is finally asking for my promotion.

Finally? I was owed it when I turned eighteen last week. The boss promised.

Like when he used to promise he'd never punch you in the face and punched you in the stomach instead.

Carefully, I pull Bunny's sleeve up, and immediately deflate.

Tiny cuts litter his arms, closed but still pink, some of them not quite scabbed over yet. He's been picking again. Just enough to expose a little blood, to use his own blood's energy to play with his science. It's why he's tired all the time—stealing energy from the body takes its toll. It's why he rages so often.

I take a deep breath and get up carefully so as not to wake Bunny, dress quickly.

One problem at a time.

The ground is still wet from last night, making the sandy stone of the square look like the bed of a drained lake. But the sun is already warm, and it'll be dry before noon. Beyond the square, a much-too-long mile off, lies the thick jungle.

Vibrant, damp, the breezes rustling its leaves. *Victoria*, it hums through my body. Part of me wants to answer that call, escape what I must do.

Escape. Poor choice of word. No one escapes the Exotic Lands Touring Company, unless one would call deciding how they'd like to die "escaping"—shot trying to climb the twenty-foot wall between us and civilization, or dead somewhere in the jungle in any number of ways exceedingly worse than a shot to the head.

I've been here since I was six, and in that time, only five people have tried running. Maron, Wiles, Liz, Benji, John. I remember their names, if not their faces. They each chose the wall, because the next day we had to look at their bullet-nested bodies in the square. Each time, the boss wouldn't let us take away their bodies until they stank of rot in the mid-day's scorching sun. Just once I wanted someone to choose the jungle . . . no bodies involved. No memories. No rage burning in my belly. I could imagine the only reason I never saw them again was because they'd made it to the other side, alive and well and living free.

Me? I'd choose the jungle in a heartbeat. And I do, without the risk of running—I spend twenty-seven days a month on the road that runs through it, and I'd spend more if I wasn't forced to take days off. Unfortunately, no one ever travels on Sundays. I'd do anything in my power to get away from the boss and Dean, and volunteering for tours is the only thing in my power.

I should take more days off—what's happening to Bunny could very well happen to me if I'm not careful. It could happen to any of us. But I *am* careful. And my science has always had more endurance than anyone's.

No, I'm not worried about raging.

Though I'd prefer that to what I'm about to do.

Do it for Bunny. When he's safe, and away from here, you never have to take another day off again.

I turn away from my view of freedom and walk toward the office, leaping over scattered puddles. The main office is about a half mile from our huts and hidden behind a lumber fence—as if the jungle isn't angry enough in the first place about us clearing a bit of its majesty away to build on. But the boss doesn't want clients seeing where we live. It ruins the touring experience, he says.

There are about forty Wildbloods in the company—half here and half on the other side of the jungle road. For the moment, Bunny is the youngest in the camp; the oldest of us, Jim, is somewhere in his fifties. He had a head injury a few years back and can't seem to keep track of details anymore, so we decided fifty-three sounded fair. I pass some of my fellows hanging laundry on flimsy clotheslines, reading, kicking a ball around. No one says good morning or wishes me luck, even though I'm certain everyone knows what I'm about to do given how many gossips there are among us.

Not that I expect them to—no one has trusted me since I was twelve years old and used my science to bust a guard's eardrum, sending blood gushing from his ear and everyone running away screaming. It was self-defense. The man would've beaten me for something as simple as getting too close to the trees, but that didn't matter to them. To them, an inability to control your science was close enough to raging to shun me—a danger to everyone who should not be associated with. As if raging is contagious and not just an unfortunate quirk of one's own body.

What they don't know—or just can't stomach—is that what I did to that guard was 100 percent in my control. I meant to do it. But I was young. I didn't know it would hurt him so badly. That there'd be so much blood. That he'd be deaf in that ear for the rest of his life. But it was me or him. He'd meant to beat me, and if any of my injuries had been lasting, the boss wouldn't have had use for me anymore.

I may be the most powerful Wildblood, but out on the relatively uneventful journey by road that doesn't matter much. The boss only allows me to go on as many tours as I do because of my looks. What he doesn't know is that on tours I wear baggy men's clothing and a wide hat to make sure no one ever sees the Rare Beauty they're getting.

I glance up at the armed guard strolling atop the stone walls. Unlike my peers, he waves as if he knows me. He's a wall guard, so I don't know his name—and with the sun glaring I'd never recognize him even if I did. I wave back, the gesture meaningless and empty. I don't want to say hello to a man who can and will shoot me if I step out of line, but better to obey and not cause a scene. Not now, when I'm so close to what I need.

Someday, when Bunny is safe, I'll defy that threatening wave by simply not responding to it.

I arrive at the office and look up at the painted wooden sign over the door. THE EXOTIC LANDS TOURING COMPANY WELCOMES YOU, it reads. Seems a flock of birds disagreed and decided to drop their breakfast on it sometime this morning, so the L and S are whited out, making it THE EXOTIC AND TOURING COMPANY.

What's exotic about Jamaica, anyway? Having never lived anywhere else, I can't say. The English seem to think it's accurate, despite having occupied the island for centuries. Strange that it isn't normal to them yet.

Now that I'm here, my stomach aches. Like every organ in me is trying to knot itself small enough to hide. I don't want to do this. After avoiding the boss for so long, it feels like a betrayal of myself to walk into the snake pit again.

God, I don't want to do this.

But Bunny needs me.

I swallow back the urge to cry then grab the doorknob, pressing my eyes closed for a moment.

Good morning, sir. I want to remind you that you said you'd promote me to tour leader when I turned eighteen. You already prepared the contract on my last birthday. I have it with me. If you'll just sign here . . . Thank you, sir.

I take a breath.

The bell on the door chimes as I push it open and step into the reception area. No one is there to occupy the ten seats arranged about the room, but even if clients were waiting Louis would find some reason to scowl at me from over his typewriter.

"Mr. Spitz can't see you now," he says. As usual, he doesn't give a reason. He's already sweating in his neatly pressed shirt and jacket as he peers over the desk at my feet. "Good Lord, girl."

My feet aren't that dirty—I avoided all the puddles—but I wipe them carefully on the mat anyway. "I can wait."

"You're going to, whether you can or not," he says, going back to his loud typing.

The boss never meets with clients this early. Louis has no reason to keep me away. And besides, unnatural sounds, like the slamming of those keys, grate on my nerves. Give me insect wings and birdsong and water dripping through leaves any day.

The opposite end of the small reception area has another doorway, leading to a hall laid with hardwood floors. Ten feet down, the boss's office door sits to the right; ten more feet to the left, his bedroom. My body is trying to revolt, but I don't have time to lose my nerve. All I need to do is get to that first room.

"Did you see that birds disrespected the sign?" I ask.

Louis immediately looks up, like I swore at him. "What?"

"Shat"—I spread my hands as if smearing the stuff on the air—"all over it."

He eyes me suspiciously. "Still legible?"

"Um, well . . ." I can't lie if I look at him, so I pretend to fix a stack of pamphlets on his desk. "Maybe. I mean, if you know what it's *supposed* to say."

"If it isn't one thing, it's another," he grumbles, shoving up from his desk. He stomps away, heading outside.

As soon as he clears the door, I rush down the hall.

I halt before knocking.

Voices.

So he really is with a client? This early? Strange.

I sigh and stand against the opposite wall to wait, teetering a bit before stepping toward the door again. If their consultation just started there's no point in wait—

I scramble backward at the shifting of wood against wood, pressing my back against the wall.

A young man halts in the doorway, and I see his eyes light up right before I drop my gaze to the floor. I hate when they do that. Gawk. Because I'm light-skinned Black. Because my great-grandmother or great-great- or great-great-great- or maybe all of them were raped by some slimy slave owner who thought no better of her than a dog, and somehow that makes me more desirable.

Or maybe I look away because this young man has skin the color of blackstrap molasses, eyes black as ackee seeds, dimples in his cheeks without even trying . . . and because I don't feel sick like I do when other men look at me.

From the corner of my eye, I see him remove his bowler hat. "Morning, miss," he says, then moves away quick with a small jerk, shoved casually by the man behind him. I look up in time to see that man sneer at me, eyebrows raised, like he wants an explanation for why I'm bothering his friend.

I'm used to that look, too.

Out of all the many races of people who live on this island, there's one thing for sure they have in common—everyone hates a Wildblood.

I watch them walk away, the beautiful one looking over his shoulder at me, and I feel myself blush at his unmannerly curiosity. Both are Black, which is strange for clients, but I have no time to wonder about that.

The boss's hacking cough carries into the hall and anxiety swims in my head.

I'm here for a reason.

I turn my attention to the office and my blush is replaced by heated loathing.

Dean has his arms crossed and is leaning against the desk, glaring at me. His skin is almost as pale as the boss's—if the boss didn't get so red in the sun—like a tree with the bark shaved off to a nutty cream inside. His gray eyes hold the same hateful, questioning expression the man from a moment ago had, tangled with panic.

I relish that panic.

We were both taken from our families younger than most, both Black, both light-skinned. Level ground, until you consider his science is next to nothing compared to mine. Level again, when you consider he's a boy and can pass as white to the whites when his hair is cropped short. The boss will always favor Dean above me because of that. Let him have it—I built a figurative altar to God the day he became Dean Spitz, lone adopted son and heir to the boss's company and fortune, and the boss finally stopped summoning me to compete for the coveted position.

But the thought that laying eyes on me can stir fear of losing his beloved inheritance, that I can torture him just by entering a room . . . I'm not a vicious person, but I hate him enough to enjoy this.

Maybe that *does* make me vicious.

But he isn't the one making my heart twist with anxiety, pound painfully in my throat.

The boss drinks his morning cup of rum, reading one of the papers on his desk. Even standing in the doorway of the room he's in makes my skin crawl. But I can't turn back now.

Louis calls my name, chastisement in his voice, but the door to the office is still open so I knock without his permission.

"Come in," the boss says, without looking up from his paperwork.

I try not to look at Dean's hateful expression as I step inside. Quickly, before I can back out. Before I'm eaten alive by nerves.

"Good morning, sir," I say in a steady stream, just like I've been rehearsing to myself all week, "I want to remind you that you said you'd promote me to tour leader when I turned eighteen—"

"Isn't it your day off, Victoria?" the boss says more than asks. *Warns* more than states.

"Yes, sir." My head hurts. I take a deep breath, collecting myself. "B-but, um, you did already—um, you prepared the contract on my last birthday. I have it with me." I take the contract out of my pocket, holding it out to him. "If you can just sign here . . ."

Dean tilts his head, raising his eyebrows slightly. *Well played.* Tour leader isn't anywhere near as prestigious as protégé, but it's a degree of freedom, a pay raise, guaranteed opportunities to get me out onto the jungle road and away from this suffocating place.

And for all those reasons, I know Dean is going to make sure I don't get what I want.

But, for now, he doesn't make a move.

The boss looks up from his papers, removing his reading spectacles. My muscles tighten painfully under his gaze. He smiles, but that's never meant anything. "I'm afraid I've already promoted someone today, Victoria." His voice is coarse from years of cigar smoking, and frighteningly calm from years of trampling on the hopes of children. "We won't need another leader for some time."

I swallow, my courage dwindling. This is not the response I was expecting. "I get very high reviews on my client surveys, sir. And you promised me."

Dean scoffs, and I hate him even more. But he's right—I used the *P*-word. To the boss that has as opposite a meaning as his smiles.

"This client is too high profile for your lack of social skills, and the tour will be off the marked path. It requires men who can stand that sort of rough environment."

My courage surges a little. "That's me, sir. I lived in the jungle for a year, you remember. I know all the dangers, how to navigate—"

"As a feral child," the boss says, and it's his turn to scoff. "Not an experienced tour guide."

"The important thing is to remember the way. I do."

I don't. That was a long time ago, and I barely remember anything before coming here. But it's better than what Dean can do. *Anything* is better than what Dean can do. He hasn't stepped foot on the jungle road for a year and has *never* wandered beyond it. And who knows, maybe certain landmarks will spark my memory.

Besides, the jungle will guide me if I continue to respect it and ask politely.

The boss has another coughing fit into his handkerchief before sighing. It only started happening in the past few months, the coughing. I told him all that smoke in his lungs would kill him one day.

God, I hope it does.

"The *important* thing," he says when he's finished, "is to make a good impression. As you know, Dean is taking over ownership of the touring company, since I have no children of my own. And the best way for him to be an effective leader is to know all the ins and outs—that includes leading tours."

I gape before he's even done speaking. "*Dean?* But sir—"

"Do you have a problem with my decision?"

My stomach turns. His tone is no longer calm. For a moment I think of the loaded gun he keeps in his desk. He's never used it on me before . . . but then, I've never questioned his decisions.

"N-no—" I stutter, then press my lips tight to shut myself up. It's over. I feel my heartbeat ticking in my wrists, and I can't be sure intelligible words will come out of me next time I speak.

"Enjoy your weekend." The boss shoos me away. "Shut the door on your way out."

I nod instead of trying to speak and turn on my heel.

The words *Bunny is counting on you* hammer in my mind to the pounding of my heart, and I stop myself before heading down the hall, taking a deep breath.

You idiot. Get away while you can.

I ignore my own sage advice and burst back into the office.

"Dean's science is pathetic," I say, my voice coated in desperation. "And he's never wandered off the marked path. How can he lead a tour to the center of the jungle? He'll get everyone lost, or worse—"

The boss presses on the arms of his chair to help himself stand, and it's like there are three gates between us and one has been thrown wide open. He's stocky, the remains of a retired boxer—a skill he's demonstrated on me enough times that I don't want him to open that second gate. But he does, by stepping around the desk toward me, and I have to adjust my breath to seem calm. If I back away, he'll never give me what I want.

Be brave. Bunny needs you.

The coaching barely helps as he comes closer.

"You foolish little girl . . ." he chides.

Please don't touch me . . . please please please . . .

When he's close enough, he takes my chin in his hand.

The third gate has been breached.

I freeze, bracing for that caress to turn into a fist. I'm taller by a few inches, but his presence is massive and consuming and I can't breathe . . . Lord, have mercy, I can't breathe . . .

I glance behind him at Dean, though I don't know why I expect he's going to intervene for me. But he could say *something.* Admit that I'm right, at least. Or do something other than grip the desk as if he's about to be beaten instead of me.

But it's been a year since I could trust him to do right by me.

"I know the jungle better than Dean," I try again. Or I think I do. The boss's touch is so repulsive, his presence filling me with so much anxiety, I might die right here and now.

"That's not the point," he says, his voice calm enough to make my stomach turn. "What would it look like if a quiet little girl who can't even speak without stammering was leading the pack? Who would hire me again, with my reputation tarnished? No, you're a follower, girl—and good at it, too. Let's not change a system that isn't broken. Besides, these are the most prestigious clients we've ever served."

My stomach swims. The one thing I know I have to offer is the thing I'm also dreading.

"Then I'll help make Dean look good," I say, silently thanking God my words cooperate.

I'd felt the beginnings of the boss's clamping grip tightening on my chin, but he pauses. Whatever I fill this pause with will mean victory or destruction.

"I'm the most powerful Wildblood," I say quickly. "And I've faced the dangers of the deepest part of the jungle. Give me my promotion, and I'll make Dean look like the best tour leader you've ever had."

I'm surprised I didn't falter during my speech. Deliberately working with Dean. Closely, as a team. After the way he betrayed me? Being torn apart by rabid dogs would be a kinder punishment. But if I can swallow my emotions and pull it off, Bunny will never have to go on another tour again.

The boss releases me slowly, and I let out a small breath of relief, wanting more than anything to tear all the skin he's touched away and burn it with my own lightning. "Now there's an idea."

Behind him, Dean stands upright, shocked and fuming. "The clients requested strong guides, not antisocial little girls."

I use those fumes to fuel my own fire. "My brand of strength is more useful in the jungle than the strongest man in the world. Besides, don't these prestigious clients deserve the best protection and service Jamaica can offer? My blood science will provide that."

The boss paces, stops abruptly. "One condition. The client has to come back singing Dean's praises and *unaware* that you were assisting."

That's two conditions, but I'm too relieved to care. "Yes, sir," I say, holding back a smile—but I do hold out my unsigned contract. He grabs his quill and signs it without question, high on his own ego. Or just high, probably—the office reeks of ganja.

Dean, wisely, says nothing.

"I want to be paired with Bunny, if that's okay," I slip in, seeing as the boss is in a good mood.

"Ask your tour leader," he says, and falls into more coughing, no longer interested in looking at me as he heads back to his desk.

I take a second to swallow before I look at Dean. He's more pissed off than usual, if that's possible, but thankfully not stupid enough to start an argument in front of the boss—not with his own promotion on the line.

"He's your responsibility," he grumbles.

I nod. "No problem." And I leave quickly, before the boss changes his mind.

I trip to a stop around the corner, just out of view. My legs tremble, and I have to grab the wall to keep myself upright. My lungs ache as I release a heavy breath, taking a few deep ones to give my nerves a moment to settle.

I did it. I actually did it.

Well, almost.

One more trip, first.

Don't screw this up, V.

The sound of creaking wood alerts me to Dean, even if his footsteps are as quiet as mine. "What do you want, Dean?" I ask, walking toward the waiting area quickly—Dean wouldn't dare try anything in front of Louis, who reports all "hooligan behavior," as he calls it, to the boss.

But I barely make it a few feet before a strong hand clamps around my wrist, his touch, his presence igniting my fighting instinct immediately. He tugs me around, and I lift my open hand just as he lifts his fist.

I feel my wild blood spark like an ember within my gut, feel the warmth of my irises shifting to a glowing red with power, but shove my energy back under the coals just as quickly. It's not worth the trouble to fight back. Not when I've already gotten what I wanted. I drop my hand, my eyes cooling to light brown again. My hate-filled stare is stronger, anyway—I know, because he twitches while his fist lingers in the air, passively.

His science really is pathetic when compared to mine. I know it, he knows it. Which is why I know to threaten him with it, seeing as, if he had the mind to, he could easily beat me bloody with that callus-hardened fist. He wasn't so much taught how to fight as forced to learn by boxing with the boss twice a week. It's why most of the bones in his face have been broken at one time or another, one cheekbone lower than the other, his nose twisted. The boss never promised not to punch *him* in the face.

We both know our strengths. All I need to do is pull a drop of blood from his pores—more easily his gums, since they're softer—and fashion it midair into a needle to drive through his eye, maybe all the way into his brain. He's gripping one of my wrists while the other is cocked away, fingers closed off from summoning his science, which puts him at a deadly disadvantage against my open hand.

I've won the round in the office *and* this one in the hall.

Overall, it's been a satisfying morning.

"Don't you ever," he says, low, because the door is still so close and wide open, "embarrass me in front of the boss again."

"You don't need my help to embarrass yourself," a braver, stupider Victoria would say. For Bunny's sake, I say nothing. When he's safe and off the island, living a life where he doesn't have to stress over long journeys and using his science, maybe I'll find some way to get back at Dean. But there's too much riding on this trip for me to make trouble now.

He releases my wrist, and I hide my trembling revulsion in my pocket.

"You'd better not mess this up for me," he says, then storms back into the office and, blessedly, away from me.

CHAPTER 3

When I find Samson, he's sitting in the sun, wavy black hair lying against his shoulder blades and dampening his shirt nearly to the hem, broad shoulders bowed over an assortment of knives that he appears to be sharpening.

"You washed your hair on a Saturday, Sammy?"

He looks up at me and grins, shading his hooded eyes with his hand. Seeing those eyes is just what I needed after that stressful meeting. Tapered on the outside ends and brown brown *brown* like the warmest, deepest, most soothing thought. "Morning, baby. How'd it go?"

I cringe, and his grin drops before I even say anything. "I have to prove myself with this next tour tomorrow."

"What the hell more do you have to prove? You're the best Wildblood in the entire company, and you've been on more tours than anyone."

"I know."

"This is bullshit."

"I *know.*" I sigh and sit across from him as he goes back, rather grumpily and with murmured swears, to his knives. "You should wear your sun hat. You know the boss doesn't like you getting too dark."

"The boss can kiss my ass." He checks a blade with his thumb. "Anyway, my hair needs to dry. I borrowed some of Ada's conditioning cream. I didn't even use that much but I'm a little worried it'll make me greasy."

"Why didn't you just use mine? Our textures are closer."

Closer? Maybe when wet. When dry, his hair is brilliant and wavy and smooth, as long as he's conditioned a little. My curls are soft and loose, but *thick,* and I have to finger-comb and deep condition for an hour for them to be defined and not frizz up. I rarely wear my hair out for that reason. Honestly, if the boss would allow me to wear it short, I would.

"You're running low. I didn't want to use it until you could make some more."

That's true, and an answer to my question, but it's a wonder I heard it with everything else going on in my head. I chew on my lip, weighing whether to say . . . "Dean was promoted instead of me."

Samson freezes. Raises his eyebrows at me. "Dean?" His voice is a mixture of disturbance and disbelief.

"The boss says he needs tour leader experience before he can take over the company."

Samson throws down his knife, the blade sticking in the ground, then rakes his fingers through his wet hair. "That means he's leading the next tour."

I lower my voice. "Part of the deal is that I have to make him look good—"

"That means he was in the room with you. Both he *and* the boss. Alone with you."

"It was fine."

"You should've come and got me before you went in. I could've at least stood outside the door."

I shush him, reaching over to touch his beautiful tawny cheek. "There was no time. Anyway, I can handle Dean."

"But not both of them."

"Everything was fine. Honest."

"Next time you come and get me right away."

I roll my eyes. Only three years older than me and already behaving like an old nag.

"I mean it," he says, taking my chin in his giant hand. "Immediately."

He's naturally heavy-handed, and I shove his fingers away before he gets emotional and squeezes enough to hurt. "Alright, alright."

He sighs and shakes his head. "I worry about you."

"We should worry more about Bunny," I say, thankful for a segue that takes the attention away from myself. "He's picking at himself again."

Samson's sigh is deep and weary. He's too young to be sighing that way. But then he's been forced to take care of himself for the past eight years—since he was thirteen. Bunny would say I'm the same way, but somehow it seems to stress Sam out more. "First Dean, now Bunny. I was having such an uneventful morning for once, did you have to pile it all on in one go?"

I shrug sheepishly. "Maybe you can talk to him? He listens to you more than he does me."

"Yeah, let me finish up with these."

"Great. I'll wake him." I jump to my feet and plant a kiss on Samson's damp head, and he reaches up and hugs the back of my head, scrunching my hair a little. "Love you, Sammy."

"Love you too, baby."

I dash off back to the hut. Bunny is the only one in there, still sleeping. I sigh and stoop down to rub his back. "Bun, you have to get up," I say. "We have a new job tomorrow. Laundry time."

Bunny groans and rolls over, and it's only a year of working closely with him that allows me to understand when he mumbles, "If you're a tour leader why do *we* have a new job?"

"Well, because I'm . . . not . . . a tour leader . . . yet?"

Each time I hesitate Bunny emerges further and further from sleep and the covers. Finally, he stares at me with raised, expectant eyebrows—his one eye wide, the other lid permanently lowered, only open the slightest bit to barely reveal an open socket. "You chickened out?"

"No." I snatch the blanket from him and stand so I can fold it. "But the boss wasn't going to give it to me. I had to cut a deal."

He buries his face in his gangly brown arms with a groan. "Why does this deal have to involve ruining my weekend?"

"Because I can't look out for you if I'm gone and you get paired with someone else come Monday." I poke him in the side with my toes. "Besides, all you're going to do is sleep."

"One: nobody else wants to pair up with me." He grabs my foot, trying to shove me off balance for the millionth time, even though he knows I've walked the uneven terrain of the jungle too many times to fall victim to that. "Two: it takes three days to travel the road to the other side. We both know you're going to take another job right away, so three more days back. By then, it's the weekend again. That's eight days I get to relax and do nothing."

"We're not going to the other side, we're going to the heart of the jungle. And you know you'd rather come with me than let the boss find you idle."

Bunny takes a moment to let out all his groaning before reluctantly sitting up.

"Who leaves for a journey on a Sunday?" he grumbles, dragging on a fresh shirt. "Bunch of heathens."

"Apparently, very wealthy, prestigious heathens, who are going to make the company a lot of money if we do this right."

"Will we get paid more, do you think? Maybe they'll tip us." He puts his bed mat away quickly and gathers his dirty clothes. "Any grandmothers? They always tip."

"I don't know," I say, grinning at his enthusiasm. "We'll find out tomorrow."

Bunny yelps as I lead the way out. "Don't move."

I want to turn to see how serious his expression is, but in our dangerous environment it's best to take the words "don't move" literally. "What?"

"In your hair," he whispers. "A Lady."

I smile and reach up to my hair carefully.

"Are you crazy, V?" Bunny whisper-yells. "I'll get some incense to ward it off."

The butterfly's wing tickles my finger with a quick flick, and I move my hand just enough so she can crawl aboard. I bring my hand in front of my face to look at her while Bunny continues to freak out.

Why they call her a Bloody Lady, I'll never know—it's not as if she draws blood when she kills you. Maybe it's because when the red-and-pink ombré of her wings, speckled in black, are fully extended they look like reddened lips.

"Why do you always end up with something dangerous following you home?"

"She won't hurt me," I say, and smile fondly at the creature. "Will you, beautiful? No, of course not."

"You're crazy. One wrong move and you're going to swell up, or *worse*."

"Start the laundry, Bun, I'll be right there."

"You don't *always* have to sacrifice yourself!" he shouts as I head out of the lumber gate toward the trees.

It's a pleasant walk, a mile or so, and I intend to enjoy every step of it despite all the chores I have to do—the most important one is done, the rest will be busywork. Unfortunately, the grounds between the wall and the trees are occupied today. Dean and four guards are fighting by the well, as they do some mornings, and I purposely give them a wide berth without making it look like I'm avoiding them. There's a covering over the well, a hut roof held up by four poles—a small space, but the whole point of their little fighting game is to stay in the shade. Anyone who gets knocked into the surrounding sunshine loses.

It's a game for the guards, anyway. They cheer and bet money and consider it a fun distraction during their morning break from duty. For Dean, it's just practice. For what, I don't know. But he's bulked up in the past year from the slender boy I used to know, and that sort of change can't be for nothing.

Or maybe he just wants to be like the boss in every way possible.

I cringe at the sound of vulgar whistling and do my best not to look like I've noticed, focus on my Lady instead.

"Hey there, beautiful," calls one of the guards, and my stomach turns. If I quicken my pace they'll see it as a challenge—

although, realistically, there's no way all four of them are on break at once, and since the boss is finished with his meeting he's bound to notice that the main wall is only being guarded by one man. Still, I can't count on them getting caught. I just have to hope they find the fight more interesting.

"Come see us, Victoria," another guard calls, while one of them makes kissing noises that are suddenly cut off by choking sounds.

I make the mistake of looking to see why and find Dean glaring at me, the guard's neck tucked snugly in his elbow, his other arm locking the man's head in place. The man slaps Dean's arm, attempting to tap out of the fight, but Dean holds him easily despite his struggle. All while he glares at me.

Of course he's pissed—I've stolen attention away from him. Our whole life we've been pitted against each other, and he can't stand when I'm better than him at something, even if it's just existing. It doesn't matter that I don't want anything to do with what he's coveting. He can keep the attention.

The man goes limp from lack of air, and only then does Dean let him drop to the ground and kick him into the sun to an uproar of cheers.

He looks at me as I pass, then turns his back to me. The message is clear, even if I'm not close enough to read his eyes. His science may be pathetic next to mine, but Wildbloods can't summon their science without enough oxygen.

I think I'll take the long way back to the huts.

I ignore the armed guard at the mouth of the road and step up to the tree line, thick with brush and vines. My sweet friend still sits on my finger but has closed her wings—I hate to move her while she's resting, but there's too much to do today to linger.

"One of us should be free," I murmur, and lay a delicate

kiss on her wing before extending my hand to a dewy leaf. She shifts over to it and I feel the loss, worse so when she takes off flying through the leaves, disappearing from sight. The jungle whispers—what, I don't know, but I close my eyes and try to listen. I want to go with her. For a moment, I want to forget everything and run.

But I can't do that to Bunny. And, anyway, where would I go?

"Victoria."

I jolt, looking over to see that Ross is the guard I ignored. He's old enough to be my father, with a sandy blond mustache and stern blue eyes, and he says my name in a warning tone I've heard fathers on tours use for their children. A little more sinister while holding a rifle, though, even if he hasn't lifted it. I don't have a father, but I imagine they don't threaten to shoot their children. So his tone doesn't mean the same thing to me, I think, as it does to him.

"Step away from the trees, lass," he says, as if he's sorry to disappoint me.

Sorry that he'll have to shoot me if I don't obey.

I hurry back toward the lumber gate, spotting Louis distributing sealed notes into our rusted metal cubbies. The assignments for all booked tours for the week will be in there. When he's finished I rush to my cubby and grab my single note. Makes sense—there's no time for another tour this week, not when we'll have to travel to the depths of the jungle and back.

Meet in the dining hall Sunday at sunrise, is all it says. I take Bunny's note, too—he won't check it himself, he never does—and go to help him do the laundry I know he hasn't started.

CHAPTER 4

Despite having lived on land surrounded completely by ocean, I have never seen it, let alone a beach. Cool breezes blow off it, soothing my skin against the sun and rustling the leaves of the jungle nearby. Distant waves crash, providing sound within the silence to lull me to sleep when the rain isn't available. Salty air provides an occasional snack to lick off my lips and adds to the humidity I've come to ignore.

Other than that, I couldn't tell you anything about it. Not the color or the temperature, not what it looks like or what creatures live in it. I only know what I've been told.

But I know the river. It travels from the high hills of the jungle down toward us, crossing under an arched bridge along the marked jungle road, ending perhaps nowhere at all. I've plunged my feet into its crisp clear depths, swum within its thrashing rapids, floated on my back along its calming flow.

For me, it doesn't matter that I will never experience the ocean, even if everyone else has. I have no real desire or need to see it. My allegiance is to the river—how could it not be, when it's the only thing on this earth ever to show me mercy?

When the River Mumma usually drowns everyone else.

Is that why I can't get to sleep tonight? Is it the anticipation of entering the heart of that whispering jungle, ruled by a spirit who drowns mortals who dare get too close?

Or is it because the thought of anyone invading that sacred jungle makes me hope she drowns them all?

We're up before the sun, birdsong our company. Well, *I'm* up. I wake Bunny, because he'll need a minute to gather the will to get going, and then I dress quickly and quietly so as not to wake anyone else. The dark is nothing to me. My clean clothes are where I always stack them, and I don't need sight to tighten the straps around my tan trousers at my waist, thighs, and ankles. I had Samson braid my long, curly hair into a crown last night—a low-maintenance style I'll do my best to keep for the entire trip—and I set my wide-brimmed, silk-lined straw hat on my head even if there's no sun to block quite yet. By now, Bunny is finally up, slouching like the walking dead but able to dress himself at least, mostly. I rebutton his plaid shirt for him, adjust his eye patch, tighten the straps on his trousers.

I lead my half-asleep Bunny by the hand into the dining hall, nearly stopping short when I see who else is in there waiting for the meeting. Nine people, including Dean. The two of us make eleven. How big is this client's party that so many Wildbloods are required?

Everyone is dressed similarly to me—light-colored cotton or linen shirt with the collar close to the neck, tan or brown trousers, some with suspenders and some without, and a wide boater or worn newsboy to block the sun. No one wears jackets or shoes. What would be the point of that? Who is there to impress out in the jungle?

Dean is the only one with extra stuff on—he wears some light, worn gloves, and a hat with a wider brim than the others, like mine. I made them for us after we spent an afternoon playing outside a few years ago and came back with tans the boss deemed unseemly. He'd beaten us, made us scrub a layer of skin off, and then kept us inside and secluded until we looked light enough for him again. More palatable. From that moment on, neither of us bothered with the sun, although I just hide my hands with my large sleeves instead of messing with sweaty gloves.

"You're lucky I waited for you slackers," Dean says, his voice echoing in the large, nearly empty room.

He says "slackers" as if he means to call us something not quite as friendly. I bite my tongue.

I sit Bunny between me and Samson, and he immediately reaches for a sugarcane. Samson raises his eyebrows at me, spooning some fluffy yellow ackee and pungent saltfish onto Bunny's plate without me having to say a word.

I'm not surprised the boss included Samson on the list. He's the only Chinese Jamaican in the entire camp, which makes him a favorite among the tourists for the same reason I am, unfortunately. As Rare Beauties, we have to be physically perfect in the eyes of the boss, who, of course, claims that his standards are what the public is looking for—lighter skin, no physical disabilities or scars, a pretty enough face, "good" hair. Nothing to do with what actually makes a person beautiful. Nothing to do with being rare, either—never mind that plenty of light-skinned Blacks own property just up the hill and that the Chinese have been here for at least forty years.

We can't have been late, because the plantains are fresh from the grease, and I pluck a few big crispy ones up with my fingers onto a slice of bread.

Samson leans around Bunny's slouching back and whispers, "You know what the hell is going on?"

Other than a client asking if he could be led into the heart of a demon-infested jungle and the boss not immediately calling him insane and turning him away?

I shrug.

He kisses his teeth, making the sound last a few seconds as he turns back to his plate.

I think the sentiment for everyone else at the table is mutual.

Clients have asked us to be discreet before, but never to this extent.

"Let's get down to business," Dean says. He's sitting on the table, thankfully at the opposite end from me. "Our client is very high profile, which is why you're only being briefed directly before we leave. No one can know who we're guiding and where. When you get back, you are not to talk about the mission until the client has left the island.

"Now I'll tell you, this mission is taking us into the heart of the jungle." There are gasps and murmurs from the group, but he moves on quickly. "If anyone has an issue with either the secrecy aspect of the mission or where we're headed, feel free to back out now."

No one moves. Why would they? What do any of us have but this?

"Our client is Laertes Thorn, a renowned goldminer from America. Along with his business partner and accountant, Hal Badger, he wants to take a team into the jungle to the Gilded Orchard. We'll be going . . ."

The Gilded Orchard? This must be a joke.

That's the last place anyone should be going. The creatures who live in the trees—and, by extension, guard them—are naturally attracted to the golden sap within the bark. All they see is the color gold. They're drawn to it, obsessed. Getting even the slightest bit on you will only draw their attention, and the attention of any monster of the jungle is a death sentence.

The room suddenly roars with voices.

"Did you hear that?" Bunny says to me, tapping my arm in a frantic tempo.

I havn't heard a thing Dean has said since mentioning the orchard, but judging by the animated protests I can only assume it was something extremely Dean-like. "What?"

"No pairing up? Can he do that?"

Dean whistles loudly to get everyone's attention. "The client has requested this," he says, though his voice barely carries over some remaining protests. "He feels it will be safer with a Wildblood paired with each member of his party. But there are plenty of us. We'll be fine."

We'll be fine?

Like hell.

"Dean," I speak up, "why—?"

"Why what, V?" He turns to me, his attempt to be casual instead extremely on edge, his eyes begging me to behave. "I just explained it. If you can't pay attention during a simple briefing maybe you should stay home."

A few in the group snicker. I bite the inside of my cheek, my hate for Dean simmering . . . and not only him. How can they side with him, laugh with him? Don't they know he's an accomplice to a monster?

"Victoria knows about the jungle, Dean," Samson says. "You should listen to what she has to say."

Samson looks at me, giving me an encouraging nod. I swallow before continuing, "D-did you tell the client that Wildbloods pairing up and taking turns using our science is essential to our survival?"

Dean sighs as if he's already sick of me—not Samson. His glare is clearly meant only for me. "There hasn't been a casualty on the jungle road for years. No duppy encounters for weeks. A record number of Wildbloods not actually having to use their science to get across." He holds up a leather folder of reports, from which, I assume, he's pulled that information. "If you have a problem with it, I'll find someone to take your place."

"That road has been cleared and secured—we're allowed that road. When we enter the trees, the jungle will instantly view us as unwanted guests. We'll be in enough danger without also being at risk of our science raging."

"Shut up, Victoria, and let Dean finish," says Nathan, high and mighty, as if he's a stolen prince instead of a butcher's son whose most useful skill is preparing meat and whose only personality trait of late is sucking up to Dean. He thinks it'll come in handy when Dean takes over, but he doesn't know Dean like I do.

Dean doesn't care about anyone, least of all his friends.

Samson leans on the table to look at him. I can't see his expression but I'm certain it's a warning look because Nathan clamps his jaw shut.

Even so, I hold my tongue for the remainder of the meeting. I can't afford to be argumentative. I need this trip. Dean knows it and I know it. He doesn't know Bunny is depending on it, but he doesn't have to. It doesn't matter. I can't afford to screw up, and I sure as hell can't afford to stay home. No one's going to listen to me with Dean leading, anyway—but then they wouldn't, no matter the leader. To them, I'm too dangerous, too volatile to ever be trusted.

If it comes down to it, Bunny, Samson, and I can band together if we run into trouble.

And we *will* run into trouble.

As soon as the meeting is over, I get up and sit by Samson on the bench, backward so I can lean against the table and look at him. He grins, not moving to prepare for the journey. We'll wait for Bunny to finish his breakfast first.

"They're never going to accept me as a leader, are they?" I say quietly.

"They won't have much of a choice," says Samson.

"But they barely respect me as it is."

"They're afraid of you. The disrespect is them trying to play it off, bring you down. You just have to prove to them you aren't a pushover."

I chew on my lip. But it's more than that, isn't it? They're superstitious, thus they want nothing to do with me. Like throwing salt at a duppy and avoiding opening an umbrella inside. Even if I were brave, they would still hate me.

Just because I happen to be more capable with an ability we all possess.

When Bunny is finished, we head out to join the others in the launch area, but when we step outside a woman is leaning against the flagpole nearby. Her skin is the color of tamarind paste, but I gather the sun added that reddish edge—despite her melanin, she doesn't seem suited for the sun at all. Her wide-brimmed hat is keeping her face in shadow, yet she still squints when she looks around. She looks dressed for a picnic luncheon, fan and all.

Samson has been at this game long enough to keep from laughing at her ridiculous choice of clothing, but Bunny has to turn his into a cough and ends up sounding like a dog hacking up rotten food. I look at Samson and he sighs, steering Bunny away from the woman with a hand on his shoulder.

"Are you waiting for someone, ma'am?" I ask when they've gone. I wouldn't have said anything, but she looks so out of place and alone. "You're welcome to sit in the reception area and get a cold Coca-Cola."

She looks at me abruptly, using her hand to add more unnecessary shade over her eyes. She still squints, as if I'm forty feet away instead of only ten. "My husband is getting the bags. Or are you here to tell me he got lost in another woman's skirts along the way?"

"U-um—" What a strange thing to say. A joke or . . . ? "No, ma'am."

She laughs. "You look so concerned, honey. Nobody wants that giant fool but me. And, to tell you the truth, I don't even want him. You know what that big idiot did?" She shifts against the flagpole to face me, hand planted on her hip. "We had this trip to Jamaica planned for months—*months*, I tell you—and the man goes and agrees to go on some expedition with his business partner. You married?"

It doesn't seem worth it to explain that no one in their

right mind would want to marry a Wildblood, so I don't. "No, ma'am."

"Don't get married. We have plenty of money, and he wants to go out looking for more. I don't care how much gold is in that jungle, if there are no boat tours or beaches or cliffs to climb, what's the point? Trees are not interesting."

"Oh, you're with the mining party?"

"I'm simply tagging along to make sure my husband does what he needs to do and gets out, so I can get back to my vacation. Ah." She lifts her hand coolly in greeting to someone beyond me. "The idiot himself."

I turn and take a deep breath, and for a moment I don't know how to let it out. The two men I'd seen yesterday walk toward us. I knew it. He's married. Of course he is. He's too beautiful not to be.

"Will you be changing your clothes, ma'am?" I ask, if only to distract myself from the disappointing fact.

"No, my bloomer suit is as sporty as I can stomach." She spins around to show off the dark blue, wide . . . trousers? They cinch in at the waist and close at her knees, revealing black stockings above her heeled boots. I must look as confused as I feel, because she raises her eyebrows. "You know, for bicycling? Women don't wear these here?"

Do they? Out of all the clients I've ever guided, I've never seen them before now. "I just mean small creatures may like the folds of fabric—"

"Badger!" she shouts to the two men, clearly missing what I said.

I need to move on, anyway. First impressions are everything, and I have to be lined up in the launch area before the clients reach it.

But of course it won't be my first impression, and that makes me more nervous than anything else.

I rush away and find my place beside Bunny. He holds open the strap of a satchel full of salt, and I slip it on while he holds its weight. Did he grow since this morning, or am I shrinking?

"You okay?" Bunny whispers.

"Fine," I murmur, adjusting the bag on my hip.

"I don't know, you're sort of curled in on yourself. Are you still upset about that argument with Dean?"

I straighten my spine quickly, taking a deep breath. "He's lost his mind."

"No, I mean, you look shook up. And your face is all red."

"We're not paired up. The boss should've vetoed the client as soon as he asked for this ridiculous arrangement."

Bunny rolls his eyes. "Okay, *don't* tell me what's really wrong then."

I scowl at him. "I don't know what you're talking about. I'm thinking about *you*."

"Don't worry about me."

Spoken like a fourteen-year-old boy who has never had to hold someone down while they rage, their mind eventually warping into eternal madness. "Just stick close, if you can. And don't use your science unless totally necessary."

"Alright, alright."

"I mean it."

"*Alright*." We straighten up as Dean and the clients approach.

"You're turning into an old ragged auntie before your time, you know that?"

"Whatever it takes to make you listen."

Each Wildblood, in addition to their satchel of salt, has exactly one waterproof backpack—dried food, a canteen, a foldable cot, extra incense, a tin bowl for catching dew for drinking water. Nothing more than necessary. Clients always bring more than necessary—tents, cookware, multiple outfits. But then, most clients stay on the road for only three days. These people will be in the jungle for God knows how long. I can't blame them for being overprepared.

Dean looks in our direction. He uses his index and middle fingers to point at me and Bunny, then moves his index and thumb in a twisting motion. Bunny and I look at each other, but the signal is clear enough. We swap places so I'm standing at the end of the line.

Starting from the opposite end, Dean walks Thorn's party down our neatly formed line, assigning each member of their team to a Wildblood. I knew Thorn and his partner were Black, but I suppose I didn't expect to find that his entire party is, as well. A nice change, to be honest—I don't know, it's just a little less tense when you're with your own. I also didn't expect Thorn to be at least ten years younger than everyone else in his group, closer to my age—he looks out of place in that way, as if he's the little brother tagging along instead of their obviously fearless leader. I didn't realize how young he was before. And I certainly never expected him to shake hands with each Wildblood Dean introduces him to.

Overall, Thorn's polite enough, but I still feel like a rotten pear on display at the market. I hate that Dean made me stand at the very end, instead of somewhere in the middle where I can be forgotten. I *really* hate that Thorn might recognize me from yesterday.

Most of all I hate that Thorn's deliberately putting us all in danger by not adhering to the pair rules . . . and yet I'm still attracted to him.

But it's not a crime to be roped in by a pair of dimples, I guess, as long as they don't *actually* get us killed.

Finally, everyone is assigned but me. Thorn's eyes light up when he sees me, that same look he gave me in the hall yesterday, and removes his hat. "Hello again," he says, and I feel my nerves crumble. He remembers me, despite my form covered in a man's shirt and a straw hat blocking most of my face.

"Hello," I manage without a stutter, but then he smiles. He has a thin gap between his two front teeth, which adds charm to his smile. He's so beautiful . . . I don't think I'll ever be able to speak correctly around him again.

"This is Victoria," says Dean, and there's something about *his* smile that is less customer-service-friendly and more harboring-a-secret-devious. "She'll be your guide."

"Queen Victoria," Thorn greets me, and my heart swells. He takes my hand and I feel it twitch like it's never been touched before as he kisses it. His hand is calloused and scarred like mine—I never expected someone so rich to be doing his own mining. He gives me that charming smile again, and I drop my gaze, forcing my breath even. I feel stupid. He's going to get us killed, I shouldn't care what he looks like. This is stupid. *He's* stupid. "How can we fail with the sovereign of England on our side?"

The queenly reference is charming even if it doesn't fit right on someone of my station.

"Y-you're very kind, s-sir," I murmur. I'm here to make Dean look good, and so far I'm doing horribly.

"Queen?" Thorn's friend scoffs. He surveys me, hat to toes. Just like Thorn, he wears the same expression as yesterday. "This satanic little mouse?"

"Be nice, Badger," says Thorn. "Or she might leave you to die in the jungle." He winks at me and squeezes my hand with both of his, and suddenly I realize he has yet to let go from kissing it. "My God, *please* leave him to die in the jungle."

The man named Badger rolls his eyes. "Such an idiot," he mutters, adjusting his pack over his shoulder as he walks away.

"Don't even make it look like an accident, just let the monsters have him," Thorn says, louder so his colleague will hear. His grin falters as he gives me a sheepish look. "I apologize for him, my dear."

"I'm used to it," I say. I don't understand why he apologized, and my hand feels sweaty now from how long he's been holding it, but it feels rude to pull away.

As if hearing my thought, he looks down at our hands and lets go abruptly. Wipes his hands on his pants. I'd wipe me off, too. "Doesn't make it right. Or nice, for that matter. We're all God's creatures, after all."

"In fairness to Mr. Badger, sir, I don't think blood science was ever in God's plan."

Thorn gives me a curious look, one with a disturbed enough edge that I think I'd better keep my mouth shut for the rest of the trip.

I hesitate, feeling helplessly stupid, before simply getting on with my job. I kneel on one knee to attach straps to Thorn's boots so they rest tight enough against his calf not to let any critters inside. Then I attach a small metal thurible to his belt and light the incense.

"What's that for?" Thorn asks.

"To deter venomous insects." My words actually worked that time. Maybe because it was related to my job . . . and because I wasn't looking at him.

"How does that work, exactly?" He wiggles his nose like a rabbit, cringing, and it's the sweetest thing I've ever seen. "Never mind, I smell it."

A man in Thorn's party coughs while vehemently protesting the smoke, and when I glance down the line, the woman I'd met earlier is holding her nose and waving the smell away with her fan. Does it really smell that bad? Maybe I'm just used to it.

I hesitate. "Would you excuse me a moment?" I rush off to catch up with Dean before he bangs the big gong in the square. "Dean."

He sighs heavily, as if this is the two-hundredth time I've spoken to him today instead of the second. "Do you annoy all your tour leaders this badly?"

"Why did you put me with the client?"

"Well, my science is 'pathetic,' and you are omnipotent." We've made it to the gong, and he finally looks at me. "Isn't that what you told the boss when you were weaseling your way into my mission?"

"So this is payback, is that what you're saying?"

"Why would giving you one-on-one time with the man you have to impress be payback?" He picks up the mossy gong mallet. "I'm giving you an opportunity to redeem yourself in the boss's eyes. Make good on your lofty claims."

"You sure it has nothing to do with the fact that he's probably going to talk to me the entire trip?"

The slightest upturn of amusement tugs at Dean's lips. "Will he?"

We both turn at the sound of arguing. I'm not positive, but it looks like the man who was complaining about the smoke is doing most of the yelling.

Dean murmurs a swear, replacing the mallet. "We can't let the boss see that."

We, he says, as if he hadn't just been acting like I was some sort of imposition. As if we're in this together. I suppose we are, but if he can't put out this small fire before the tour has even begun, he has no business leading, anyway.

Still, we rush over to the scene, where Thorn seems to be trying to reason with the man. Dean joins him, while I go stand beside the other Wildbloods.

Samson grins and leans closer so I can hear him over the yelling. "You've got a little friend on your hat."

I push his face away, eyeing him with good-natured suspicion. "Don't you dare."

"I'm not going to flick your hat in the dirt again." He chuckles. "My black eye is finally gone from the last time."

"Serves you right, dirtying my hat."

"Serves me right, sneaking up on you. Next time I do it head-on." He stands next to me and hangs an arm around my shoulders. "No, I mean you literally have a Lady sunbathing on your hat."

At the mention, Bunny bounds to my side. "Not again," he fusses. "Is it the same one from yesterday?"

"Oh." I can feel myself beaming. "You were serious about the 'little friend' part."

"Would I lie to you? Bunny, leave it," Samson says, as Bunny approaches me with a stick. "We're protected by the incense. Let it be."

Meanwhile, the great thurible debate doesn't seem to be concluding—the man has removed it from his belt and dumped the incense on the ground, stomping it out. We're wasting valuable minutes. The more time we spend here, the less daylight we have to travel under. Dean should tell the man he either wears it or stays back, that he can't step foot onto the jungle road without it.

Which gives me a bit of an idea.

"Samson," I whisper, "go tell them about the butterfly. Seeing one might help sway him."

"Tell them yourself, tour leader," Samson replies, and I can tell he's smiling even if my hat is blocking my view.

I take a deep breath. Some days I hate his confidence in me to function properly.

I remove my hat, allowing the Lady to crawl onto my finger as I step up beside Thorn.

The man stops yelling abruptly—he seems a bit confused by my presence. I don't look at Dean, but if I know him—and I do, sadly—he's pissed.

But a leader handles situations, and if the boss finds out we've yet to leave because Dean lacks the capacity to problem solve, there goes my promotion.

"Do you see this butterfly, sir?" I ask, holding my hand up to show him.

"It's called a Bloody Lady," Dean cuts in. He glances at me, his expression a mix of gratefulness and annoyance, then looks back down at my hand balancing one of the most dangerous weapons this side of the West Indies. "One bite will swell up every pathway in your body until you can no longer breathe and your blood stops flowing." He looks at the man again. "The smoke and smell from the incense are the only things that will deter it, or any other venomous creature in the jungle, from biting you."

"A *butterfly?*" The man lets out a bark of a laugh. "If you were trying to scare me you should've used a snake."

What's scary about a snake?

He throws the thurible, and I instinctively lift my hat to block it, the Lady fluttering from my finger. I gape as Thorn steps in front of me, huddling close, taking the impact of the little metal censer on his back. I grip my hat in my hands—the only thing separating his strong body from mine.

"Have you lost your mind?" Thorn demands, over his shoulder, before turning back to me. "Victoria," he says, his voice quieter but no less intense. "Are you alright?"

I am, physically—nothing hit me. But I feel awed, and I'm sure my face isn't hiding it. This handsome stranger . . . stepped in the way. *Protected* me. Why would he do that? Doesn't he know Wildbloods are the scum of the earth?

Still my heart is racing, drawing up a blush that burns my cheeks.

Unless I'm being stupid, and it's just the sun.

I put my hat on and step away from him. "I'm fine, sir, thank you—"

The man who threw the thurible suddenly yelps and grabs

his neck, then throws something on the ground. I gasp, almost choke. My Lady lies crumpled at his feet. Her wings twitch. Why did she do that? There's enough smoke around that it should've deterred her. And Bloody Ladies don't bite unless they're provoked.

The man clears his throat. Clutches it. Gasps.

He was without incense for less than a minute and is already suffering the consequences.

Thorn's party is in chaos. They crowd him, coach him to breathe, call for medical attention, ask for antivenom. There is no antivenom. Nothing on earth could ever reverse the swelling fast enough to save him. His face goes from red to purple, eyes bulging, blood vessels bursting into crimson tears. He's dying.

And I can't find it in myself to feel sorry.

But that beautiful creature, who did nothing to anyone but live . . . this land is still hers, even if men have cleared the trees away. I take deep breaths, pushing down the pain. Bunny's hand slides into mine and I grip it.

You can't break down, V. Not over a butterfly.

But she's more than just a butterfly. With all this smoke around, she should've been docile. Flown away from us, not toward. She had . . . no, it sounds crazy when I put words to it. But I swear, she went after the man *on purpose*. He threw that thurible at me, tried to hurt me, and she avenged me.

Just a butterfly.

The man is dead, but I'm so used to death that I barely process it as a sad event. Mourning takes emotional energy, energy that can't be wasted on annoying jerks I barely met a few minutes ago. I used to cringe at the cruelty of my own thoughts, but they've become so necessary for my survival that I think nothing of them now.

The only thing I'm worried about is how a casualty before we've even left headquarters will affect Thorn's overall report.

A few Wildbloods carry the body away, followed by another member of Thorn's party to look after the dead—two less tourists to worry about wrangling in the jungle. Thorn's party is still a bit shaken up. Shaken up, uncomfortable, but not mourning. Not really, anyway. Sorry, but no crying, as if it's an unfortunate thing but no one knew him anyway. All except Mrs. Badger, who has buried her face in her husband's chest as he holds her. She shouldn't be here. None of them should, but her especially. A literal tourist about to step into a death trap.

I catch Thorn's eye and he gives me a reassuring smile.

"Well," he says, with a bit of a shrug, "I suppose that's what happens when you hire an explosives expert who just finished ten years in prison for armed robbery and arson."

I blink at him. "That is . . . a joke, I hope."

Dean manages to not look entirely annoyed as he orders, "Everyone keep their thurible on," before storming over to the gong. I rush to scoop up the crushed butterfly in my hands and take her to the tree line. I only have time to reach in and place her in the brush before the gong's metal vibrates the air.

A simple mercy.

Time to go.

CHAPTER 5

The jungle road is made of ugly concrete, maybe twenty feet in width to accommodate the space if wagons or carriages ever need to pass each other. A great convenience, the boss always says, that the clients can take in the beauty of the jungle without the danger of being too close to the trees. Convenience, he calls it. I call it a shame, and sad. That so many trees needed to be cleared so some dumb tourists don't have to walk like the rest of us . . .

But the jungle doesn't need me to fight its battles—the River Mumma, in all her grace and wisdom, is petty enough for the both of us. Over the years, the roots of the trees bordering the road have gradually crept underneath the concrete to reach the soil, lifting and cracking it in parts, mostly along the edge but often extending far toward the middle. I've seen plenty of broken wagon wheels due to those raised cracks, and even more complaints of an uncomfortable carriage ride.

You killed my friends for this ugly thing? the jungle seems to say. *Good luck using it.*

Thankfully, Thorn's team at least knew enough not to bother bringing anything with wheels. The ten reliable Wild-bloods walk closer to the outside, taking turns sprinkling salt along the edge of the road from the giant satchels at our hips. We need more than usual. Last night's rain has washed the previous tour's salt away. Dean stays in the center with our clients, pretending to know where he's going. To be fair, he does know the road well enough. We all do. Most of us have traveled it hundreds of times, maybe more.

But I doubt Dean knows where to go once we turn from the road and enter the trees, and I'm not sure how to help, how to make it look like my suggestions are due to Dean's "stellar leadership skills" . . . especially since Thorn is walking right next to me instead of in the center of the road with the rest of his party.

It's adorable, in an extremely anxiety-inducing way.

"Salt, right?" Thorn asks, pointing to my satchel.

I rub my white, parched fingers through the pebble-sized crystals. "Yes, sir."

"Thorn is fine. What's it for?"

"To keep the duppies away."

"Duppies?" His expression looks skeptical, as if that can't possibly be a word. "And those are?"

"Um . . . ghosts, I guess you would call them."

"Ha!" His eyes sparkle. "I wonder if American ghosts hate salt, too. It would've made that haunted mine we found a year ago so much easier to navigate. Hey, Badger!" he calls, and I wince at his volume. "They use salt to keep ghosts away!"

"I don't care," his companion calls back without even looking his way.

Thorn chuckles. He pulls out a compass. I don't know why, since he isn't the one navigating. "So, Victoria, how long have you been with the company?"

"You don't seem to like each other," I say instead of answering. He doesn't really want the truth, and no one's ever asked me before, so I've had no time to think of a convincing lie.

"Friendly rivalry, that's all. Nothing to worry about."

"That's *friendly?*"

"On my end." He raises an eyebrow, summoning me with a sly finger—and I don't know why, but I feel myself hanging on his words as he lowers his voice and says, "Let me tell you one of the secrets of life, Victoria: the person in the rivalry who seems the most bitter is usually the one who's losing."

I feel myself grin, which seems to please him, because his smile lights up my soul.

"The salt is delightful," he says. "Look, watch this." He looks over at the group again. "Madelyn! The *salt!*"

"They need to salt some fish while they're at it." She laughs. "These ghosts are out here eating better than me!"

Thorn laughs heartily, and even I can't help grinning. He has the sort of laugh that could sway the command of kings. "See?" he says. "Badger's just salty." He winks. "Get it? *Salty?*"

"U-um . . ." I shrug, feeling a little sheepish. I don't know that I see it as funny but smile for his sake.

He's going to do this the whole trip, isn't he? Part of me hates it. The other part will do anything to see that beautiful smile, even if I have to sit through a hundred jokes I don't quite get.

That part of me might be an idiot.

"Tell me, Victoria," Thorn says, with barely a pause, "do you enjoy your work?"

I hesitate. "I like being in the jungle."

"We have that in common—well, the woods. This is my first time visiting the tropics."

What part of his comment should I ask about? Will he think I'm impolite if I don't ask anything at all?

I settle on "Do you like it here?" just as he asks, "So, why do you do this if you don't like it?"

He chuckles. "Apologies, I don't know when to shut up. You were saying?"

"Um . . ." I don't want to answer his question. I was taken when I was six and forced to work or die. The jungle is the only place where I can escape the threat of abuse. It's the only place where I feel safe, as crazy as that sounds. But I have to make a good impression, if only for the sake of my promotion, and none of those answers will achieve my goal.

I shake my head. I can feel myself blushing—and I know for sure I am, because Thorn gives me a reassuring smile.

"I hope you don't feel like I'm pressuring you," he says. "But we're going to be on the road for quite some time, and it might pass easier with conversation."

I look down at my salt. "You may want to pick a different conversation partner. I'm not very . . . good at this sort of thing."

"Nonsense. You're perfectly charming."

I tip my hat lower to make sure the shade hides my blushing, which is becoming uncomfortably warm mingled with the heat of the day.

"Perhaps we just haven't found your subject." He looks up at the jungle's canopy for a moment, the branches of the trees on each side reaching out to each other across the road, shading while also providing pockets of light. "Tell me about your magic. I'm sure you could talk for hours about that."

If you count every time I've been asked about it on every trip for over a decade, I'm sure I *have* talked for hours about it. "It's not magic. It's biological."

"Uh-oh, what's the punishment for offending a queen?" Thorn's teasing grin turns into a smile of enthusiasm. "I think we've found your subject."

I look out into the jungle, heat climbing up my neck. How is it possible for someone to be equally entrancing *and* annoying?

Or is it only annoying because his beauty and spirit make me nervous, and I *know* my words won't cooperate if I'm forced to string more than five together?

"Biological how?" he prompts.

"I-it's—" I swallow. Pretend to pay attention to my surroundings so I can avoid his kind, genuinely interested expression unraveling my nerves. "Samson is better at explaining it."

"You're doing beautifully," he says, and the sweetness in his smile and encouragement in his voice makes my stomach flutter.

"Um, it's . . . it's energy that comes from . . . um, life. In the blood."

"Then what powers the human body also powers your—" He pauses. "What would you call that?"

"Hematothermy." Except no one calls it that. Physicians, maybe. But there's too much of a stigma surrounding us for anyone else to use a respectable, scientific name. To everyone else, we're witches. Demons. As if biology has nothing to do with it. I shrug off the thought. "Blood science."

"I am in the presence of a woman of science," Thorn says. "I have to say, I'm awed and honored."

I almost choke on my next breath. Awed and honored? To meet *me*? He couldn't mean that, and yet his tone sounds perfectly genuine, nothing sinister creeping underneath like the way Dean always sounds when I know he's up to something.

We continue forward in silence. Even from the corner of my eye I can tell he's looking at me. "So, what do you do with it?"

"With our science?"

"Yes."

"Shape it into things. Weapons."

"Wait a second—you shape *blood* into weapons? How do you . . . I suppose this is a stupid question, but how do you get the blood out?" He chews on his lip, then answers for me, "Not cut yourself?"

"Usually. But we can use animal blood, or . . ." I look in Dean's direction and imagine stabbing him, then using every ounce of blood in his body to form a giant blade to stab him again. "The blood of our enemies."

"What if you need something other than a weapon? Like a spoon?"

"Well, we only use it in emergencies. In case of danger. So . . . I don't know. You can use your hands or a leaf in that case."

I venture to look at him. He has a silly grin on his face that makes my heart skip. I swallow down my churning nerves. I've never felt this way before, I've never had a reason to, and I have no idea why I'm feeling this way now. His spirit coats my heart like warm honey. So sweet . . . so inhumanly sweet, and he's wasting it all on me.

Why is he wasting it on me?

The tiniest of flashes catches the corner of my eye. Anyone inexperienced with blood science might think it's the sun briefly bouncing off a boot buckle or knife. But I immediately look at Bunny.

My heart slams inside me uncomfortably.

"Please excuse me, sir," I say quickly.

"Oh, yes," Thorn says, his tone slightly confused but friendly. "Of course."

I hurry to the other side of the road, trying to seem casual as I lace my fingers through Bunny's. He doesn't look at me as we walk together, hand in hand.

"Please don't do that," I say.

"Do what?" he says. Still won't look at me.

I sigh. "Make me worry about you."

"You do that to yourself," he grumbles. Despite his words, his slender fingers squeeze my hand tighter. "I won't do it again until there's trouble. Just needed a little . . . courage."

"Get it from me and Samson. We're here for you, Bun."

"I know." He shakes his hand from mine, lowering his voice to say, "But don't mother me, okay? Not in front of all these tough miners. Makes me seem like a baby, and I'm fourteen, you know."

You're a baby to the jungle. You've only been here a year.

I don't say any of those things.

Instead, I look at Samson. He nods. Bunny says he won't summon his science unnecessarily and pretending to believe him is the only thing that makes him continue to confide in me. He won't do it again today, that's all I know. Not on the open road.

For now, that's good enough.

We travel for a couple hours before our pace begins visibly slowing. I don't mind. It gives me more time to enjoy the view. The zip and buzz of insect wings are like percussion to the surrounding trees. I used to fall asleep in those trees, lulled to sleep by the sounds of their music.

"My feet hurt," Madelyn whines. It's no wonder, in those heeled boots.

"Yeah, this road is terrible," one of the men agrees.

"Come on, now, spirits up!" Thorn says. "How about a song?" He starts one without waiting for a reply.

"In the merry month of June from me home I started
Left the girls of Tuam nearly brokenhearted—"

"Boo!!" shouts one of Thorn's men, and Thorn laughs instead of letting it discourage him. But maybe that's the joke and I've missed it, because two of his companions pounce on him, laughing, attempting to shut him up. But he won't, and I admire him for it—and so does Madelyn, who laughs and joins in the singing, clapping along.

"Then off to reap the corn, leave where I was born
Cut a stout blackthorn to banish ghosts and goblins.
A brand new pair of brogues, rattlin' o'er the bogs—"

When he sings a line, "'Frightenin' all the dogs ...'" he punches Badger in the shoulder playfully. I press my lips together to conceal a grin, tucking my chin. How could anyone want to mute someone so charismatic?

They don't, clearly, because by the chorus they're all singing along with him heartily:

"One two three four five!
Hunt the Hare and turn her down the rocky road
And all the way to Dublin, Whack fol lol le rah!"

They continue on that way for a while, finishing the song and starting another, then another. I'm relieved to be away from talking with Thorn, if only for a mile. But the river runs across the road up ahead, with only an old wooden footbridge to cross over, and . . . well, if we're going to run into trouble on the road it'll be there.

"Okay, everyone," Dean announces, walking backward so he can face the group. "For safety reasons, keep your arms and legs within the boundaries of the bridge. Walk quickly, and do not touch or look into the water."

That announcement always seems too short to me. It's the standard, but I've always found it to be too vague and not very helpful. The best way to get silly tourists to mess with the river is to deliberately tell them not to mess with the river. The worst part is, the boss emphasizes not telling the clients *why* they shouldn't. But if they knew an ancient river spirit with a penchant for punishing the humans who invade her jungle lived inside, maybe then they'd think twice.

As it stands, I don't have to field questions today. The river is impossibly violent, roughed up as if by a storm even though the day is calm. If the Lady was the first warning to stay out of the jungle, this is the second. The bridge is old and creaks at each step, covered in fungus and a little rot, but it's far sturdier than it looks. Thankfully, the clients don't know that and are eager to get across quickly.

All except Thorn. He pauses in the middle of the bridge to let his team go across first, to keep account of everyone. I finally look up to his face and see he's looking down into the river.

I roll my eyes. It never fails—there's always one tourist who doesn't follow directions. If I had been taking bets I would've won.

But he's too still. Entirely, terrifyingly still.

"Mr. Thorn, don't stare at the water."

I peek over the rail of the bridge and, there in the rapids, I see her. The indistinct, but very present, face of a woman looking up from the depths of the untamed river.

I step in front of Thorn right as he goes to lean over the edge, take hold of his arms, and shake him, hard. "Thorn," I say, but he won't look at me, and sudden panic rises in my throat. I take his face in my hands, try my best to block his view of the river with my body so he can look at nothing but me. "Thorn!"

His eyes focus on me and my breath catches. He blinks. "Victoria?"

I don't let go of his face, just to be sure he won't look again to the water and fall back into a trance. "We have to get off the bridge."

"Yes, of course," he says, but he still seems disoriented. I take his arm, one hand at his back, and guide him across the rest of the bridge to safer land. Dean has paused the group and is rushing toward us. "Yes, you did tell me to walk in your direction, I should pay better attention."

I try not to show alarm as I look at him. "W-what did I say to you, sir?"

But maybe I'm not hiding my emotion as well as I think, because he looks at me as if deciphering what I mean. "You said . . . 'Come to me.'"

"Mr. Thorn." Dean takes over, planting a hand firmly on his back and gesturing to his party as he escorts him forward. "Please continue this way toward the rest of your group. We still have a few miles to go before making camp . . ."

Dean lets Thorn walk a bit ahead, and when Dean looks at me it's confidential—there's thankfulness in his eyes for successfully doing my job but with such an edge of wild concern that I know I'm going to have to hear about this later.

I look back at the river, take a deep breath. That was the second warning the jungle offered. I'm sure of it.

If it has to send a third, I have a sinking feeling it'll try its hardest to make sure no one leaves the jungle alive.

CHAPTER 6

After a full day of walking and far too many rest stops, we finally make camp for the night, securing the area with a large ring of salt. Thorn's team brought tents, which most travelers do, but we won't be on the road beyond tonight. Dean should've told them tents are ridiculously impractical for the uneven floor of the jungle, especially the unnecessarily large wall tents they brought. But despite how commonsensical it seems to me, not everyone would consider that. So I keep my mouth shut.

For the record, I forgive Thorn's team the ignorance, not Dean.

As for me and my fellows, we unfold our simple cots—who needs covering with the jungle's canopy for shelter? All anyone needs is their incense, which we wear constantly anyway. And there's nowhere here to bathe, unless you're fool enough to attempt to go near the river, so lying out with no covering means you're bathed in the excessive amount of dew the jungle creates the next morning. Clean, refreshed, and dry again by midmorning.

To be honest, I'd much rather sleep in a tree than anything. But, seeing as I have to keep such a close eye on Dean and Thorn, the cot will do.

"I figured it out, V," Bunny says, grinning as he sits on his cot and crosses his bare feet underneath him.

"What?" I ask, raising a curious brow.

"What had you all riled up this morning." His grin widens as he wiggles his eyebrows at me. "It starts with a T-H-O-R—"

"Stop." I throw my backpack at him, embarrassment flaring across my face—not only because he figured it out, but because it took me so long to figure out what he was spelling. "He had nothing to do with it."

He tosses my pack back, and I put it on my cot. "You two have been joined at the hip all day. I think he only left your side a few times."

"Half the day, at most."

"That's still a long time. *Hours!*"

I glance over at Dean, who is clearly listening as he unpacks, side-eying me with the slightest frown. Dean's curiosity is never a good thing, but I can't imagine what he'd do with this foolish information. "That was all him. He doesn't stop talking."

"You like it."

"I hate talking."

"But you like to hear *Thorn* talk."

He laughs as I pretend to pummel him in the head. "Shut *up*, Bunny!"

"Victoria." Dean's voice sounds behind me, and I jolt, turning to him quickly.

"Dean," I say coolly.

He's taken off his gloves for the day, letting his hat hang on his back by its string around his neck. "Walk with me." He starts walking without waiting for a reply.

I blow out a heavy breath and follow.

"After everything that's happened today, I hope you're thinking of turning around," I say, because honestly I don't want to know what he planned on saying.

"Turning around?" He scoffs, glances at me. "Are you not having a good time, Vicky?"

"I *was*," I mutter.

"See, *that* is why the boss hasn't promoted you yet. You can't even speak up with me, let alone strangers."

I don't want to talk to you, traitor.

But I quicken my steps to walk beside him so as not to make a scene. "That's not the reason, and you know it."

"I didn't want this, believe me," he says, and I do. He sounds genuinely annoyed. He glances around to make sure no one is looking, then lowers his voice further. "We can't go back now, and you know why—you know what the boss would do to us. All we can do is speed things along and get us home as soon as possible. Which is why we need to talk about tomorrow."

So he actually *wants* my help? After giving me such a hard time about it, too.

We reach the salt barrier and I turn and lean my back against a tree quickly. "This is far enough."

"What are you afraid of?"

Something thick and sick rises up in my throat, and I can barely swallow it down. I can't believe he would ask me that, as if he doesn't remember what he did to me to earn his holier-than-thou position as protégé. I press my hands together to keep from shoving him or using my science, but I also keep my fingers straight in case.

What am I afraid of, he asks?

You. Stabbing me in the back.

"*What* about tomorrow?" I ask impatiently.

Instead of answering, he walks past me into the trees. I close my eyes for a moment. This is the last thing I want, the last thing I should be doing. I remind myself that he's not going to do anything. He can't. People saw us together. If anything happens to me, they'll know he did it. Besides, he clearly needs me for this tour to be a success. It's fine.

I don't think about it anymore, just turn and step into the trees to follow.

Even the jungle's whispers don't do much to ease my anger. If anything, they encourage it.

Why does this trespasser disrespect you, daughter? Kill him and we shall consume the remains.

"Don't tempt me," I murmur.

We walk a small distance, every foot forward setting my nerves on edge, until Dean finally stops and crouches, leaning back against a tree.

"Is this necessary?" I ask. *I hate you*, my tone says.

He knows that tone and acknowledges it with a tip of his chin. "The boss specified that no one can know," he says.

I nod reluctantly, sitting across from him in a bit of moss and leafy ground cover. My back against the tree feels warm and welcomed, and I take my courage from it—from the life inside, warmth, traveling up and down deep inside the bark like a circuit. If Dean could feel the pulse of the jungle like I can, would he dare allow this trip to continue?

Yes. He would. Appeasing the boss is all that matters to him.

"First of all," he says, "don't worry so much about the other members of Thorn's party. Thorn and Badger are the only ones who matter. How you saved Thorn today? Keep that up."

"What's the point in endangering all of these people if—?"

"That's not our concern," he says, flinging his hand carelessly. "They chose to bring along a large party, against my advice. It's unrealistic to expect everyone to make it back. All that matters is the ones paying us."

I release a heavy sigh, biting my lip against a sharp remark.

"We break the tree line tomorrow," he continues. "What are your thoughts?"

I lay my hand in the dark green moss, burying my fingers in its soft dampness. It's cool. Comforting, compared to the rest of this situation. "In general, the spirits mean us no harm if we leave them alone. So unless we're attacked first, we should just give them space and not engage."

"Simple enough. Anything else?"

I nod. "We should walk in single file, to disturb the jungle as little as possible."

"Two lines," he says, drawing them in the air with his pointer and middle finger. "I lead one, you the other. It'll be easier to keep track of everyone. We've already had one casualty, and I don't trust these reckless Americans not to do anything else stupid."

"Well, we shouldn't expect anything too dangerous tomorrow—most of the bigger threats tend to steer clear of the road."

"What about twelve miles in? We have to cover at least that much."

I chew on my lip. "That's ambitious for this group; we only hit ten miles on level terrain today."

"We don't have much of a choice, unless we want to spend a month in here. Day one has already been a mess, and the more days we can shave off the trip, the easier it'll be to keep things under control."

I don't point out that he keeps saying "we," that he's given up on antagonizing me. As much as I hate the idea of it, we need to work together in this. "We'll have even less control once we breach the tree line."

Dean's jaw shifts as he chews on his cheek. He looks genuinely pensive. "I can already tell these clients are going to be prima donnas once we enter the trees."

"They're not the worst we've seen," I say with a shrug.

He raises his eyebrows as if I must be joking. "Throwing thuribles?"

"Not quite that, no. Smoking—" I look up at him, fighting the urge to smile, because we said the word at the same time.

Dean smirks. "Remember that—what was he?"

I kiss my teeth, roll my eyes. "A 'banker,' he *insisted*."

"Swindler."

"Remember he stole coins from the other travelers and then acted—"

"—like they were from his own pocket, to tip us." Dean laughs. "Like we hadn't just watched him nick it off someone else."

"And he put the incense stick in his mouth like a cigarette."

"'Why's smoke coming out the back end,'" he says in a

stunningly accurate London accent, "'if I ain't supposed to smoke it?'"

I find myself laughing without thinking. For a moment, Dean looks different . . . how he used to, when the two of us were alone, away from the boss's cruel scrutiny. When we could finally relax and not be rivals, pitted against each other for something neither of us truly wanted. It was the only time I'd see a smile brighten his face, in the few hours before bed, finding new ways to make each other laugh. And then sweet sleep would finally arrive, and I'd hold his hand like I do Bunny's.

We did it, he'd say.

We survived, he meant.

But now our laughter drifts off, and with it the memories. And I feel a creeping resentment fighting its way back toward hate.

Back to the present.

"Wish we could go back to being that way," he says, watching a forty-leg minding his business as he crawls across the ground between us.

I watch him too, the long, cylindrical arthropod with antennae like mini creatures themselves. There's the slightest shadow of red blood sloshing around inside his exoskeleton. Normal forty-legs don't have red blood like we do, but this parasitic one can function on anything. His bite is painful, and the venom he injects to keep his victim's blood from clotting makes for a slow recovery. He takes what doesn't belong to him to use for himself, leaving behind an open wound. Remorseless.

The steady rhythm of his alternating legs is the only thing keeping me from screaming.

"I never want to go back," I murmur.

From the corner of my eye, I see Dean look at me, as if sensing the shift, too. When I fully look at him, his brows are lowered, but it's not quite a glare. Maybe he can't pull himself from the memories as easily as I can, and why should he? Lingering in them holds no horror for him.

Which only reminds me that I shouldn't be here when he comes to—we hate each other enough that being alone together too long might result in something neither of us can control.

His death, ideally.

Before I can stand there's a sickening crunch, and I look down to see the thick, red fluid of the poor forty-leg rise up from his shell, which has been cracked all the way down the center. Dean's hand dances slowly and small crackles of light follow, manipulating the blood into a liquid sphere, a cylinder . . . a long needle.

His eyes burn bloodred. He drops his wrist like bouncing a ball, and the needle stabs into the empty shell, pinning it to the dirt.

Tearing liquid through a thin exoskeleton isn't an advanced skill for a Wildblood, especially because insects don't have veins or bones or layers of skin to get through.

But we both know that's not the point.

"Back to work, then," he says, his eyes shifting back to a cold stone gray. He shoves to his feet and walks back to camp, leaving his bloody weapon to splatter on the ground, bathing its lifeless victim.

Dean used to cry a lot. We were children, after all, and being punched in the face or smacked with a horsewhip or screamed at over nothing would make even a grown person cry. Not me, not anymore, but . . . someone who hadn't grown up with it. Badger, probably.

But Dean would cry over small things, too. A disappointed tone, or in anticipation of punishment before he'd even failed the task given to him. There was a span of a few months, after the boss started boxing with him, when he'd cry when the man simply entered the room, even if it was only to grab a piece of paper.

I should've known something was wrong the day Dean stopped crying.

We were sixteen. He'd just finished a boxing session. His nose was bleeding, and he was bruised up, tears streaming down his cheeks.

"You're not bleeding as much as usual," I said, bandages ready like every time he boxed.

"I'm sick of him beating me," he said.

"You're getting better."

He sniffled. "Not good enough."

I paused then, I remember. His tone seemed off to me. "He used to get paid for this. I don't think he expects you to win."

"You would say that," he grumbled. "Little Miss Favorite."

"I do as he says, when he says," I said, a bite of annoyance in my voice. "If that makes me the favorite, so be it."

"You're good at everything he asks of you."

"I observe, I listen, I keep my head down. Besides, I'm not good at *everything* . . ." *I'm just better than you are.* I didn't say that of course. It was petty and pointless. Dean was my only competition. I was good at things through practice, but I didn't *have* to be good, so long as I performed better than him. "And, anyway, if he ever challenged me to a fistfight I wouldn't be able to beat him, either. So don't drag me into it."

Dean sighed. "Sorry, V."

"What's really bothering you?"

"As long as I keep losing, I'm no use to him. I'm no use to anyone." Dean dabbed his nose with the back of his hand and stared at the blood there. "I just . . . I want to do something right for once."

He usually sat, let me bandage him, then laid down and cried until he fell asleep. But that day he only stood there. For about a minute he stood, rubbing his eyes, getting rid of any sign of tears as they forced their way out. Finally, he looked at me, his gray eyes wild like he wanted to kill something. And stormed out of the room.

"Dean," I said, as I caught up, "don't do anything stupid."

"I'm going to do something right for once."

Since when was challenging the boss the right thing for anyone?

"He'll be tired," I protested. "He might be sleeping and angry that you're bothering him. He'll beat you *for real* for that."

But the boss wasn't sleeping. Even worse. He was at his desk, working. He was still sweating from the fight, and the undershirt he wore was speckled with blood.

He looked at us like we'd stepped on sacred ground. "You'd better have a good reason for disturbing me."

"I'm not done with you," Dean said.

The boss planted his hands on his desk and rose to his feet. I could feel myself trembling even though I wasn't the one who'd made the threat. "You . . . what?" he asked, in his calm tone that makes my skin crawl.

"You heard me."

"I don't think I did." He stepped around the desk, approaching Dean. "You want to say it again to my face—?"

Instead of repeating himself, Dean punched the boss square in the jaw, making him stumble back.

The boss gaped up at Dean, paying no mind to the blood running out of his nose to his chin. He let out a single laugh, shook his head. "Now that's how you throw a punch, boy," he praised.

I should've enjoyed seeing the boss get decked—after everything he'd ever done to us, a bloody nose was the bare minimum he deserved. But for him, it wasn't a punishment. Dean and I had been pitted against each other since we were six, and this was just another of his tests. A test that Dean had just passed with flying colors. One I could never best him at, even if I'd wanted to.

And, for that reason, the satisfied grin that slipped onto Dean's lips made me sick to my stomach.

CHAPTER 7

When I arrive back in camp, it looks like a small settlement. Thorn's team is working on putting up a fourth wall tent, with a fifth waiting to be assembled. I head to the cots, where Bunny is already dozing and Samson is sitting, sharpening his broad-bladed cutlass with a stone.

He's angry. He sharpened all these blades yesterday. But it's busywork, and he can imagine killing someone as he occupies his hands. As I insisted, years ago, killing someone in his imagination is all I'll allow him to indulge in.

Killing someone outside his imagination will only get him executed. I could never bear to live with that.

"You went off with Dean, alone?" Samson asks, slightly vexed.

I shrug, playing off the fact that my heartbeat has only just started to climb down to a normal level. "I didn't want to make a scene."

"Are you alright?"

I shush him and look around—thankfully the area is clear.

"We have to make a good impression for the client. You can't . . . *imply* things in public like that."

"All the more reason for you to not go off alone with him. I mean it. Stay where I can see you."

"I hate when you get overbearing. I'm eighteen now, you know."

"*I* hate when you put yourself in dangerous situations," he says, sheathing his knife. He stands, holding my upper arms gently. "Anyway, you shouldn't have told me how he threw you to the lions if you didn't want me to worry about you."

"Sammy."

"It's that simple."

"Well, for the sake of securing my promotion, I'm asking you to *please* make sure the client thinks he's a saint." I smirk and wrap my arms around his waist. "Besides, he's my nemesis. Get your own."

"Aren't you two sweet," Thorn says—I only know his voice because he's been talking nonstop for hours—and I spin to look at him and accidently bump into Samson, who wraps his arm around my shoulders like a warm cloak.

Sweet? Normally I'd fall asleep in his arms, but today I squirm out as quickly as possible. Thorn will think we're a couple now. I don't want that. I don't want to give him a reason to think it's inappropriate to talk to me.

"Oh, apologies," Thorn says, holding up his hands briefly in surrender, as Badger looks on, brooding beside him. "I didn't mean to startle you. Only, we need firewood, and I wasn't sure if I was allowed to ask anyone who wasn't assigned to me."

"Firewood?" Dean should've told him it's better to bring dried food that doesn't require cooking. But he let him have eleven Wildbloods. And he allowed him to think going into the jungle in the first place was possible. At this point, I shouldn't be surprised.

"Victoria would love to go," Bunny says, popping up on his cot. I glare down at him. Trust him to be sleeping when there's work to be done and faking it when I need him to keep his mouth shut. "She knows how to find firewood better than anyone."

"Excellent," says Thorn. He holds out an escorting arm toward the side of the road. "Shall we?"

"Take someone else with you," Dean says, and I raise my eyebrows at his uncharacteristically pleasant tone as he approaches us. "You shouldn't spend more than twenty minutes in the jungle away from the group, and an extra set of hands should help speed things along."

I don't think I can raise my brows any higher. Twenty minutes? He pulled that number from his ass. The jungle doesn't keep a schedule of when it will or won't kill you.

But we'll probably only need that long anyway, if Thorn and Badger are efficient at chopping. Bunny was right in saying I'm the best at finding firewood. To be fair, I'm the *only* one who knows, since regular trips where the road is taken the whole way through usually involve a supply car with wood brought along.

"Good man, Spitz," says Thorn, and slaps him on the back.

Dean winces at the impact of Thorn's hand, and his discomfort brings me indescribable joy. I shouldn't be so vicious, but I don't care. He deserves to feel helpless, if only for a moment.

But viciousness begets viciousness and, as if sensing my pleasure at his pain, Dean looks at me. His gray eyes demand obedience, yearn for the vengeance against my silent laughter he can never get away with reaping in front of Thorn.

"Be safe," he says, his voice low, calculating . . . sinister. Or maybe it only sounds that way because I know him so well. He steps closer to me, and my stomach lurches as his strong hand holds the back of my neck, my muscles stiffening painfully as his lips press against mine.

My science flares in my stomach, and I close my eyes so it won't show. But I don't fight back, don't shove him off, don't move, even though my body is practically vibrating with a rabid desire to get away. I can't give Thorn any reason to bring the boss a poor report. Bunny's life depends on it.

But I don't want to settle into, let alone open my mind to consider, the familiarity of his lips. The same lips that used to comfort me after the boss's punishments, that made me feel there was something right in the world, now being used as a weapon of manipulation. I hate that I remember his lips so well. I hate that he's simultaneously conjuring memories and destroying their beauty, turning them into something warped and wrong.

He had kissed me that night, too—the night he betrayed me. With those lips that made my soul want to follow him anywhere. That healed every hurt inflicted by the boss.

The kiss that night was a manipulation, too. A trick to make me follow him without question.

Backstabber.

His lips release mine, and I gasp, as if he's sucked life from me. His lips still invade my space as they shift to my ear to whisper, "Did you really think I'd let you have him?"

My heart pounds. He's punishing me. *In front* of people, no less, for not accepting his olive branch earlier . . . for not forgiving him and forgetting the past.

For not submitting.

I hate you, I want to say.

Instead, I let my science burn away the tears at the backs of my eyes before pressing it down and opening them.

I glance at Bunny, who's gone back to dozing, which I'm glad of. I *don't* look at Samson, and simply pray he didn't see what happened. Except, even though I told him not to make a scene, maybe this time I wouldn't have minded. Because this time I wouldn't have had to witness the look on Thorn's face— shocked, disturbed, disappointed, all within a second before he turns away.

But I can't contradict my tour leader in front of a client, no matter how much I hate him.

Dean's thumb presses subtly against my throat, right below my jaw, with just enough pressure to hurt without bruising, and I don't know if I'm feeling my elevated pulse or his. "Don't do anything stupid."

He releases me with a smile, leaving me to go check on the rest of Thorn's party.

I want to cry. Scream. Worst of all, my stomach burns with rage, and I can't do anything about it.

Dean's become more like the boss in the past year than I realized. I'll have to be more careful.

"Ready?" Thorn's voice knocks me from my loathing. When I look over, Samson is standing with him, gripping his cutlass. It's for the firewood, but from the way he looks at me, he's currently thinking of cutting something else with it.

Today I want to let him.

But life hasn't cared about what I've been going through since I was six years old, and it moves on, Thorn and Badger making their way to the tree line. We've nearly breached it when Madelyn rushes over to us with small, quick steps. "Where are you going?" she asks.

"Firewood," says Thorn. "We'll be back soon—"

"Oh no no no, sir, I have been holding my urine for hours."

"Ask your guide to take you."

"A *man* other than my *husband?*" She hooks her arm with mine, grinning at me. "You don't mind, do you?"

"Um . . ." I look at Thorn, a bit sheepishly. "Maybe we can all go together."

"Great." She tugs me along impatiently. "Shall we?"

"So, I can come?" Thorn says, raising an eyebrow. "I don't count as 'a man other than your husband'?"

"Of course not, my dear. Your name is Laertes. There's no danger there."

"He killed Hamlet."

"Hamlet killed *him.*"

"He was also an Argonaut."

Madelyn gives him a teasing look of mock pity. "It's too bourgeois to incite fear, sweetie. Just accept it."

Badger silently rolls his eyes.

"Don't waste your salt," I say to Samson, as they continue to argue good-naturedly. "We'll walk in single file."

"You're the leader," he says.

It feels real when he says it. Official. I almost laugh.

I clear my throat, trying my best to capture a pause in their conversation. "We should go before it starts to get dark."

We probably won't have to go far to find appropriate wood—with so much hard rain the soil tends to soften and run off, and with nothing to grip their roots to the thinner trees usually fall over.

I lead the way, spreading salt in my path to walk on. "River Mumma," I whisper, "I need firewood, please." My soul pulls me west, and I follow its lead.

"How far do we have to go?" Madelyn asks impatiently—can't say I blame her if she's been holding her urine literally all day. "There are plenty of trees here to chop up."

"We can't use standing trees," I say.

I *don't* say that you should only ever injure a standing tree if you want the jungle to eat you alive.

I trip to a halt, wincing at the explosive *bang* of a gun. My heart sprints in my temple, the shot echoing back to us as the jungle voices its displeasure in squawks and rustling of leaves as creatures retreat, mixed with a swell of angry energy down the trees and through the ground.

"You big oaf!" I turn in time to see Madelyn hit the side of her fist against Badger's chest. "Are you trying to make me wet myself?"

"What was it?" Thorn asks.

Badger looks a little red-faced. "Something moved in the trees."

"You know what *won't* move?" Madelyn says, snatching the rifle from her husband. "You, after I kill you for making me ruin my pants." She clicks the safety in place and pulls out the magazine, dumping out the bullets before shoving it back at her husband. "I mean, honestly! Why do I let you handle weapons?"

"This place feels cursed," he mutters.

"It's just up this way," I say quickly, continuing forward.

As promised, we come to the edge of a small gully with a tree lying at an angle to the muddy bottom, its top half being held up by the branches of its fellow trees, its roots still halfway in the ground on one side.

Thorn whistles. "You led us here like you knew exactly where this tree would be."

"She did," says Samson, and slides down the muddy edge without having to be told.

Thorn looks at me. "Thank you, Victoria."

I feel myself blushing, but don't have time to find words I know won't malfunction on me before Madelyn is dragging me away.

Urinating is more annoying than getting rid of duppies. I light my flint to purify a small spot of shrubbery and make sure it's safe to squat, then sprinkle salt around the area.

I turn my back, giving Madelyn a little space to do her business. For the first time since we left headquarters, I can pretend I'm alone. I can pretend the fresh scent of wet leaves that offer me their blessed shade is all that matters.

I touch a nearby tree, smiling as the warmth rolls under my hand like a cat's purr. *Welcome home.* I feel the whisper in my soul. *We've missed you, daughter.*

I close my eyes to better soak it in. *I've missed you, too.*

But like a swarm of bees identifying an intruder, I feel the warmth in the tree turn hot and needlelike as it races down the trunk into the roots beneath the earth, beneath my feet, leaping in the direction of Madelyn like a sudden violent hiss.

"Leave her," I whisper quickly.

"Did you say something?" Madelyn's voice sounds from behind me.

I swallow; thankfully the vengeful energy retreats as quickly as it lashed out. "No, ma'am."

We've already been warned twice about leaving, first the Bloody Lady, then the raging river. I think . . . no. I *know* I have to say something to Thorn before the third warning comes. Tonight, without Dean around. Thorn has seemed receptive to everything I've had to say so far. He'll listen to reason, even if Dean can't.

Because if it goes past the point of a third warning, we're dead. "I meant to say this earlier," Madelyn goes on, blithely unaware of my mental crisis. "That Dean is a handsome one, don't you think?"

I retch a little, unable to contain the reflex. "You think so, ma'am?" I say quickly, hoping it covers up my initial show of disgust.

I used to think Dean was the most beautiful thing I'd ever seen. That's part of what makes me so sick about it now. To me, people with mucked-up souls can never be anything other than ugly, no matter what they look like on the outside.

Maybe my cover-up is convincing, because she adds, "Well, maybe not for me. But you two would make a lovely couple."

Would make. So she hadn't seen the kiss. This time I'm ready for her response, and say evenly, my relief only coming through a little bit, "He's my superior, Mrs. Badger, so I don't think so."

"Ah, yes. What a shame."

Blessed silence.

"I apologize for Thorn," she says. I hear fabric rustling as she messes with her ruched trousers. "He seems to be laying it on thick with you."

I take a deep breath, blowing it out slowly, rub the calluses on the pads of one hand with my thumb. The silence was nice while it lasted. "Laying it on thick?"

"The charm." She chuckles. "He's usually not so blatant about the flirting. I suppose he feels there are less restrictions in the wilderness."

I turn in time to see her step out of the salt ring, unconcerned. But not on the side where we'd already stepped, not on the side I'd already sprinkled salt. Does she not understand she's in the jungle now? The disregard—the pure disrespect of her surroundings—annoys me.

You don't have to respect me. But, Lord have mercy, respect the jungle where it can see you.

"You are pretty," she continues, fanning away mosquitos, unaware of the danger she's potentially put herself in as she adjusts her bloomers. "I'll give him that. He could certainly clean you up and pass you off as one of us. You may be light-skinned, but you're still working class. He knows your station is beneath him. I just don't want you to get your hopes up."

Hopes up for what? If she had mentioned my status as a Wildblood, her words would've been true. But I make an honest living while Thorn takes gold that doesn't belong to him, and *that* is the reason I am beneath him?

I don't bother with a response. Her words don't affect me. I've heard far worse. But I can't argue—I *am* beneath Thorn, if only because he's my one hope of getting my promotion. I am at his mercy until the end of the trip. And if he wants to talk my brain to mush, I'll let him do it. That doesn't mean we're doing anything wrong or indecent.

Besides—and I hate to admit that Bunny is right, but—I'm enjoying his attention.

There's no sense in standing here since Madelyn is finished, so I turn and head back to the gully, with Madelyn tight on my tail.

"I'm only telling you," she says—Lord have mercy, she talks as much as Thorn—"because every time Thorn leads an expedition, he finds some unsuspecting girl for a fling. You seem like a nice girl, which is why I'm warning you. I discouraged him before he invited you to go wood-chopping, but it all went in one ear and out the other, it seems. So it would behoove you to decline him a few times until he gets the point."

I raise an eyebrow, looking over my shoulder at her. "Be . . . hoove me?"

"Do you understand what that means?" she asks.

"I'm here to serve the client," I say simply. "He can do whatever he likes."

"He cannot do *whatever* he likes, dear girl." She charges ahead to get in front of me, tripping over the uneven ground, and I do her the favor of catching her. She wobbles as I steady her and fixes her hair. "Believe it or not, I'm trying to help you. He needs to understand what he's doing is wrong before he initiates something that may ruin you or himself. Besides, don't you have a beau? This isn't fair to him, either."

My gut tightens in an uncomfortable way. "He's a sweet man."

"I love him to death as a friend, but would I ever let a girl I know consider him as a real prospect? He's an absolute scoundrel.

A libertine. But he's handsome and wealthy, so he can get away with a wild week of sex in the jungle and then go home and think nothing of it. You, on the other hand, may be left with his consequences."

I understand what she's saying. That I would be his mistress while he's here. That I could become pregnant, and he'd refuse to have any claim to it.

I understand everything, except that she said a week. Does she really think we can reach the gold, mine it, and leave the jungle in only seven days? "I don't think he wants sex."

"All men want sex."

"So do women, if that's the case."

As long as the right to consent isn't torn from us . . . The very thought makes me irrationally angry.

Madelyn gapes at me. I didn't even say what I was thinking, which means she looks horrified and scandalized based only on the fact that women can want sex—strange that a married woman doesn't know that better than I do. "What are you saying? You'd *give* it to him?"

I wouldn't give him anything. He wouldn't take anything. We would be doing something together.

But now I can feel a blush flaring. Why am I even thinking of sex with a man I hardly know, in the middle of the jungle no less?

Besides, I don't want that with Thorn.

I want more than that.

Instead of replying, I press forward to reach the gully faster, knowing that she won't dare continue the subject with others nearby to hear. And sure enough, like the rich, well-mannered lady she is, she's tight-lipped when we reach the edge.

"Welcome back, ladies," Thorn says, swiping sweat from his brow with the back of his hand and beaming.

Madelyn looks around impatiently. "Aren't you done yet?"

"Nearly there. If you help it'll go faster."

"That mud and these bloomers? You must be joking."

I don't have a tool, so I slide into the gully and grab some vines clinging to the fallen tree and use them to bundle the wood that's already been chopped.

When I come to the end of the available vine, I sit on my pile to watch them work. I've never seen a tourist so well suited to chores as Thorn—though it shouldn't be surprising, since he mines gold for a living. He's rolled his sleeves up above his elbows, the muscles in his forearms contracting as he adjusts his grip on the axe. My God, the strength in those arms . . . so beautiful. He lifts the axe and brings it down quickly, sending a cylinder of wood into the mud with one strike.

That simple action stirs something inside me, and I quickly look away, my pulse throbbing at my throat.

I've seen plenty of people chop wood. It's a basic chore we do daily. Why the hell does it feel different when Thorn does it?

And why do I simultaneously feel exhilarated and like I should repent?

"Can we hurry it up?" Badger grumbles. "These trees give me the creeps."

Thorn rolls his eyes. "We're on a beautiful tropical island, sourpuss. Relax, will you?"

"I don't know how anyone can relax in this place."

"Just reminding you, dear husband," Madelyn says, with a silky-smooth smile that doesn't match her tone, "we could've been sampling wine on the coast right now instead of sitting in the dirt in a sweaty jungle." She crosses her arms, looking at her surroundings cautiously. "I really hope your precious gold mine isn't a myth."

"It's not a myth," Badger says harshly. He pauses, turning to level a glare at Thorn. "It better not be a myth."

"It's not," he says firmly. "We both know it's not."

"From books? From hearsay? We don't *know* anything."

"It's not," I confirm, hoping to help alleviate the tension. Instead, Badger turns his skeptical glare on me, and I want to disappear.

"Have you seen it?" he asks dubiously.

Thorn looks at me too, in curiosity and encouragement.

"U-um—" I swallow. "Well, I—I—" I clamp my jaw down, knowing the next word isn't going to cooperate with my tongue. I don't understand why, since I'm used to aggression like his, but I also know that talking to people who are annoyed with me never really ends in my favor.

"Well, you what?" Badger says with clear irritation, his sharp voice making me jolt.

Thorn reaches out and flicks his wrist at Badger, like shooing an obnoxious gull. "Let her speak."

"It's . . ." I swallow. "It's not a mine, exactly. It's an orchard of mythical trees, guarded by the man-eaters."

"So it *is* a myth," Badger says, throwing up his hands.

His impatience aggravates me, and "All myths have truth to them" slips out before I can wrangle it.

Thorn whistles. "Found another favorite subject, I see." He beams at me, and I'm grateful for the pile of wood to distract me. "Educate us, Victoria."

The truth is, you're lucky the jungle is being patient enough to let us live this long.

"No one has found it and lived to tell their story," I say finally. "But I've seen it from a distance. I know the river that runs through it, nurtures it. If we follow the river's path, we'll make it there."

Badger exchanges a look with his wife. "What do you mean, 'No one has lived to tell their story'?"

"It means what it sounds like," Samson finally chimes in, rescuing me.

Madelyn's hand covers her mouth. "Is it because of those monsters guarding the gold?"

I shake my head. "I doubt they made it that far. To reach it you have to follow the river upstream, and well . . ." What's the most tactful way to say it? "The River Mumma is only merciful to children."

The three glance at one another, and I'm positive my report is going to be tarnished—telling the clients they're facing certain death is, at the bare minimum, poor customer service.

I clear my throat and stand, holding up a bundle of wood to occupy my fidgety hands. "We should probably go before it gets dark."

CHAPTER 8

The night is exquisite.

Silver streams in through the gaps of the leafed canopy, a soothing contrast against the brash campfire. Our tin bowls are all laid out to catch the dew that will settle the next morning.

Thorn must wear many hats back home, because he conducts a church service while we eat. I let a dried mango slice soften in my mouth as I listen to his beautiful voice read a few poetic psalms. Normally, I wouldn't eat with the clients—there's nothing comfortable about sitting around an open flame in the sticky, humid warmth of the jungle air, especially when we're deep enough into the jungle that the trees block out the ocean breeze.

But Bunny looks so interested, how can I leave? Although now they're taking out a banjo and a violin, and a few other small instruments—otherwise known as more unnecessary things to lug along with us. They're for sure going to sing, and while I'm sitting here I may be forced to join in. Not that I hate music, I just . . . hate the sound of my own voice. And social activities.

Sure enough, Thorn starts us in with a hymn:

"Crown Him with many crowns
The Lamb upon the throne
Hark! How the heav'nly anthems drowns
All music but its own!
Awake, my soul and sing
Of Him Who died for thee
And hail Him as thy matchless King
Thru all eternity . . ."

God, his voice is beautiful. I'm honestly not surprised. I've only ever heard this hymn sung solemnly, but the instruments add a playfully rhythmic quality to it. And, as everyone joins in to sing with him, it's almost strange how the atmosphere changes. Even Badger seems less uptight, less intent on masking his fear with anger.

Finally, Thorn closes the service out with a prayer. The men remove their hats, the solemnity returning. But only while Thorn prays, because as soon as he's finished he calls to his friend, "Greyson! 'Arkansas Traveler'?"

It's an invitation his friend accepts wholeheartedly, racing his bow across the strings of his violin as quick and wild as the river. Another man plucks the banjo, and all the men whoop, clapping in syncopation and dancing along.

Thorn plays a mandolin, one of the few instruments I know of, but only because I once guided a luthier across the jungle road. A smaller stringed instrument, with four pairs of doubled steel strings, plucked with a small pick. It suits Thorn, to be honest. The notes he plucks speak as rapidly as he does, but their tones match his gentle heart. If joy and kindness were an instrument, they would be a mandolin.

Still, I shrink against the commotion. It's too loud. I'm sure they're having fun, but growing up I had to condition myself not to see it that way—because no one wanted to be around me, I'd largely been excluded from any group activities. Eventually I decided they were pointless and noisy.

And besides, as much as I love spending time with Thorn, I'm tired of people. Even Thorn. Even my boys. And it's so *loud* I can barely hear myself think, far more noise than we should ever be making in the jungle. I wish I could climb a tree to escape. I need to do *something*, before someone asks if I want to dance or sing.

Familiar fingers lace through mine. I grin up at Samson, his slightly lowered brows scrutinizing me. I wish he wouldn't worry, not over this. I stand, he follows my lead, and we sneak off to our cots.

"Crowds?" he asks when we've settled down.

"Just crowds," I reply, reveling in the stars overhead. "You can let down your guard now."

He kisses his teeth, as if I've said something ridiculous, and I can't help smirking.

I close my eyes, pretending to fall asleep until I'm certain Sam has.

The songs of insects settle in my ears, like a party talking over each other—much like the party I'm trying to ignore, but with conversation I'm interested in. The rustle of leaves joins them, and I wonder what's scurrying up there, leaping from branch to branch.

I used to climb up to the canopy where the fuzzies nest, attempting to chase lizards through the trees. Not once did I catch one, and the fuzzies would always clap their tiny rodent hands with high-pitched little screams, like they were laughing at me. But then they'd feed me afterward, and I'd snuggle up there with them to sleep.

Why'd that memory pop into my head, of all things?

My eyes shoot open as something weighty touches my hair.

"See?" says Bunny, and he sounds like he's smiling even if he's leaning over me, and I can't quite see him. "She's not sleeping."

"I could've been," I mutter.

"You never fall asleep before me." He settles down on his cot. "You and Samson missed a lot of fun. Look at you, leaving early like an old married couple."

"Well—" That's Thorn's voice now, and that one word rushes me to my feet. He holds his hands out to me, a lit lantern in one of them, as if trying to hold me back. "Oh no, I'm sorry, Victoria. I didn't mean for you to get up."

"Bunny's right," I say. "I can't sleep unless I know he's safe in bed."

"Thanks, Auntie," Bunny teases, rolling over before I can bend down and flick him in the forehead.

"That's very sweet," Thorn says, and his voice sounds honeyed when he says it, enough to make me blush.

"U-um—well—" I bite my tongue. Should I thank him? Tell him not to say that? Neither seem like the right response. "Did you need something, Thorn?"

"Not if you're tired."

"I'm fine. Honest."

"It'll be quick. If you could just help me with the campfire."

I glance at Samson to make sure he's still sleeping and follow Thorn to where the fire is still burning a little.

This is just what I needed anyway. A moment alone with Thorn, without Dean. And to think, I nearly foolishly daydreamed through my opportunity.

This is far too important to dwell on sweet memories, Victoria.

"I didn't realize Bunny is your brother," Thorn says before I can open my mouth. He kicks dirt onto the fire, putting it out without much help from me.

It's obvious the conversation was what he wanted more than the help, but there's no harm in that. "Not by blood."

He grins reassuringly. "I'd still call that a brother. I've got plenty of friends like him. Sort of have to, as an only child."

"Honestly," I say, "sometimes he feels more like my son than anything."

Thorn chuckles. "Adolescence is the pits. He'll grow out of it."

Not before it kills him.

I try to smile, but I'm not fooling him, because he asks, his tone curious, "Or not?"

He's prying. Normally, I'd divert to a different topic, or find some reason to excuse myself. I don't know why I say, "It's nothing to do with his age. This sort of life doesn't suit him, and he . . ."

He uses his wild blood like an escape drug.

I know that moment. You summon energy, feel the blood move like threads pulled by your fingers . . . in that moment, lightning itself is at your command, even if it's only a product of the blood's energy. It's a power few possess, awesome and awful at once. Blood and energy, in your control.

I get it. It's the only thing he *can* control. It feels good to wield such power, even if that power could one day be his end.

But how can I explain that to someone who isn't a Wildblood and have him understand? That Bunny is slowly killing himself in order to feel, for just a moment, that he is the master of his own life?

"He expresses his stress in unhealthy ways," I finish.

Thorn nods. "And that worries you."

"I wish I could help him. I'm afraid for him. Both me and Samson look out for him, do what we can to keep him out of trouble, but sometimes it's still not enough."

"Well, is there any other work he enjoys? Anywhere he can be apprenticed?"

Thorn is a sweet man with too much heart. I don't want him handing in a poor report just because of a sad fact that no amount of talking will change.

I shake my head.

He frowns, then nods. As if he understands without me revealing anything. "But you do get paid?"

"Yes. It's not slavery."

"But it isn't freedom, either."

I shrug, and I'm sure I have a stupid, sheepish look on my face. What does he want me to say? That the armed guards aren't there to protect the tourists who pass through? That we're paid barely a living wage simply as a loophole? That we're only here because we were kidnapped?

"The job takes us into the jungle," I say instead. "The jungle is freedom."

"To some," he says, and I know what he's implying.

"To some," I agree.

Not to Bunny, who only came here a year ago and knew a life outside the walls of the company unrelated to the jungle. Who had parents who loved him, not the equivalent of an overseer who makes him fear each day. Who wasn't raised in situations requiring the same kind of fortitude as near-slavery on one side and a vengeful jungle on the other.

But all this makes me wonder what Bunny told Thorn to prompt this conversation.

"Well," says Thorn, "Greyson—the man Bunny's guiding— he's a nice chap, farmer-type, lots of kids. I can ask him to keep Bunny busy."

"I'd rather you didn't," I say quickly. "Bunny wouldn't like that I told you any of this. He might suspect something."

Thorn taps the side of his nose with his index finger and winks at me.

I feel the corner of my mouth twitch into a grin. "Thank you."

"Of course." He stretches a little, arching his back. "I should probably let you go to bed, we have a big day tomorrow. Although," he adds, and I hesitate, only half turning. "I've been meaning to ask you this all evening, ever since we went for firewood. Do you mind?"

I force myself not to panic. He's not going to ask anything personal. I'm positive I dodged all the personal questions today. Even so, I nod.

"River Mumma?" he asks.

"Oh." Relief washes over me like a hug. "She's the river spirit."

His brows lower. "River spirit . . ."

"Yes."

Thorn chews on his lip. "That was her, wasn't it? Who spoke to me. On the bridge."

"Um . . . yes."

"I think she . . ." He shakes his head, his expression a mix of confusion and discomfort. "I think she tried to drown me."

"She did, sir. It was a warning. The jungle normally gives three warnings to scare mortals off, offering them a chance to reconsider before entering."

He whistles. "No wonder no one's ever mined the gold."

I feel my nose scrunch. "Gold is not the wealth of the jungle."

"Then why is she so protective of it? You said yourself no one's ever made it that far."

I try my best to force back annoyance that won't listen to reason. "The jungle is a massive expanse. *You* are the only one preoccupied with gold."

"I've driven you to passion again." He chuckles. "Is this River Mumma a favorite of yours? Like the butterfly?"

I freeze, my mind blank of any coherent response. I don't open my mouth to even try. I'll just fumble stupidly. But something about what he said doesn't sound mean-spirited or condescending. He . . . I think he might . . . understand?

"Forgive my rambling," he says, putting my poor brain out of its misery. "We can talk more tomorrow, if you'd like—"

"We shouldn't continue, Thorn," I blurt out, before he can fully turn away.

"What have we started, Victoria?" he asks, and I feel myself blushing at his playful tone.

"I—I—" I fumble with my words. "I mean, you almost drowning was the second warning. The Bloody Lady killing that man in your party was the first. If the jungle is forced to deliver a final warning and you don't heed it, no amount of Wild-bloods accompanying your party will be able to save you. Aren't the lives of so many men worth more than gold?"

Thorn is quiet. He looks at me as if trying to suss out a lie and keeping eye contact with him is unbearable. "What do you suggest?"

All my breath releases in one massive huff of relief. "That we turn back. Go back to headquarters without entering the jungle."

"Victoria, dear . . ." Thorn sighs. Rubs his temple. "I mean a suggestion that won't hold up the expedition."

My heart drops into my stomach. "Sir, if we step into those trees, everyone will die."

"My men are well equipped for the wilderness. I would never have allowed Madelyn out with us if we weren't." He gives me a reassuring smile. "It's been a long day. Let's head to bed, and I'll speak to Spitz about it in the morning. Try not to worry, Victoria. Okay?"

No. It's not okay. Because Dean doesn't care about the warnings. He'll deny them, play them off as me being silly and superstitious. He's never been beyond the trees far enough to do anything but piss, so, for him, the wrath of the boss is more real than the threat of the River Mumma.

The difference is, the boss can't kill us all and still run a business. And the River Mumma has more in her arsenal than guns and fists.

"By the way," Thorn says before I can make order to my words, "do I look forty?"

"U-um—" I blink at him. "No."

"Then stop calling me 'sir.'" His grin sends warmth crawling up my neck. He backs away, raising his hand in a motionless wave. "Good night, Victoria."

"Good night, Thorn," I barely gasp, as he turns away toward his tent, and part of me wonders if it's the last night I'll get to say it.

I jolt awake at the sound of a crash, and with it, a sick feeling in my throat, like bile from the urge to vomit. I scramble from my cot, the realization of what that sensation means only hitting me as I watch a stake from one of the tents pop up from the ground, float in midair for a moment, and drop.

"Duppy!" Dean shouts, before I can even open my mouth. "Everybody up!"

I shake Bunny awake before grabbing my satchel of salt.

"Which one of these idiots pissed on the salt barrier?" Samson grumbles.

"Should we take bets?" I say, rolling my eyes. It's happened enough times throughout my many tours that it's no longer funny.

Samson kisses his teeth, long and unhurried.

It's tedious to have to wake so suddenly, and maybe wake too widely to ever get back to sleep peacefully, but we've all done this before. All we have to do is herd the duppy toward an unsalted area and clear an exit for it. Dean is already in the process, pouring water on a small area near the tree line and swiping it with his foot. If you throw salt at random, you may not be able to keep track of where it is or trap it at the center of the campsite. We form lines without having to be asked, throwing salt like scattering seeds. Easy.

At least it should be easy, straightforward. Usually they just pull hair, whip up little cyclones of papers, throw food. But this duppy seems overly ambitious, and a tent launches into the closest tree, sending a screaming man with it. The crash I'd heard earlier was an entire wooden chest of food supplies, splintered and scattered. Campsites are not usually so large, don't contain so many tents, so we have to hurry, or it will destroy everything.

We work quickly, narrowing toward the opening, screams and mayhem lingering despite Dean escorting the clients to the salted earth where it's safe. The duppy is agitated, knowing its fun is over but determined to cause as much trouble as it can before being banished from camp. It whips up a wind, and I blink dirt from my eyes.

All at once, the air is still. Not quiet—there is enough commotion in the camp to wake the jungle—but still. Only human movement. The duppy is gone.

I've never experienced a duppy like this before. With this sort of aggression, it has to be the third warning. One last warning to stay on the road Mumma has allotted us. What the jungle sees, it whispers to Mumma, and I'm sure now that there's not one inch of this jungle that isn't aware we are here. If we ignore this, if we enter the trees tomorrow . . . there will be no holding the jungle back.

Thorn is helping one of his men lie on the ground, yelling to some of the others to start cleaning up camp and take stock of what supplies are left. The man on the ground is grunting and groaning. I recognize him as the one who had gotten thrown into the tree.

We've gone from one problem to another, it seems.

Dean goes to check on them, and I follow—if it's a certain kind of injury, I may know of a plant out here that can help. Dean kneels to examine the man's back, checking for anything out of place. He's not a doctor by any means but has enough experience with injuries to at least get an idea. "Nothing broken," he says. "Might be some muscle trauma from impact."

I bite my lip. Not much I can do about muscle trauma. Hot compress? I'm not sure how we'd manage that out here.

"What does that mean for us?" Thorn asks, very business-like.

"You're down another man, I'm afraid," Dean says. "The travel will be much less straightforward once we break the trees. I couldn't in good conscience allow him to face potential danger in his condition."

"Just give me a few hours," the man says, his voice an agonized wisp as he winces with every breath. "I'll be in fighting shape by the morning."

"I don't recommend that," says Dean. "This is not the kind of injury that can be cured by rest. He'll need medical attention. I can have one of mine escort him back to headquarters."

"I agree." Thorn pats the man on the shoulder when he tries to protest. "Face it, Billups, you're no use to anyone in this state. Look at you, you can barely sit up straight."

"It's settled." Dean stands. "You should prepare him to leave immediately. The journey will be long in his condition."

Dean heads back to the Wildbloods waiting for instruction, and since I'm no use here, I follow again.

"One less person to share the gold with," I hear Badger murmur as I walk by.

"Hal, that's awful," Madelyn chastises, shoving him in the

arm, but her smirk is a little less merciful before they both share a small chuckle.

"Nathan," Dean says, as we make it to our group, "escort the gentleman back to headquarters."

Nathan freezes, like when an animal is caught in a trap before realizing where it is and the thrashing starts. "But I wasn't assigned to him."

Dean levels a stern look at him—not a glare, like he would me, but the look of a leader. "I'm assigning you to him now."

"With all due respect, Dean, I'm of much more use to you out here."

Dean looks at him squarely, now. I know *that* look. The one that says he'd rather argue with his fists, but he's allowing one more chance to obey. More subtle than his glare, so maybe Nathan has never seen it before. But then, Nathan couldn't think of a bad thing to say about Dean if you paid him and told him he could worship Dean's shadow for the rest of his life. "You're of use to me where I say you're of use to me. You will escort Mr. Billups back to headquarters. Gather your things."

Nathan hesitates. Rushes off. Wise choice, if only that he'll be spared a worse fate than missing out on pay for an unfinished tour.

"The rest of you," he continues, "secure the salt barrier. Then you can go back to bed. Maybe we can have at least a few hours of peace."

I can feel the collective sigh of relief, even if none of us will dare voice it, as they rush off to do just that.

Bunny leans on Samson's shoulder, but Samson pushes him back to his feet sternly.

"Oh no, you don't," he murmurs.

"Come on, Sam, I'm tired," Bunny fusses, as Sam leads the way to our cots.

"You're taller than me now. No more piggybacks."

Bunny may be tall, but he's still as scrawny as he was before his growth spurt. His weight is taken up by all his limbs. But I see Sam's point.

Even so, he's still a child . . . even if he won't always be.

I take Bunny's hand as consolation, and we grab handfuls of salt to fortify the shield along our quarter of camp.

The man Billups can hardly stand up straight, but he can walk, which is good enough. I watch the shadows of Nathan leading him back the way we came. The road is already salted. It'll be long and tedious, but safe enough.

But why should he be the only one to leave? Why should he be the only one to get out of this alive? Bunny tugs on my hand to prompt me back onto my cot, and I rock between allowing it and running toward Dean and Thorn, who are still chatting together.

But I don't think I could forgive myself if I refused to say something that makes a difference because I'm too nervous to drum up the courage.

"I'll be back," I say to my boys in general without really looking at either of them.

"Where are you going now?" Sam asks, chastisement sharpening his tone.

"I'll stay in camp," I insist, and rush away before he can say more.

Thankfully, Dean's back is facing me, so I'm able to step into their circle without any interception.

"Thorn, that was the last warning," I say, the words pouring out of me. I don't want to excuse my interruption—it'll give Dean the opportunity to shoot me down, and I *have* to say this. "Remember last night when I said the jungle would give us three warnings before it—"

"You're *tired*, Victoria," Dean cuts in, giving me a pointed look. *Another word and you'll get it*, say his eyes. And now that I know he doesn't mind punishing me in front of Thorn, my words falter for a moment.

But it's enough time for Thorn to say, "Aren't we all," his tone unaware of what has just passed between Dean and me. Or maybe he agrees with him, that I'm crazy and must be silenced, because he takes my shoulders firmly—Thorn's grasp doesn't clamp any harder than a polite handshake, but my muscles still freeze against the kind of hold that usually brings pain. No pain comes, only a gentleness in his touch and tone I can't for the life of me process. "Don't worry, Victoria. Please don't worry. Get some rest. Everything is going to be fine."

Dean waits until Thorn walks toward his tent to lean over me, close enough that the feral child in me wants to bite his face off.

"What the hell are you doing?" he whispers harshly. "You practically begged to come on this trip."

"Neither of us will be promoted if none of the clients come home alive," I hiss back.

"You sound unhinged, you know that? Is that what you want the man who will decide our future to think you are?"

"You know the jungle speaks to me. You know what I'm saying is true."

There's a falter in his glare, his jaw shifting. "If the jungle likes you so much, then tell it how much you need this. Tell it to back off."

He leaves me quickly, and I don't make a scene by rushing after him. Instead, I go back to my cot and lie between my two boys with a heavy sigh. Down three clients—two before we even left headquarters, one before we wandered off the road.

This does not bode well for tomorrow.

CHAPTER 9

I awake with the dawn, damp with dew and oddly invigorated.

On regular trips, the jungle road is never as dangerous as one thinks it might be. Stay within the salt barrier. Keep your thurible lit. Don't shout too much. It requires no work on the client's part, except to inform one of us if their incense smoke is thinning out. The jungle has generously allotted us this road, but its charity stops here. And things like yesterday . . . all the warnings . . . rarely happen on the road during regular trips.

But this isn't a regular trip. The jungle knows we mean to invade it.

Still, I'd decided to take Thorn's advice and not worry—it was the only way I was able to get any sleep. And besides, Dean was right. Thorn is who matters. He's my priority. If I can't convince him, I'll just have to protect him.

We pour our collected dew into canteens and leave as soon as the sun is high enough to see our surroundings beneath the canopy.

A contented feeling takes over me as soon as we break the tree line. The canopy of branches and leaves overhead is thicker than on the road, blocking out most of the sun but bathing everyone and everything in a kaleidoscope of scattered light and shadow. Insects buzz and chirp, birds shout, gossiping like bored tourists. The humidity brings out the various smells of plant life—mucky, musty, fresh, fragrant. The morning dew has settled like little jewels on the faces of leaves, ornamenting spiderwebs that reach between branches. I smile. This place feels like magic.

This place feels like home.

Dean sticks with the plan we'd discussed yesterday, thank God—two lines, one led by him, the shorter one led by me. He's doing a better job leading than I'd like to admit, navigating the jungle floor barefooted like the seasoned Wildblood he is, with a spark of his old self that I hate myself for noticing.

I shove the fond memories away to focus on the present.

The present being our clients, with their travel boots, trudging through broken sticks and crunching leaves like clumsy cows compared to us. We've barely gotten an eighth of a mile from the road and this already feels like a horrible idea. The jungle, much like the boss, does not like to be disturbed.

"It's so peaceful here," Thorn muses from behind me.

"Peaceful?" Badger fusses behind Dean a few feet away. He looks around, paranoid. "This place gives me the creeps."

"You've been shut up in that office for too long, Badger. Give me the wild outdoors any day."

I glance over my shoulder and find Thorn smiling at his surroundings.

God, he's so cute.

He doesn't talk as much, now, and it's slower going because his party needs to look at their feet a lot to keep from tripping. But at least we haven't run into any trouble. After how yesterday went, it's honestly a miracle. Although Thorn's party is complaining a lot more about their feet hurting on the uneven terrain, about the incense burning their eyes, about the stifling humidity.

But I'm not team leader yet, so I ignore them.

A doctor bird zips by, her bright green wings a lightning-fast blur, then back the other way again. I smile and whisper, "Good morning, my darling."

She flies backward in front of my face, showing off, before hovering there, keeping pace as I continue walking. When I lift my hand, she lands on my finger. The feathers of her breast are white, speckling into black, bright green flowing like a painting into warm orange. She kisses my hand with her long, needle-width beak.

"Magnificent," Thorn breathes.

I almost trip as I stop, his whisper close. He's broken formation, nearly beside me, and is looking over my shoulder at my friend. His closeness is alarmingly lovely.

"How did you get her to land on you like that?" he asks.

"I . . . didn't," I say honestly. Stupidly. Dean has halted his line, too, but the rim of his hat is low enough that I can't tell if he's pissed or not. Safe guess is *yes*.

Thorn reaches his hand toward mine. "May I try?"

I hesitate, then hold my hand closer to him so he can reach it.

"Hey, baby," he says sweetly, and makes kissing noises, as if a wild bird will respond to a pet call. "Come on, baby. Sweet thing . . ."

His finger barely touches mine—a warm brush that runs

tingles up my arm—before the little doctor bird sends her wings moving a mile a minute again and hovers, seeming to assess Thorn, before flying away.

Thorn groans in disappointment. "I don't have the touch, I guess."

"You're too loud," I say. "You have to blend in. Become part of the scenery."

"But I like being noticed," he says with a charming grin.

I quickly lower the rim of my hat to keep him from seeing how much that one small action has flustered me, before pressing forward.

Something bobbing in the brush up ahead catches my attention, and I watch to make sure I'm seeing it correctly. Our clients' booted, inexperienced steps are so noisy I almost can't hear the movement rustling up ahead. But of course there's no natural sounds.

Spirits don't interact with their surroundings like we do.

A little hand pushes forward out of the brush to reveal a line of children walking in single file, holding hands in a long chain.

Pickneys.

I look over at Dean. He nods.

"Don't engage," he orders, loud enough for everyone to hear without being disrespectful to the jungle. "Just let them pass."

There are at least twenty pickneys, some taller than others, all dressed in what they'd died in. Simple trousers or play dresses from current and long-ago decades, one even in her christening dress—unless they were here as a result of a miscarriage, in which case they look like toddlers clothed in all the finery the jungle has to offer, vines and leaves and brightly colored flowers. Medicine has a long way to go . . . about half are miscarriages, even if none of them look younger than three years old.

Little girls and boys, taken from this world too soon.

Thorn's presence hovers a bit closer to me as the pickneys approach. "My God," he murmurs.

They are an unsettling sight if you aren't used to them, the poor sweet things.

All of their faces are nothing but blank, brown canvases, excluding every single feature humans should have on their faces.

But then, they aren't human anymore.

The only one with a proper face is the line leader—and proper is putting it sweetly. A pair of eyes, ears, a nose, a mouth, have all been pressed into her blank face, like lodging stones into a lump of clay. Arranged by the hands of blind children, her eyes are a bit lopsided, one ear higher than the other. The thought of her peers crowded around, putting a face on for her with their tiny hands, is endearing. Until I remember they have to steal a face in order to gain one.

The nose and ears are pale and slightly sunburned, eyes a shifting green, lips thin and pink—their victim had been a tourist. Or maybe even a soldier. Once in use of the pickneys, the features don't age, don't fade with time or decay. Who knows how long ago they had been stolen.

"Excuse us," says the line leader, her voice like a broken music box tinkling only sour, raspy notes. Dean and I keep our lines moving and out of their way. Madelyn lets out a disturbed sound, and someone shushes her harshly. The air is thick with tension from the clients and Wildbloods alike, with fear. They seem to have interpreted "Don't engage" as "don't draw attention in any way." They don't realize that not one of these little ones can see or hear them, none except the line leader, and she's busy.

But that's okay. Let them fear. It will make my job so much easier.

Finally, the pickneys are behind us, but still, no one in our party says a word. It's over a minute before I feel Thorn's hand on my shoulder. I tremble at his touch, warmth traveling through me. Or maybe that's just disturbed sweat making its way down my arm.

"Those were children," he says. He sounds somber, and it makes my throat tighten. I don't want him to be upset.

"The jungle harbors many lost souls," I reply.

"They're . . . dead?"

"Don't worry," I say, giving him a reassuring smile. "They like exploring."

"I want to believe you, but . . ." He hesitates before letting me go. "Poor babies."

"Do you have children?" I ask, to distract him.

"Mining can be dangerous, it's better if I don't have anyone back home worried about me. Besides, plenty of time for that later." He's quiet a moment. "Do . . . you have children?"

"Only Bunny."

He laughs, and I don't interrupt the beautiful sound lightening my steps as we proceed deeper into the jungle.

We didn't travel nearly as far as we should've. Thankfully, most of the food that required cooking had been ruined by the duppy, so it wasn't too difficult to convince the group we didn't need a campfire. Most of us agree it was too hot last night, not to mention it would attract night hunters now that we're in the midst of the jungle. Still, we will need to find some source of food pretty soon.

The tree spacing makes for awkward tent positioning, and God bless Thorn's team if they can find a spot that doesn't require them to lie on tree roots. Even with three fewer members, they somehow still require five tents. Americans must not like sleeping near each other, because the ten of us Wildbloods could probably all fit in one of those tents and sleep fine, even using each other as pillows.

"I'll be back," I tell Bunny, leaving my packs on my cot, including my satchel of salt.

"With Thorn?" he asks slyly.

I sigh, shake my head. "To piss."

He scratches beneath his eyepatch. "Just don't let anything dangerous follow you back to camp."

I smirk. "No guarantees."

I step out of the salt barrier and rush away until I can hear more of the jungle than my travel companions, until I can smell fresh leaves and sap instead of incense. The murmur of the jungle envelops me, and I close my eyes to listen. My thurible has long burned out, but I don't bother relighting it. I want the jungle to see me, to recognize my scent.

For me, the smoke is only a show anyway, an attempt to pretend I belong to the life that's been forced upon me.

I relieve myself, and then walk through the trees, slowly. I touch each one I pass, feeling the jungle's heartbeat. A branch snaps, and I pause.

Someone in Thorn's party is coming toward me—I know because the brush of leaves and smell of incense and the distinct weight of the steps tell me it's human. No creature in the jungle would move so loudly at night. No Wildblood, either.

I brace myself to see Badger step out of the shadows. Not the one I would've expected, but unnerving nonetheless.

"There you are, Victoria," he says.

The only words we've spoken to each other since leaving headquarters were yesterday while chopping firewood. It's a wonder he knows my name, but not such a wonder he's using it, and in a far less aggressive tone than he's used the entire trip.

It's obvious he wants something, and I honestly don't care to find out what.

"You shouldn't be out here without your guide, Mr. Badger," I say.

"I'd prefer to talk to you without prying ears."

I freeze. "Any concerns about your tour experience should be taken up with your tour leader," I quote from the handbook, and I'm amazed I can manage that many coherent words with my throat closing tighter and tighter as he stares at me. I walk quickly, trying to leave enough space in between us, but he grabs my arm and drags me back, cornering me against a tree.

I suddenly feel like soaked-through wood after a storm. Useless. My science stands by, but I'm afraid to use it. I'm afraid of what might happen if I do . . . how easily I can lose the chance at my promotion if he tells someone, and he will.

So I stay silent, don't make eye contact, keep my expression as neutral as I can. Maybe then he won't see me as a threat and want to attack.

Unless he's the type of animal who is only scared off by aggression and a display of power.

If that's the case, I'm screwed.

Badger leans closer, scoffing when I wince. "I won't hurt you, little mouse. Just as long as you do exactly as I say." He reaches down and waiting for his hand to resurface where I can see it is like torture. When his hand comes back into my eye line, he's holding a wad of bills. Lord. More money than I'd ever seen at once in my entire life.

"See this?" he says. "This can be yours—and it's only half of what I'll give you. The other half you'll get after we reach and successfully mine the gold."

I turn my face away, my breath stumbling as his hand moves toward me. I feel the paper money brush my cheek, slide beneath my nose. It smells dirty and sweaty, and like it was sharing a pocket with cigars.

"All you have to do," he goes on, "is not be so good at your job." I feel my eyes widen as I look his way again, and he lets out a low laugh. "You heard right. I need you to neglect Thorn a little. And if he happens to meet an untimely death on your watch, hey . . . the jungle is a dangerous place for travelers, now, isn't it?" He shakes the money at me. "Go on, take it."

I reach up slowly and take his money, but not because I want it. It's because he's already told me, even if I haven't agreed to anything . . . and he only agreed not to hurt me if I do as he says. So I take it and hold it to my chest in both hands, waiting for him to release me.

"This is between us," he says. "I hear about it elsewhere and I'll know it was you."

I nod quickly. Satisfied, he steps aside, and I immediately rush away. I don't wait for him. He can die in the jungle for all I care.

I didn't have the time or sense to count the money, but it

looked like enough . . . maybe just enough, added to what I've already saved, to get Bunny off the island. But not enough to start a life once he gets away. Not enough to live on.

What am I thinking? I can't follow through on this to earn the second half. That would require failing at my job. What he's offering isn't enough to suffer the boss's punishment, let alone Dean's wrath at messing this up for him. My promotion is on the line.

Besides . . . I don't think I can bear to see harm come to Thorn.

So, Victoria . . . ?

Earn enough money to send Bunny away and have the boss or Dean murder me for neglecting the client, or secure my promotion and possibly be murdered before I make it out of the jungle?

Either way, I'm going to die.

I slow down as I approach camp so as not to alarm anyone, but Dean locks eyes with me as soon as I enter the salt border.

"Where have you been?" he asks, approaching.

Bitterness vibrates through me, and on top of my unease from the conversation with Badger, I feel sick. "I had to piss."

"Takes that long?"

I kiss my teeth. "I can't just whip something out of my trousers and water a tree."

"Next time tell me where you're going. I don't want you abandoning Thorn, he's the whole reason we're out here." His eyes shift beyond me, and I know he's probably watching Badger enter camp. "That what took so long?"

"You don't care."

"I do if whatever happened impedes your performance."

Rage blossoms in my gut at his implication. At the irony and hypocrisy of it. I glare up at him, and he winces. But it's not as satisfying as usual. I want to figure out which bone in his face hasn't been broken so I can do it myself.

"Your concern is grimly comical," I say.

His throat bobs a few times, as if he's having trouble swallowing. "Right now, unless you're escorting the man paying us, it's in your best interest to keep the field trips to a minimum. You can be a petty little girl holding a grudge when we get home."

I feel heat surge in my veins, but people are watching and wondering what we could be discussing. I haven't hidden one emotion on my face. The Wildbloods, at least, know Dean and I hate each other—or at least that I hate Dean, and they all hate *me* for that fact. But I don't know what everyone else must think.

What Thorn must think.

Either way, for Bunny's sake, I can't make Dean look like an antagonist. Even though he is. Even though I hate him in a way that feels poisonous.

"Then stop breathing down my neck," I say. "I'm here to make *you* look good, after all."

"And one poor report from me will crush your tour leader dreams forever. We need each other, Vicky. The boss has been pitting us against each other so long you forget who the real enemy is."

"I know who my *enemies* are," I say, leaning away. "Don't pretend you're some team player just because there are clients around."

Dean grips my arm above the elbow, tugs me back to him as I try to step away, and everything in me but my voice screams so loudly that I can barely hear what he says next. "If this mission goes south, both our necks are in the noose. We live or die together. Remember that."

He's not wrong, but that doesn't make him right. I feel my blood wake with fire, only the thought of protecting Bunny stopping me from turning it into a weapon. But without my science, tears try their best to break through.

You sick traitor.

I feel anger crawling up my stomach, making its way to my throat.

Let go of me, my body pleads.

"Is there a problem here?"

I jolt, looking over quickly to see Thorn standing in front of us. He's the last person I want to suspect, well, anything. But seeing him so suddenly kicks warmth up my neck and into my face. And I think Thorn notices and translates it as something else, because he narrows his eyes slightly.

"No problem," Dean says, but doesn't release me, a subtle show of power that makes me want to stab him in the throat. Because if there's no problem, if I'm fine with his touch, why should he have to let go?

A *snap* interrupts us as Thorn presses his closed fist with the heel of his other palm, cracking his knuckles—a threat, even as he smiles at Dean. His sleeves are rolled up to his elbows, and the muscles in his forearms twitch at the movement. Those forearms could tear down mountains . . . "Good. Should we get some sleep, then? Big day tomorrow."

"Indeed," Dean says, and looks at me.

If you kiss me again this won't end well for you.

My eyes do the talking, even if my mouth isn't permitted. The good thing about being rivals since we were six is it doesn't take words to communicate—there were times, far too many, where speaking aloud would get us beaten by the boss. Our eyes were all we had. Married couples can't read each other's eyes as well as we can—and I've seen hundreds of couples, if not thousands, during my short stay on Earth. It's not something I delight in. It's a fact.

But Dean hates me, so even if I ask him he may very well spite me.

Instead his eyes say, *Please make this work,* and his expression is so like Little Dean—uncertain and a little scared—that I want to both sigh in nostalgia and tear his eyes out so he can never do it again.

I do neither. I wrap my arm around his neck and pull him in for a hug, feeling him stiffen before playing the game. He no longer feels familiar—most of this muscle was gained after we were off hugging terms. But he smells the same and I hate myself for noticing, so I shove him in the chest. Quickly, away from me, but still trying to appear playful. So his aggressive grip he'd had on my arm seems less, well, aggressive. So I can shove back the memories of lying beside him on our bed mat, his scent familiar and lovely and soothing me to sleep.

"See you tomorrow," I say, while my eyes say *Never again.*

"Sleep well, Victoria," he says, his eyes returning with *We'll see.*

I should've kissed him. It would've been just my lips, then. Now I feel like I need to rub my entire body against the roughest tree I can find. The skin would grow back eventually.

"Good night, Mr. Thorn," I murmur. I don't look at him. I don't think I'm keeping the anger off my face, and all the work

I've done will be wasted if he sees it. I rush by him, cringing as I hear his heavy boots follow.

"Are you okay, Victoria?" Thorn asks, low, as he joins beside me.

"Of course." My voice squeaks slightly, but at least I don't stutter.

"I know he's your . . . well, *one* of your lovers," he says, and I have to force myself not to gag.

"*One* of my lovers?" I ask, raising my brows. "Who's the other?"

"Samson . . . Or did I misread that? You're very sweet together."

"We're just friends."

"Does *he* know that?"

I feel myself blushing. I don't know why. It's just . . . I don't know, *embarrassing* to think of Samson as my lover. Do Americans not hug their friends?

"Anyway," Thorn says, sighing, "I don't like the way Spitz was holding you."

I swallow. "How was he holding me?"

Thorn narrows his eyes, unconvinced by my false ignorance. "I'm used to working with the unsavory type. I know an abuser when I see one. He was obviously keeping you in check."

"We were playing," I say, my heart thudding in my throat. "Besides, you were the only one flinging warnings."

"Me?"

I raise an eyebrow. He's not even trying to sound innocent. "Dean is a skilled fighter, and a Wildblood."

"So it'll be doubly humiliating when I kick his ass."

I grin a little, even though I shouldn't. But it ignites his smile, which makes the betrayal of my team leader in front of a client all worth it.

"Whatever it looked like, he was just concerned because I went off alone."

"Yes, you shouldn't do that. We have a paired system for a reason."

I have a Wildblood pairing system for a reason, but you don't seem to be worried about that.

The last thing I'm afraid of is being alone in the jungle.

But he's right. After what Badger asked me to do, I don't think I can leave his side for the rest of the trip. Because if I don't follow through with the kill, Badger might.

I manage a reassuring smile. "We're stuck like glue for the rest of the trip. Promise."

Thorn beams. "Excellent." He touches my arm, a gesture I don't realize I actually enjoy until he's already moved away. "I'll see you tomorrow, partner."

For a moment I don't know how to respond, or if I should or *can* for that matter. His touch had felt so nice, not marred by cruel memories or ill intentions. Such the opposite of Dean it makes me want to cry.

I can't kill him. I didn't want to, but now I know I never can. What kind of monster would it make me to let harm come to a man who can touch Wildbloods like they're human, like they're equal?

Who can touch a Wildblood, hated by all other Wildbloods, like she means something to him?

CHAPTER 10

I wait until I'm sure everyone is sleeping before sneaking away from my cot and over to Thorn's tent. I hate to wake him when we have such a long journey ahead of us, but when else will I be able to speak with him alone without drawing suspicion?

I take a deep breath and open the flap of his tent. It's so dark, I can barely make out his outline. "Thorn?"

"What?" I hear the blankets rustle in the shadows. "Victoria, is that you?"

I hear the glass door of a lantern open and rush over. "No light. Please. Our shadows against the tarp will give away that I'm here."

"What's wrong?" He sounds serious all of a sudden, and my stomach twists. There's no going back now . . . not that going back would be any more pleasant. Either way Badger will want me dead.

Despite my warning, Thorn lights the lantern, and I drop

to my knees so I'm not visible from the outside as the tent fills with firelight. I feel myself blush as I look at his strong, shirtless torso, grateful I can see the beginnings of his trousers at his waist so at least I know he isn't naked down below. He looks gravely concerned as he kicks the blanket aside, scooting closer.

"Victoria, what's happened?" he asks, reaching out to me.

I don't know what to do with his reaction. Only a few people in my entire life have ever . . . *cared* before, and never an outsider. For a moment I feel stuck, as if this interaction isn't even real.

But then Thorn touches my face, and I know he can feel me tremble because I certainly can.

"My God," he says. "You're pale."

"Nothing happened," I say quickly.

"You can tell me." He tightens his lips and takes a deep breath, and the next time he says, "You can tell me," the edge in his voice is gone and it's nothing but soothing.

Soothing is an understatement. I've never heard that tone from anyone. Not toward me. *Never* toward me. Tears burn at the backs of my eyes. As much as I love my boys, not even they have ever sounded like this. Wildbloods aren't used to comfort. We love, but it's different. There is a razor's edge to most of us that no amount of love can ever undo. I didn't realize an easy tone like this could even be produced until Thorn spoke, all soft lines and warmth.

"I—I—" I stutter, stumbling on my words. Thorn doesn't tell me to hurry up or call me stupid. He sits patiently and waits when all I want him to do is slap me and make me shut up.

"I-it's Badger," I say finally.

Thorn's brows drop. "What has he done to you?"

I don't know if my words will work again, so I pull out the wad of money instead and hold it out to him.

"He propositioned you," he concludes.

I nod.

"For sex."

I shake my head quickly. "To let you die," are more words than I can manage right now, so all I say is, "Kill you."

And then all I can do is gape, because the first thing Thorn does is roll his eyes. "Not again."

"U-um—" I blink at him as he kicks the blanket away farther to drag on his boots. "Again?"

"This motherfu—" He transitions his word into an annoyed grunt as he stands. "Forgive my language, dear. Yes, this has got to be at least the third time since I've known him."

"Why are you still partners if he wants you dead?"

"Because we work well together. We're both the best at what we do." He snatches up his rifle from his travel gear. "Do you know how long it took to find a competent business partner?"

I get to my feet nervously. "I thought you said you work well together."

"We do." He looks down at the rifle, as if just realizing he's loading the thing. "No, don't worry, Victoria. I'm not going to kill him." He snaps it shut and gives me that charming grin. "I'm just going to scare him a little."

I follow him out of the tent, hugging myself to keep my insides from turning over. "He's not going to like that I told you."

Thorn slows his pace enough to look at me. "He threatened you?"

I don't have to answer, apparently. Or maybe my expression

does it for me. Because Thorn narrows his eyes and presses forward, throwing open the flap of Badger's tent.

Madelyn is awake and lounging with her head on her sleeping husband's chest, a silk scarf tied around her hair. She looks up from her book quickly, her eyes tired in the lantern's light. She drops the book and pulls her blanket up to her chest, her eyes widening as she gets a good look at us. "Thorn, what's happening?"

"Hey. Bastard." Thorn shoves Badger in the side with his boot—not hard enough to be a kick, but enough to send the man jolting from sleep. "Get up."

Badger blinks the sleep away, then stares at the gun, realization of what it is slowly dawning on him. "What the hell is this about, Thorn?"

"You know exactly what it's about." He slides something back then out again under the long barrel with a loud click and holds the rifle steady at its target.

"Laertes, put the gun away, you're going to kill someone!" Madelyn orders, while Badger frantically demands, "What the hell? What the *hell*, man!" all while Thorn lets the joke go too far with, "Give me a reason not to shoot you in the head!"

All I can do is fruitlessly shush them and wish to smother their sound in a blanket. There are creatures far scarier than guns lurking in the surrounding jungle that don't like their sleep disturbed.

Dean shoves the flap of the tent open and halfway steps in and—I can't believe I feel this—I'm relieved to see him. But as soon as he turns his glare on me, I remember I'm supposed to make him look good, and a client holding someone at gunpoint will definitely not look good on the report.

I Ie charges into the tent, grabbing the barrel of the rifle and redirecting it. "If your aim is to attract every predator on the island, keep shouting."

Thorn lowers his rifle immediately. The joke's over, and I'm glad he has sense enough to know when to turn it off. "I take full responsibility for my actions. It won't happen again." His tone hardens despite his smile as he looks down at Badger. "Will it?"

Dean blows a slow breath through his nostrils, his glare settling on me, and I wisely step out of his way instead of challenging him as he storms from the tent.

I hear him ordering everyone back to bed. I'm sure he blames me for this, and now that I know he's not afraid to punish me in front of people, I'll have to keep my eyes open for when he's ready to retaliate.

"Laertes, stop it!" Madelyn sobs as Thorn half kneels and grips the front of Badger's shirt in his fist, twisting the fabric.

"Threaten Victoria again, my friend," Thorn says, his voice low and dangerous, "and I will kill you."

I cover my mouth with my hand. I've never heard him use so few words to get his point across and it's chilling—that part isn't a joke, even if the rest of it was, and everyone in the tent senses that fact keenly. Maybe he hears me gasp, because he looks at me quickly, his expression softening as he releases Badger and stands.

Thorn protecting me has become a pattern, one that both thrills and unsettles me.

I turn away just as quickly and exit the tent. Everyone is settling back onto their cots, in their tents, but there are a few stragglers looking in our direction trying to suss out what happened.

Samson is sitting up on his cot across the camp. I can't see his face with only the sparse moon as light, yet I know he's waiting for me. Bunny is still fast asleep, but that's not surprising.

"Are you alright, Victoria?" Thorn has hung the strap of his rifle over his strong shoulder, and with the event over, I suddenly remember he is very much shirtless. "You looked a little shaken in there."

I bow my head, mostly so I won't look at him and lose my wits. "I'm fine, thank you."

"I'm glad." He makes an odd sound in his throat. I look at him and his lips tighten against a smile—but it doesn't seem to work, because he stifles a laugh in his hand.

"You had a little too much fun," I say, and I can't help smiling. "That could've gone so poorly."

"But the look on his face!" He just stands there and laughs, then leans over to support himself on his thighs. I don't know why I find myself grinning along with this beautiful man and his sadistic sense of humor.

"You're horrible," I say, and his laughter is contagious, although I manage to bite mine back before it gets too far.

"I am," he says, finally catching his breath. "I'm sorry Madelyn had to be involved, poor girl, but Badger deserved it."

"How are you so brave?"

And joyful and beautiful and kindhearted . . . and out of my league . . . and, Lord, I work for you.

I drop my chin to hide my blush in the darkness, pressing back my thoughts.

"Doesn't take courage to deal with rats," he says. Our laughter has died, and I sense him looking at me. I make sure not to return his gaze. "Are you sure he didn't hurt you?"

"I'm sure."

"Can you look at me when you say it so I believe you?"

"No, thank you," I murmur. I'm not lying to him. I'm not even afraid. I just feel myself blushing far too much, and the last thing I want is for him to see.

He's quiet a moment. "I specifically requested no women guides on this trip—you can't always trust all the men on your team to be decent, and I can't be everywhere at once. Dean told me there had to be one, because of Madelyn. Fair enough. But you weren't even assigned to look out for her. So I don't . . ." He sighs heavily. "I honestly don't know what's going on."

I venture a look at him through my eyelashes, watching him chew on his lip in thought.

Finally, he says, "I know that was scary for you, defying Badger's threats to tell me about his plan. But you might've saved my life, Victoria. You've done nothing but look out for me since we entered the jungle. So I hope you don't think me patronizing when I say I want to look out for you, too. I don't want to leave your side for the rest of the trip."

My blush is burning uncomfortably now. I press my fingers to the back of my hot neck, letting my elbows go forward to hide my face even more. "I like that idea," I blurt, like an idiot, then bite my tongue to shut myself up.

He chuckles. "Excellent. You put it best earlier this evening—stuck together like glue. We could even tie ourselves together with some rope to get the genuine experience."

"We'll look like monster bait," I say, and he laughs even

more. I don't know why he's laughing—monster bait is an actual thing—but it makes me feel so content that I hope he'll never stop.

"My tent is open to you, if you're comfortable. There's enough space that I can—"

Finally, I look at him, my heart pounding.

And that irresistible gapped-tooth smile instantly slips away. "Sweet girl. You're blushing. I didn't mean to imply anything lewd. We'd stay on opposite ends of course."

Lewd? To offer me shelter from those who might hurt me? How could I ever translate that as anything but . . .

I drop my face again, and now I feel I may cry.

. . . *as anything but undeserved.*

"Why are you so kind to me?" I ask.

I can't bear to look at him when he asks, "Do I need a reason to be kind?"

"No one is kind to . . ." I swallow. *To a Wildblood,* I should say, otherwise he'll think I'm pathetic. But I've seen kindness shown toward other Wildbloods. Not often, but it happens. I've just never experienced it myself.

Maybe that's my fault, for staying away from people as much as possible.

"There's always a reason," I say instead.

"Maybe I like you," he says, and I feel myself blush even more.

"A real reason."

"The Bible says kindness is one of the fruits of the spirit . . . also, I *really* like you."

"That's . . ." I hug my arms, fumbling for a coherent sentence. I settle on "stupid."

"I disagree."

His tone is too sincere. I grip my arms tighter to keep my hands from trembling. "Ill-advised, then."

He pauses. "Now that might be true, considering we've known each other . . ." He looks up briefly, as if contemplating the math. "Two days."

I swallow, shuffling my feet. "Madelyn told me you have a new sexual conquest every time you go on an expedition."

Thorn's expression goes through a cycle of shock, confusion, exasperation, and annoyance. "Madelyn doesn't know what happens on expeditions; this is her first. Why would she say that? I'll have a talk with her."

"You don't have to, no harm done," I say quickly. Honestly, the lie isn't that strange. Thorn is rich and accomplished, and I'm poor with next to no social status. I could easily be seen as an opportunist from a distance—although, if she knew him well enough, she had to know that he was doing most of the talking.

But I also . . . I also hadn't denied that I would sleep with him if he asked.

"Still," he says, "she should mind her own business."

"So this doesn't happen often?"

"By 'this' do you mean falling for someone in two days?"

I gape, words lost, heart pounding. The longer I stare at him the bigger his smile becomes.

"No," he says gently, "that's never happened before." He clears his throat and looks out into the trees at the sounds of chirping insects. "Anyway, Madelyn married Badger, so she's not really the authority on relationships."

"They seem okay together."

"They are, oddly enough." He seems to think about it for a bit, then shrugs. "Makes you wonder what a sweet woman like her sees in that scheming grouch."

What do you see in me? I want to ask. Instead, "I should let you get some sleep."

"Ah, you're right. Look at me talking your ear off. I'm sorry, Victoria, you're probably exhausted."

He's sorry . . .

He's *sorry?*

He's sorry?

And yet there's a simmering heat deep in his eyes that makes my legs momentarily feel weak.

"It's okay," I manage.

"Seriously, tell me to shut up anytime."

"I like listening to you. Your voice is . . . comforting."

"Comforting?" He looks surprised. Chews on his lip. For a second, I imagine he's blushing as much as I am. "I feel I might say something inappropriate if we continue, so . . . I'll bid you good night."

I want him to keep talking to me like this. If I go to sleep I might wake to realize this whole lovely exchange was all a dream, and I want it to last forever. I want him to talk to me forever.

But I can't protect him if I don't get enough sleep, so I nod. "We do have to get up early."

I want to accept his offer to sleep in his tent . . . except it's too late for that, I've already turned away . . . but I—

"Victoria?"

I turn back quickly at Thorn's voice, sweet and confident.

He takes a deep breath. Pauses, for so long it worries me. Finally, he shakes his head. "Good night."

Ask me to share your tent again.

God. I can't say that.

"Victoria."

My heart skips and I turn back to Thorn, who stumbles to a stop in front of me.

"I just wanted you to know that you're beautiful," he says. "Beauty as wild and awesome as the jungle itself."

I've been called beautiful my entire life—usually as a prelude to using it against me. Or as a fact—it is my job, after all, to give the tourists something to look at. I've never heard it said as incredibly wholesomely as Thorn just did. My hands tremble, but I can't help smiling the slightest bit. "I-is that the inappropriate thing you shouldn't have said?"

"Was that inappropriate?" he asks, with a grin dangerous enough to make me brave. "Then you don't want to hear what I was actually going to say."

I cup my trembling hands around my face like horse blinders, living and dying both at once. My face is burning, but hearing Thorn's laughter makes it even worse. "Good night, Thorn," I say, needing to get away before I embarrass myself further.

"Your Majesty," he says, with a tip of his head, his voice still holding the edges of joy from his laughter but also smooth and confident and . . . enchanted.

He meant what he said. He likes me.

Part of me shivers at the thought of what Dean might do if I reciprocate. The other part has never wanted to kiss another human being so badly in my life.

"What happened?" Samson asks as I approach.

I shrug. "Just a . . . practical joke."

"Didn't sound like a joke," he says, his voice on edge.

"Everything's fine." I sit on my cot, facing him, so I can see his skeptical expression. "Honestly."

"Every time you're out of my sight something bad happens."

I roll my eyes. "Oh, hush."

"No, seriously." He sighs. "You don't speak up, Victoria. I don't want you to end up alone with someone and unable to protect yourself."

That almost happened with Badger, but I keep that to myself. Instead I kiss my teeth, a spark of annoyance tapping at my temple. I lie back on my cot, staring up at the moonlit cracks of the canopy. "I've been taking care of myself since I was six years old, thank you very much."

"Well, I've been with you for the last eight years—"

"Seven and a half."

"Only because the first six months you didn't trust me."

I sigh. Sit up. "You were thirteen and already *huge*. Of course I didn't trust you."

"And now?"

"I don't know what I'd do without you. You know that. But that doesn't make me incapable."

We're quiet, until he draws in a ragged breath. "I love you, V," he says, "and I *know* you're capable. I love you even more because of that. But you have to be smart about this."

"Don't patronize me, Sam."

"Then don't stray from my sight for the rest of the trip. Check in with me if you have to leave camp. Be *safe*."

I narrow my eyes at him. "You know, Thorn suggested the

same thing, only he didn't make it sound like he intended to leash me like a dog."

"I'm not trying to leash you, I'm trying to protect you."

I stand, as if he's holding a physical leash and threatening to use it. "I know this jungle better than anyone, and yet—despite knowing next to *nothing* about the inner workings of the jungle—*you* want me to stay or go when *you* say. You're trying to control me, just like every other man. Just like the guards at the road who won't let me near the trees. Just like the boss. Just like Dean."

I turn to leave—I need to take a walk, brush these awful feelings off—but Samson steps in my way.

"Take that back," he chokes, distress creasing his brows.

"Why? It's true."

"I am nothing like the boss or Dean. I would never hurt you."

"Then stop being overbearing." I shove his hand away as he tries to touch my cheek. "A wild soul should not be leashed by the ones who love her."

He steps closer, his voice low, desperate. "Do you know how frightened I was to find you and Dean vanished from camp yesterday? I didn't know where you were, what was happening . . . the last time I let you go off alone with Dean he led you straight into a trap."

"Stop," I whimper, my stomach twisting.

"How many more times are you going to put yourself in danger because you 'don't want to make a scene'? It was only a year ago that the boss raped—"

"I know what he did!" I snap, rage burning in my gut. Samson reaches for me, and I stumble backward, nearly tripping over both our cots. "Don't touch me. I need air."

Samson steps back. At least he can do that much for me.

People must be looking now, but I don't think of them. I think of Thorn—of how he dealt with my aggressor, protected me, despite barely knowing me. Of how he said we should protect each other, work as a team. Of how he never once made me feel helpless.

I look up at Samson, finally catching my breath enough to say, "If you want to protect me, then protect me. But *do* something, rather than trying to hold me back."

We look at each other for a moment. I'm waiting. Waiting for him to say something . . . to do something. Anything to show he respects my wishes. Anything to prove that he's not like them.

"Are you done with this little marital squabble?" Dean demands as he approaches, giving us a grimace of a smile before landing a steady glare on me. "Because I need you to check the perimeter of camp and make sure the ruckus you caused didn't attract any pests."

"I didn't cause it," I say.

"Let's hope to God you didn't," he says. Warns. Too much like the boss for my comfort.

Samson grabs his satchel of salt. "Alright, Dean, relax."

Dean scoffs, "Not you," and glares at me, holding out a lantern. "Since you claim to be so eager to help."

"Gladly," I say, taking the lantern from him. I'm tired, but I'll do anything to escape this conversation with Samson, not to mention get away from Dean.

I walk slowly around the outside of camp, once, then blow out the lantern and head farther into the trees to make a wider circle. I don't need the light, and it's more than obvious the jungle is slightly annoyed by the disturbance—judging by the harshness of its whisper—but not enough to cause trouble. I slow my pace further. Now I'm just waiting until the camp falls asleep again.

It's moments like these—when Bunny is sleeping and Samson is being obnoxious, or there are too many strangers around . . . when I truly feel alone. It's these moments when there's nothing to be done but sleep, or else break down into fragments of myself that I barely know how to put together again.

Samson will wait up for me, I'm sure, but he can keep waiting. I sneak back into camp on the opposite side and tiptoe to Thorn's tent to sleep by the entrance. I don't want to face Samson again tonight, and maybe my presence will discourage Badger from retaliating against Thorn.

Only slightly louder than the whisper of the jungle, Thorn's voice drifts quietly through the tarp.

"Sometimes I feel like I'm almost done . . ."

Thorn is usually a ball of energy and joy. I've never heard him sound so . . . so *pained*. The melody is slow, mournful, almost to the point of haunting the air.

He repeats the words, and my stomach cramps like I may vomit. I can't help but feel that these words are all too true for him. A third time, and his voice breaks, and God, I feel his pain as if it's my own. I whimper, press my hand over my mouth to shut myself up.

He's hurting, and I have no idea what to do. Comfort him?

No . . . I can't. He doesn't know I'm out here. And anyway, I'm a stranger. What could I possibly do to help, even if he'd let me?

From the sound of it, he's as messed up as I am.

"A long ways from home . . . a long ways from home . . ."

Those words are even worse. Because I am. Even right here, in the midst of the jungle I love, I feel so far. Because I can't stay . . . I can never stay here. Even though it whispers my name. There are too many people counting on me to answer its call.

He's softly killing me and doesn't even know it.

Even so, I cling to the pain of his voice, holding it to my own pain like a mirror.

Two kindred spirits unable to sleep, both fighting for the strength to bury the heartache where no one can see.

The first time I met Samson, I was sitting on my bed mat struggling to braid my hair. I remember when they shoved him into the hut, that he didn't seem afraid like new recruits usually did. Later I found out that he'd lived across the island and his trip here had been long enough that maybe he'd had time to accept his fate. But I didn't know that then. I thought maybe he wasn't fazed because he was some sort of criminal.

He certainly looked like one—almost as tall as the doorway, long scruffy hair, angry shifting eyes. His face looked young, maybe just into puberty, but I kept my gaze down anyway. I didn't want him to notice me. He'd killed someone in his young life, I was sure of it. How else could he have been so calm after being kidnapped?

I'd cried for days after being taken. I remember that now, too. To the point that they'd had to tie me to a stake in the ground to keep me from running.

But Samson showed no signs he'd been crying, no proof that he'd fought tooth and nail not to be here. He had the demeanor of a veteran Wildblood without the actual experience.

"Mum always told me," he said, looking around—was he . . . talking to me?—"that I'd end up here if I didn't take my cod liver oil." He shook his head, dropped his bag in the corner. "Hell of a thing to be right about . . ."

And then he'd sat *next* to me, which horrified me to no end.

"I'm Samson," he said.

"Hello," I whispered.

"You got a name, too?"

The bottom of my braid had gotten knotted, my skinny little fingers fighting to dig it out. "What you gonna do with it?"

He kissed his teeth. "Now what kind of question is that?" He waited for an answer I was never going to give. "When did you get here?"

"When I was six."

"Six?" To my ten-year-old mind that seemed to make him more angry, more bloodthirsty—the first, anyway, was correct. "These people are crazy, taking kids. Man, if I had a knife . . ."

I knew it. He's a murderer.

"Hey, listen," he said, "you're the only other kid I've seen around here. We should stick together, be friends."

Kid? He was *gigantic*. And "friends"? The very word baffled me. Wildbloods didn't have friends—the closest thing they had was the one they paired with for tours, and I would come to learn even that wasn't reliable.

"You need help with that?"

I scrambled to my feet and away from him. I don't even know if he had attempted to touch me or my hair, but now that I was convinced he was a killer, it didn't matter.

"I have three little sisters," he said. "I braid their hair all the time."

I left the hut without a word to find comfort in someone familiar. I went to look for Dean.

Makes me sick to my stomach to think of now.

Six months later, Samson, the one I had feared, had become my rock—not to mention he's been braiding my hair almost every week since.

Eight years later, Dean, the one I trusted to comfort me, the one I thought I knew best, is someone I can never—*will* never—trust again.

CHAPTER 11

*O*w.

I wince at a sharp pain in my shoulder, pushing myself up before I've even finished opening my eyes. I look around briefly. Maybe I got some sleep after all, because I don't remember anything after I sat down outside Thorn's tent.

I get up quickly and walk toward my cot. The last thing I want is for Thorn, or anyone else for that matter, to see me leaving his tent in the wee hours, even if I was only outside of it.

When I reach my cot, Samson is lying awake, watching me. I cringe and lie down on my cot beside him.

"You look tired," he says. When I don't say anything, Samson reaches over and pulls my cot closer. "Do I dare ask where you've been?"

"Not now," I murmur, drowsily. *Not ever, thanks.* "Sorry about last night."

"You were upset."

"That's no excuse to compare you to the boss or Dean. That wasn't fair to you. I'm sorry."

"It's okay, baby."

We fall quiet.

"What do you think," I ask finally, "of Thorn taking Bunny along when he leaves for America?"

"Bunny has no survival instinct. It takes two of us to look out for him as it is. Imagine him alone, in a whole new country?"

"Well, he can't stay here much longer. It'll kill him."

"We have time to decide."

We settle into silence again. Samson wraps an arm around me, pulls me closer.

"Is that what you were doing?" he asks, and his voice booms too loud with my face against his chest, even if he's whispering. "Talking to Thorn about Bunny?"

At the mention of Thorn, I immediately think of his devastating song from last night. I wonder if he's okay, if he slept any. "No," I sigh.

". . . but you were with Thorn?"

More like I was sitting outside of his tent like a paranoid idiot.

But I don't have the brain capacity right now to say all that. Besides, he hasn't apologized.

"Time for sleep," I barely whisper, my strength for talking waning.

He pauses before saying, "Goldminers are nothing but thieves, stealing resources from land they don't own. You love nature. He's not a good match for you."

"We won't see him again after this tour, Sammy." I groan. "Anyway, it's not as if I'm in love with him."

"You're not?"

I roll away from him and cover my face with my arm. I don't want to think of my frustration with Sam or try to translate my feelings for Thorn or think of where to send Bunny when this is all over. There's a little over an hour left to sleep, and I'm taking full advantage.

The hour made about as much difference as a leaf floating on a puddle's surface.

I lead my line in a haze, nearly losing my footing more than once within the first hour. And it must not be as subtle as I think, because after the third time Thorn asks if I need to stop and rest—which pisses Dean off to no end, as evidenced by his glare when no one is looking.

I feel so foolish. Why did I lose sleep over this man I just met? Never mind that he's kind to me and his smile makes me . . . feel things. Never mind that I felt more connection with him through that song than I've felt with any other human being. He's nothing but ammunition for Dean to use against me, and he made Samson and me argue. And now I'm tripping over things like an idiot, while my promotion hangs in the balance.

I have to be mad at someone. Might as well be him.

"Seriously, Victoria," Thorn insists as I press forward. "We can stop for a bit."

"I'm fine," I grunt out. I hesitate, then add, "Are *you* okay?"

"I'm energized," he says. "But sweet of you to ask."

He doesn't know you were there last night. Of course he's not going to talk about it.

I try my best to push it from my mind.

I hear Madelyn scream, and when I look over she's shaking

the puffy legs of her trousers while her husband uses his canteen to knock something off her. I force myself not to roll my eyes as a lizard falls to the ground and scurries off.

I tried to tell her. She should count herself lucky it was only a lizard. Although, around here, you can't always count on the lizards to be harmless, either.

While she's recovering, Dean looks at me and gestures to a big tree. I huff out a heavy breath, but barely take a step before Thorn says my name.

I look at him, but he's looking at Dean. "Is this one of those times where we should be stuck like glue?" he asks.

I grin, despite what he's implying. It's just so very sweet. "No, it's okay. I'll only be a minute."

"What's happening?" Dean asks when I join him.

I raise my eyebrows. "What do you mean what's happening?"

"You, sleepwalking. Does it have anything to do with the ruckus from last night?"

"Well, I didn't get much sleep—"

"What was that about, anyway?"

I pause. *This* is what he cares about, not my lack of coordination. "You could've asked last night if you weren't so intent on blaming me."

He rolls his eyes. "Just tell me what happened."

"Ask your charge. It's his fault."

Dean pauses. "Badger?"

"He tried to pay me to kill Thorn."

I can see his jaw tick, like he's clenching it. "That's a little far-fetched."

"Ask Thorn, if you want. Apparently it happens a lot."

"I'll handle it." He stops himself from rubbing his face,

cracking his knuckles instead—though, in all honesty, it doesn't make him look any less flustered. "Your job is to protect Thorn from the jungle. Don't get involved with his personal matters."

"We don't get paid if they kill each other."

"Let me handle it." Dean sighs, then a slight grin slips to his lips. "You really did look like a baby animal over there."

I hate that his smile is genuine, teasing. I hate that I've missed that smile. I hate *him*. What business does he have being happy, knowing what he did to me and not even sorry for it?

"I know," I grumble, a tic of annoyance in my temple.

"Get it together."

"You're one to talk. You look exhausted."

He shrugs. "I've been functioning on little sleep for the past year. It's probably slowly killing me, but at least I'm not tripping over my feet."

I bite my lip against a laugh—his words are depressingly relatable. Still, I don't want him to think that gives him permission to get friendly with me, to pretend his betrayal never happened. To speak to me as if he isn't the enemy. And so I make sure there's no fun in my tone when I say, "Is that because you can't sleep alone?"

I don't even know if what I said is offensive. Maybe he did find a new bedmate after me. I mean, he sleeps away from the rest of the Wildbloods while we're at headquarters, but he could've. Maybe I'm childish for assuming he has no one to rely on after I was out of his life.

I'm the one who everyone hates, after all, not him.

But my words must've hit some sort of mark, because any playfulness in his eyes crystalizes into something colder. Not quite a glare, but something I know must be closer to the truth.

"Get it together," he repeats, and heads back to his line.

CHAPTER 12

After a few more hours of travel, a mass of light lies before us. The trees are sparser, making less of a canopy overhead, allowing the golden sun to shine down.

I have no memory of this place . . . but I can't tell if that's the reason I feel uneasy, or if it's something else.

My unease only grows as we come closer to the clearing—dozens upon dozens of trees have been knocked over, snapped, splintered, *crushed*.

It's not a natural clearing at all.

Lord have mercy . . . *it's a graveyard.*

Something in the way Dean's steps slow tells me he didn't see it coming, either.

"Ugh!" Madelyn fusses, her face contorting. "What is that smell?"

"What the devil . . . ?" Badger murmurs.

"What happened here?" asks Thorn.

His entire party swarms to the edge of the clearing to gawk at it, while Dean and I look at each other.

Turn around, I urge him with my eyes.

The muscles in his jaw twitch at my request. *You didn't know this was here?*

"This wasn't here thirteen years ago," I say aloud, my patience for his attitude razor thin.

"Stay within the trees," he announces. "We'll go around the clearing."

But the curiosity of the Americans is too powerful, and Thorn's party has walked into the clearing before Dean can even finish. A few of the Wildbloods follow, me included—I'm not going to let Thorn get a splinter from these mutilated trees, much less be eaten by whatever creature did this.

Although I may be more likely to get a splinter with my bare feet, tough as they are. Some of these trees are torn up enough to resemble spiny torture devices, and the ground is littered with wood chips and shards, although most of them are slightly softened by the recent rain. I step carefully, following Thorn.

"We should go back," I say.

"What happened here?" he asks again.

I can't answer that question. I've never in my life seen anything like this.

One of the few standing trees nearby is soaking wet and literally steaming, a pond-sized pool encircling it and lazily flowing downhill.

Urine. And recent, too.

Well, that explains the smell.

I try my best not to rush and draw alarm as I walk over to Dean. "Dean," I whisper, "we have to turn around and go another way. It would be foolish to go up against a creature that can hold that much piss."

"The only other way," Dean says, "takes us too close to the river. I'd much rather deal with a giant *killable* monster than try to prevent a large group from being hypnotized and drowned."

"At least we know the threat at the river. You would risk the lives of our clients on an unknown? Especially one that can decimate so many trees?"

"You're here to help, not tell me where to go. Now gather your group and tell them to be quiet. The less noise we make and the sooner we get moving, the less likely we are to attract any beasts."

I bite my lip to silence my next protest, and instead walk over to Samson.

"Pass the word around to our peers to be on their guard," I whisper.

"Why don't we just get away from this area?" he asks, but his tone is vexed to the point that I know he's going to cause trouble.

"Dean doesn't want to go near the river—"

Sam is kissing his teeth before I can finish, my attempt to hold him back by the arm futile as he storms over to Dean.

"You obviously don't know where you're going," Samson growls. "Just swallow your pride and listen to Victoria."

Dean glares at him. "Stay out of it, Sam."

"I've kept my mouth shut the entire trip—"

"Good," Dean bites back. "That's how it should be. You are a—"

"—but she is literally the only one of us who's been out here before."

"—Wildblood assigned to my team. You don't get to have opinions."

"It's not an opinion if it's true."

The restraint Dean shows in not punching Samson in the face is impressive. Maybe I was wrong, he doesn't follow the boss's example in everything. Still, there is a strange, calculating look in his eye that makes me want to take everything good I just thought of him back—serves me right, anyway, attributing any honorable trait to that backstabbing prick.

"Is there a problem?" Thorn demands, touching my shoulder and whispering a quick, "Excuse me, Victoria," as he inserts himself between me and Dean. "This seems like the worst possible place to argue."

"It is," Dean says, glaring at me—as opposed to Sam, who I wasn't sure if I should glare at as well for jeopardizing my promotion or hug and never let go for defending me. "We have to get out of this clearing and keep moving forward."

Moving forward.

"Dean," I try.

"We're leaving. Herd everyone back to the trees."

A deep and massive rumble echoes through the trees, rattling the broken wood and immediately shutting up every single one of us. Even the jungle seems too quiet, startled by the disruption. We look around, the location of the sound so vague, I'm not sure which direction it came from. All I know is, we need to go. *Now.*

The ground shakes and, in the middle of the clearing, a pile of trees shift, a giant bull rising from beneath the rubble.

Twenty, thirty, forty feet—I have no idea, but his massive size is less important than how if we don't get away from here, he's going to trample us like he did these poor trees.

But now realization dawns on me. I know this creature—or I've seen him. He was only five feet tall then and didn't have horns the length of a mature tree. If memory serves, we had a few playdates, but somehow I don't expect recognition from him at this point.

I see my fellow Wildbloods whip out their knives, prepping to access their blood. This could be a disaster if everyone is forced to use their science at once.

"Partner up!" I say, without waiting for Dean to give the order, but Dean's command is louder when he shouts, "Don't you dare leave your charge!"

I gape at him, but he doesn't see me. He, like the others, has his knife out and ready.

This isn't efficient. This isn't safe.

But there's no time.

The bull lets out a bellow and I clap my hands over my ears at his volume, the leaves and branches surrounding us quaking at his power.

"Bunny!" I call. I don't care what Dean says, I'm not letting either of my boys face this alone—although at least I know Sam won't use his science more than necessary.

Giant hooves scatter splinters in the air as the bull charges, and with it the sounds of gunshots and shouting men. A bloody harpoon flashes into the bull's shoulder, another against its stomach, with no success.

"Bunny, take cover!" I shout, but I've lost sight of him. Part of me panics, but I can't let that affect me. Blood and bullets are flying, men shouting in pain and fear. Some are running for the trees rather than face the danger. *The trees won't protect you, idiots!* I want to scream at them. *Why do you think all these wood chips are here?* But nothing is of any use but to act.

"What is the beast made of, steel?" Thorn exclaims. He shields me from a spray of wood as the bull skids around to charge again.

I tuck close, gripping his shirt. I'm grateful for the protection— for the thought of it, anyway—but I don't want it. All I want is my boys to be safe.

And the quicker I kill this poor creature, the better their odds will be.

My science burns. "Aim for the eyes!" I call. I don't know who hears me, but I see the flash of the sun bouncing off a rifle from the safety of the tree line and a gunshot from that direction, and it hits the mark along with my bloody weapon.

The bull's sounds of pain are haunting, and I fight the urge to cover my ears a second time.

"Stay here," I say in Thorn's ear, and before he can stop me, run ahead to square off with the animal.

My eyes burn red, my gut pulsing with lightning as I reach my hands out to the bull.

I realize it as it's happening—as *I'm* doing it—the blood pulling on invisible strands from my fingertips, coaxed by my power. The bull's eye socket is bleeding, but not a main entryway to the rest of the body. With one last surge, I pull my fingers into a fist as my invisible thread pulls the blood from the beast's body via the softest place I can think of—inside his mouth. And then my fists summon it to a halt.

A lake's worth of red liquid hovers in the air, lightning

flashing around and through it, suspended by the command of my hands. The bull stumbles to his stomach, rumbling the ground, shoving his collection of shattered trees out of the way as he skids to a lifeless stop five feet in front of me.

What am I doing?

My God . . .

What have I done?

And like that, my confidence turns to awe then to horror before I can fully process each emotion.

My ears are still ringing. Blood pulses hot through my veins, in my gut.

I let out a trembling whimper and drop my hands. The blood drops with them, bathing the splintered forest in carnage. I want to scream, looking at the bull, the poor creature who had never asked us to invade his territory, who had only been defending what was his. Tears burn my eyes as I reach my hand out, touching one of his massive horns.

And maybe I am screaming, because my ears are slowly clearing and I hear it, even with my mouth closed. But it doesn't—

"Victoria!"

Someone grabs my arm, and this time I know it's my own frightened scream, as I'm tugged around to face a frantic Thorn.

"Victoria, can you hear me?" he cries, shaking me by the shoulders. "Something's wrong with Bunny, what do we do?"

My heart drops into my stomach. I shove away from Thorn, racing and stumbling over to Bunny. I grip his shirt, at the same time tripping his foot out from under him, trying my best to control his fall so he doesn't slam face-first into the wood chips.

"I told you not to fight," I murmur, uselessly, as I press down on his back. "Why did you fight, Bunny?"

He can't answer, and I wouldn't want him to, anyway. His answer would frighten me far too much.

"Get away!" I shout as Thorn approaches. He takes a few steps back. The only man I've ever seen listen to me the first time I say something, without question, and I don't know why he does but I'm glad. Bunny's science could never burn me, but I don't know what it could do to someone without wild blood.

"What do you need?" he asks, and I can barely hear him over Bunny's screams.

"There's nothing you can do." I shift my feet to adjust my weight. "Help everyone else. Attend to your men. Go!" I demand, when he hesitates.

Finally, he rushes off toward his party.

I breathe out, slowly. I hadn't meant to be so short with him, but I just need him away from here. The last thing I want is for him to get hurt.

I wish I could tell him that. But now isn't the time.

Finally, Bunny collapses, and I nearly on top of him. He fusses and pushes me away, his face red as he sits up.

I take his chin in my hand. "Why do you like to scare me, Bunny?"

"Don't baby me in front of everyone," he mutters, pushing himself to his feet despite his fatigue. For a moment, I remain kneeling in the wood chips as he walks away, but I know my emotions will get the better of me soon.

The world seems trapped underwater—silent and wrong—as I get up and walk away from the group without a glance.

I pass the giant bull, slowly. His flesh is already beginning to crumble like sandstone, revealing parts of a giant rib cage, a hollow eye socket, a leg bone thicker than a tree. In an hour or two he'll become a shadow creature, a wandering spirit full of more rage than Bunny . . . and may very well remember who killed him. Not the kind of duppy that responds to salt. We need to be away from here before then.

But I have a minute, at least, to find someplace to get my crying out before we head off.

"Victoria." I hear Thorn's voice coming up behind me, and it pushes me forward faster. I don't even want to look at him— who cares that he tried to be helpful when Bunny was suffering? He's the one who put us in this situation.

Well, Dean did. But we shouldn't have been here, deep in the jungle, in the first place, and that's Thorn's fault. They're both arrogant idiots, but it's easier to release anger when it's directed at someone specific, and I don't have time to be choosy.

"Victoria," he says again, this time closer.

"You should make sure your party is ready to go in the next five minutes," I say without turning around, without stopping. I storm deeper into the trees, away from the clearing, away from everyone. I don't want them to hear me cry.

"I'd rather make sure you're okay."

"I want to be alone."

"You shouldn't go off alone when you're this upset—"

I turn to him and blurt out, "Why are you doing this?"

He pauses, as if he didn't expect my anger. "To make sure you're okay."

"The jungle gave us every opportunity to turn back. We should've never left the road." I don't want to cry in front of him, but I can't hold back anymore. I swipe my eyes with my sleeve. "You know, Bunny almost died back there."

A tender look creases his brows. "I didn't realize. I'm so sor—"

"Putting people in danger—your own people included—all for some gold. I thought you were a Christian. Isn't this a prime example of the love of money being evil?"

"'For all have sinned' is in there, too." He shrugs. "I'm certain Jesus understands that there's a learning curve. I've only been walking with Him for a few months, so I'm still not solid on all the rules."

I shake my head, for a moment at a loss for words. "Well, let me give you a hint: you're not supposed to *keep* sinning."

"This is how I make my living, Victoria, so I don't know what you want me to do."

"You're selfish."

Thorn tightens his lips. "Victoria . . ."

I move to turn away, then change my mind and add, "It's not even your gold. You have no right to it."

"It's okay, to be upset about Bunny. You don't have to make it about other things."

"Well, none of us would be here if it wasn't for your obsession with gold. It belongs to the jungle—everything here belongs to the jungle, and the jungle belongs to no one. So what makes you think you can just two-step in and take it?"

"Why *shouldn't* I take it? You said so yourself it's no one's."

"That doesn't make it right. You're wrecking natural environments, places where beautiful creatures live. I had to kill one to protect you, in his own territory. What about any of this seems right to you?"

Thorn sighs. "My parents weren't rich—they couldn't leave me with much. I had no real education, no particular skill other than music, and it was purely by chance that I discovered I had a knack for mining. I would've been playing on the street for coins otherwise."

"Forgive me for not feeling sorry for your freedom in choosing what you do for a living," I snap, and I know what I've said is wrong as soon as it leaves my mouth, but I can't stop it.

Thorn bites his lip, huffs out a heavy breath, the glisten of tears forming in his eyes. "Fine. You're right. I'm not asking for sympathy. All I'm saying is I'm not a bad person, Victoria. I don't run people out of their homes or steal or murder. I worked hard to be where I am today, and I'm not sorry for it. I am sorry it makes you uncomfortable, but I'm proud of what I've accomplished."

"Don't you understand? You *are* stealing. Just because it's not from humans doesn't make it yours."

"What do you want me to say, Victoria?" he says, taking a step closer. "I don't know what the right answer is. All I know is the earth was given to us to use, so I see no reason to feel guilty for taking from it, especially things that would otherwise just sit there."

"What makes you think the gold is just sitting there without your help?" I feel my fists curling. I should shut up, drop the subject, submit to Thorn's leadership—standing up to people, in general, rarely ends well for me. But Thorn holds nothing over me, no violence, no threats, no power . . . no power but that smile, that laugh, those dimples, the way my heart pounds when he looks at me. But I . . . I cannot submit to that.

Can I?

Still, my fingers relax.

"My apologies," he says, but he's smirking a little. "I didn't realize trees used gold for currency, too. I am learning so much on this trip."

He pauses long enough that I'm sure he's hoping I'll laugh. I don't. "Everything is a joke to you," I say, and turn away, storming through the brush.

His steps through the plant-life are loud and inexperienced as he follows. "Victoria, wait. Wait." His tone has sobered. I almost stop. "I'm sorry about what happened to Bunny. I don't—well, I don't even know *what* happened to Bunny!"

I hear him stumble. He doesn't fall, so I keep moving, and he continues to follow.

"What can I do, Victoria?" he asks almost desperately. "I can't change who I am or what I do. But let me help you. How can I make this up to you?"

I take a deep breath and turn to him, abruptly, and we almost collide. I step back from him quickly. "When Wildbloods use their science too many times in a row, it can become too much for their bodies to handle. I need you to reinstate the correct procedures and let the Wildbloods pair up."

Thorn's brows lower, and he purses his lips. "The correct procedures? This isn't how you normally do it?"

"No." I pause. "Didn't you request this?"

"Spitz Senior told me this is how it's done. I didn't ask questions."

"*You* didn't ask questions?"

Thorn smirks. "You used sarcasm, Victoria. I'm so proud."

I step back a few more steps, that charming grin threatening to draw me in and make me do something I shouldn't.

But maybe Thorn translates it as discomfort, because he clears his throat. "Um . . . about what happened back there . . ."

"With Bunny? That's what I was talking about, his body couldn't take it."

"No, I mean . . . when you pulled the blood from that bull's body." He shakes his head, as if all words have left him, if that's possible. Then, abruptly, he looks at me, and my hope withers. My hope of ever being accepted by him, ever being . . . loved by him . . . gone. Because I recognize that disturbed look I've seen so many times before.

The look my peers gave me before they turned their backs on me for good—because how could someone with power like mine not die young and raging . . . and take everyone in her path with her?

"Don't look at me like that," I choke out.

Thorn blinks a few times, as if I'd knocked him from a daydream. "It was horrifying."

"I know," I say, because I don't know what else to say, and then rush away.

Thorn grabs my wrist from behind, and I yelp like a frightened child and trip to a stop. His grip loosens as his hand slides down to mine, holding it softly . . . so softly I look down at our hands to make sure it's happening, that this is real.

"I'm sorry," I whisper.

"Why are you sorry?" he whispers back, and I suddenly realize he's leaning closer.

He's only a little taller than me, so I keep looking at our hands so I won't accidently look in his eyes and die of anxiety. "For killing it. For . . . upsetting you."

"Please don't apologize for saving my life. I mean, unless you regret it."

I pull away, even though my skin is itching to get back to him as soon as I leave. "How can you say that?"

He sighs. "It's a joke, Victoria."

I'm an idiot. A hopeless, messy idiot with apparently no sense of humor. A hopeless, messy . . . lovesick idiot.

Who's just given herself away.

Thorn steps toward me and touches my cheek. I close my eyes against it . . . but his hand never turns harsh. "Sweet girl," he murmurs, and his voice is so gentle, so soothing, I want to turn into his hand cupping my cheek and cry. Why do I feel this way, so overwhelmed all of a sudden?

He leans closer. I don't know if I can have what he's offering me, I don't know if I deserve it, I don't know if . . . if I can handle what will happen next, even if I want it.

But I do want it.

Before I can piece together my feelings, he presses his lips to mine.

I feel myself trembling and force myself to stay put. My body is so used to panic, to bracing for pain, that it doesn't know I want this.

But Thorn's touch is a sanctuary, a safe haven, and after a moment, my muscles give in to the rapture my mind has already accepted. My lips soften, part the slightest bit, and Thorn makes a small sound of praise and awe, like a wordless swear. He kisses me fully now. I still tremble, but it means something different.

When we finally part, I'm panting. I open my eyes, blinking my vision clear of tears so I can see Thorn.

His gaze shifts over my face. "Why are you crying?" he whispers, the back of his hand streaking tears across my jaw.

"That was so nice," I choke.

"God, you're a darling. Did you think it wouldn't be?" He smooths away the rest of my tears, laying a gentle kiss on my nose. "Consider this my official audition to become your primary lover."

I gasp, my muscles tightening painfully, and escape backward, my shoulder slamming into the closest tree.

"Please don't run," he says quickly. "I'm sorry, that was a bad joke. I'm so sorry—"

"W-what are we doing?" I say, gripping the tree, my heart pounding like it plans to kill me, butterflies bursting to life in my stomach. "We can't do this. You can't kiss me."

"Too forward?"

"'Too *forward*'?" I cover my face to hide my blushing, but it only deepens when I hear him chuckle. "It's not right, Thorn. I work for you."

"That's a good point, actually." When I peek through my fingers he's chewing on his lip nervously. "I'm sorry, Victoria. I swear, I don't ever do this. But I've also never met anyone like you."

I shove my trembling hands into my pockets, even though I'm sure my face is still red from the way it's burning. "Like me?"

"You're incredible."

My stomach hurts and I like it. "No, I'm not. I'm just a Wildblood."

"And I'm a goldminer. Nice to meet you."

"Stop." My throat feels tight with something like a sob. "Stop acting like we're equals. We're not."

"Yes, we are. Especially since you're the new leader of our expedition."

I gape. For a painful breath I can't get words out. "W-what?"

"I'm demoting Spitz," he says, almost too simply, while my heart thunders through me. "I'm not pleased with his performance."

"B-but you c-can't—" I'm stuttering again, barely able to make it through that small sentence. Thorn steps toward me, concern written all over his beautiful face, and I stumble beyond the tree to keep him at a distance.

He halts, mercifully. "Why does that make you anxious?"

"You're going to get me in trouble."

"I'm the client. My report of events will matter more to Spitz Senior than his son's. And if I tell him my people were dying and starving on his watch—"

"It won't make a difference," I snap.

"You're telling me your boss would punish you for something I implemented?"

I don't answer. Can't. Breaths go by that I can barely catch. "If Dean doesn't give a good report, I'll lose everything," I murmur, finally.

Thorn is quiet. I don't want to look at him and see why.

Finally, he takes a breath. "What you did back there with the bull, do they teach you to do that?"

"No one teaches us to use our science. We have to figure out our limits ourselves."

"Can all Wildbloods do what you just did?"

"No." I shrug. I feel sheepish, almost arrogant, admitting to Thorn that I'm more powerful than the rest. So I add, "I don't know. I've never seen it."

"Not even Dean?"

I scoff before I know what I'm doing. Bite my lip too late to take it back.

Thorn chuckles. "I take it that's a 'no.'"

"He's a good leader."

"We both know he's not. Out of the two of you, which one led us in the wrong direction only to nearly get us killed by a gigantic bull, and which one *saved* us?"

"It's not his fault," I bite back, desperate to cling to something to redeem Dean—if he goes down, so do I. "This is why we stay on the marked road."

"But you knew what to do. Spitz clearly didn't. I'm not going to let him lead us into another disaster."

"But it scares me, what he might do if I—Thorn, please . . ." I resort to begging. Because this beautiful, stubborn boy doesn't understand my world. How could he? "Please, don't do this. I'll be in such trouble. Please . . ."

My tears are falling too freely now. Thorn looks like a mass of color as he steps closer. This time I don't run. I let him wipe away my tears with his thumbs. "I won't let him hurt you," he says. "I promised to look out for you, didn't I?"

"He punishes me in ways you can't stop," I murmur, then freeze.

Oh my God . . . I said that out loud?

"I made Badger stop."

"Dean isn't afraid of guns."

"Then he's never been shot. I can amend that." He holds my face, and I want so badly for him to kiss me again. "Why are you afraid of him, and not the other way around? You can draw every ounce of blood from a gigantic beast in a matter of seconds. Mere mortals should quake at the sight of you."

I jerk away from him, wiping at my face—not because of tears, but because I can't bear the sensation of his sweet hands lingering. "I have people to look out for. I can't afford to be selfish like you." I straighten my shirt, giving him what is hopefully a confident glare. "And just because I have this power doesn't make me a murderer."

It doesn't, Victoria?

You killed an innocent creature without a thought.

I rush away. He follows—of course he does, it's not safe for him out here alone—but at enough distance to give me space.

"I didn't mean it in that way," he says.

I ignore him. Hear his footsteps pick up until he overtakes me, faces me, looks me dead in the eyes.

"I'm sorry, Victoria," he says, "but I'm invoking my right as a client to call the shots. I need to do what's best for my team, and what's best is if you take the lead."

What's best is if we turn around and let the men go home, gold or no. But Thorn is more stubborn than that poor bull I killed. So all I say is, "Yes, Mr. Thorn."

Thorn winces, as if I'd slapped him in the face instead of responding respectfully. "Don't hate me, please. I want to do what's best for everyone. What about a small gift from the gold we uncover? Would that make the change more palatable for you? A bit of a bonus, for going above and beyond."

He still doesn't get it. He never will.

How do you enjoy spending gold when you're beaten close

to death, your leash tightened, your promotion denied . . . any hope of helping the boy you consider a brother crushed?

But maybe . . . if I could send Bunny away with the gold first, it would all be worth it.

"That would help," I say.

Thorn sighs, wiping sweat from his brow. "But you still hate me."

"I'm not the only one," I say, and continue walking. Oddly— or not so odd with Thorn—I hear him laugh as he follows. Despite everything, I grin. "You know, it is pretty incredible that Badger hasn't retaliated since you threatened him. Usually my enemies don't give up so easily."

"Well, I've shot him before, so . . ." Now he's beside me, so I see him shrug from the corner of my eye. "Not with a rifle. And it was only a flesh wound, nothing serious. But he knows I'm crazy enough to do it again."

"You're not crazy," I say, looking over at him. "You're sweet."

"I tell you I shot someone and you tell me I'm sweet?" He looks at me and trips almost immediately, laughing it off before going back to watching his step.

"When you aren't being a selfish prick."

He swears. "I hope that's not the impression I've been leaving. I'm trying my best to impress you, Victoria."

"Why would you need to impress me? You're the client, I should be impressing you."

"I think it's pretty obvious."

His expression is unmistakable. I press forward faster to keep him from seeing my blush. "I've never in my life had someone threaten a person's life for my sake. It was very . . . touching."

"I'd do it again, in a heartbeat. I meant what I said, Victoria. I really like you." His eyes tell me more than his words dare to. I'm enjoying it more than I should. Once more, I find myself hoping he'll kiss me. In that moment, I think he might. We move as one, closer, and he glances down at my lips before quickly biting his own. He clears his throat, looking away. "Though, you know, I suppose I can't threaten Badger next time, seeing as I told him that next time I'd kill him. The threat becomes flimsy if you don't follow through—"

"We should really hurry back so we can gather the team and get moving," I interrupt softly.

"Yes, of course." He pauses. "I hope I haven't offended you, Victoria. I hope you don't think less of me because of . . . You can still like me, can't you, even if we have differing opinions? I hope?"

I nod, the corner of my mouth pulling upward a bit. "Of course. It's a relief, honestly. I was beginning to think a little too highly of you."

"Really?" Thorn trips again, this time barely catching himself before falling on his face. He rolls onto his back with a slight groan. "You can keep going. It's fine. I live here now."

I laugh, and he smiles at me like I've given him the greatest gift the world could provide. I hold out my hand and he takes it, letting me help him up. "We have to get out of bull territory."

"Oh, gladly." He's still holding my hand, and I'm keenly aware of his calloused thumb stroking my knuckles. "Lead the way, tour leader."

"About that . . ." I take my hand back, even though I don't want to, as we continue on our way. "There's too much to think about right now, what with navigating and making up for lost time . . . and it's better to tell Dean away from the team. So maybe let's not tell him until after we've made camp? That way he'll have a night to sulk about it."

"I can't wait that long. I demand competency *now*." He smirks—I suppose that must've been one of his jokes. "If that's what you want to do. There's not many travel hours left today, anyway."

"Thank you."

"Of course."

I love how he says "of course" instead of "you're welcome." "Of course." As if there's no other viable option. He's not doing as I request to be polite, he would simply never choose a different response.

When we get back to our party, no one seems to be in any rush to leave. I spot Sam and Bunny and look at Thorn . . . I don't know why. I'm not asking permission to go see my friends. It just feels strange not to acknowledge him after that . . . after we . . . I mean, *did* we? Of course we did, but I—

Thorn gives me a bit of a skeptical grin. "You alright?"

I feel myself blushing. "Fine."

He looks more radiant than ever now, if that's possible. "I won't kiss you in front of everyone if you'd like us to maintain the appearance of professionalism. But I'd like to kiss you again sometime, Victoria. Would that be okay?"

I tug down the rim of my hat. "That would be okay," I manage, although I really want to ask him *why* he's asking. I didn't know men asked ahead of time, like marking it on the calendar.

"Excellent." He touches my arm and I take a deep breath to remain poised. "Let's go gather the troops."

I head toward my boys while Thorn goes to get his party organized. They're sitting by the edge of the trees, Samson is leaning back against a trunk while Bunny kneels over him. Something about that looks . . . off. I quicken my pace and find Samson with a bloody strip of blanket around his thigh.

"What happened?" I ask, joining Bunny to examine it.

Samson waves it off, like a bleeding leg means nothing. "I fell on one of these mangled trees."

"Don't take it off," Bunny fusses as I mess with the bandage. "I just got it to stay."

"Were there any contaminants?" I ask. "How deep is it?"

Sam covers my hands with his to keep me from fidgeting. "Not deep."

"Still, I'll find you an herbal remedy as we go."

"*If* we go," Bunny says, rolling his eyes.

I look over my shoulder at Thorn's group, still gathered in a circle. I sigh and walk over to them. Madelyn is standing on the outskirts of their circle, looking extremely uncomfortable as she paces. Actually, the closer I get, the sicker she looks.

"Can you please tell them we need to leave?" she says.

I nod and join their circle. Someone in Thorn's party— forgive me, Lord, for not bothering to learn anyone's name— lies on a pile of broken trees. Blood runs from his mouth and from multiple holes in his body where the jagged parts of trees have impaled him. He's dead, that's certain. Why everyone is standing and staring at him remains to be answered.

I clear my throat. "We really shouldn't linger," I say, and some of Thorn's party look at me as if they've never seen me before.

"Yes, you're right," says Thorn. "But can we take thirty seconds to pray for our friend, Reginald? We should at least do that much, since we can't bring his body home."

The men remove their hats in prayer. I've never wanted to shake my fist at a group so badly in my life. A giant monster bull is decomposing into a spirit beast. God will understand if we pray on the way out of here.

"Victoria," Dean calls.

My body revolts against the very sound of my name from his mouth.

But I have to go to him. This time we're in the middle of a clearing, with nowhere else he can take me—not that it matters, now that I know how good he is at punishing me out in the open.

But I go, because I have to.

When I reach him, he murmurs, "We have deserters."

"How do you know they're not under the rubble somewhere?"

"Because I saw them run the way we came during the ruckus." I see him move to rub his temple, then stop himself. "Cowards."

Cowards for saving themselves from a terrifying, unnecessary situation? I say more power to them. Not everyone is built for this life of monsters and blood.

"If anyone asks," he goes on, "they were lost in the attack."

I bite the inside of my cheek. "Got it."

He looks off in the distance, and I follow his gaze to the bull, whose bones are starting to glow and smoke like embers. "Let's get the hell out of here before that thing wakes up."

CHAPTER 13

Samson's wound is a little pink around the edges, but no real sign of infection. Still, things can change very quickly in the jungle—there's bacteria here that live nowhere else in the world, I'm sure, and some of them can get pretty hungry for open flesh. I apply a salve using a large, waxy leaf, careful to keep my fingers out of it as I cover it with moss and tie the leaf in place on top with a vine. He needs better medical care than an herbal numbing concoction and medicinal mosses, but it's the best I can do for his pain under the circumstances.

"Is my leg okay?" Samson asks, attempting to sit up from his cot to look at it. I put my hand on his chest, prompting him to lie back again. "Why does it smell like rotting bananas?"

"That's just the salve, Sam. Do you feel anything?"

"Nothing from the thigh down."

"Good, it's working."

"Well . . ." He sighs heavily, closing his eyes. "My value has plummeted."

"Don't say that," I chastise, but I'm glad he can't see me chew on my lip. "I don't think the limp is permanent."

I don't want to say he's right . . . but he's right. He's marketed as a Rare Beauty. Rare Beauties are not supposed to walk with a limp.

"It's the pain causing it," I insist. "When you're healed, everything will be fine."

Sam says something within a yawn that I can't understand. I'm glad—now that he's numbed, I hope he'll sleep heavily. Walking on that leg today must have been rough, even with Thorn's and my help.

He reaches for me, eyes still closed, and I take his hand, squeezing, and fight my hardest not to have a panic attack as I look beyond our cots and watch Thorn approach Dean.

"I love you, Victoria," Samson says, and I turn back to him. "I don't think I tell you enough."

I pat his hand gently. "Stop talking like you're on death's door. Your injury isn't as bad as all that."

He's attempting to sit up again, so I press on his chest once more to ease him down. In turn, he holds the back of my head with his large hand and pulls me closer.

I freeze in his grasp for a moment, moving where he takes me. I'm not afraid of Samson, but this firm, desperate grip . . . this scares me. "Sammy, what's wrong?"

He shushes me, then lowers his voice. "Listen to me, V. I have to tell you something, and I don't want you to fight me on it. I want you to trust that I know what I'm saying. Do you trust me?"

"You're scaring me," I gasp, and I grab his hand at the back of my head with both of mine as he pulls me closer. What else was in that numbing agent to suddenly make him go crazy? "Samson, stop. Just tell me what's wrong."

"Do you love me?"

"Yes."

"Do you trust me?"

"Yes," I answer, but feel frustration building in my head, and my voice comes out with a bite of anger. "But I'm getting ready to punch you in the face if you don't stop scaring me and get to the point."

His brows lower slightly, his grip easing to a caress, as if he didn't know his own strength. "I need you, when this mission is over, to leave with Thorn for America."

I freeze. That isn't what I expected him to say at all. "Leave?"

"He's proven himself to be a good man. He'll take good care of you—"

"I don't need to be taken care of," I cut him off. "And I'm not going anywhere, especially not while Bunny is still on the island."

"I can look after Bunny."

"I can take care of myself," Bunny butts in, half asleep, barely lifting his head from his cot.

I feel tears irritating the backs of my eyes. "If you really loved me, you wouldn't suggest something like that. You wouldn't make me leave everyone—every*thing*—I love."

Samson studies me for a moment. "But you love him, too, don't you?"

Despite my trembling I manage to break away from his grasp. "I—I barely know him, Sam."

"I watch you two interact. You love him, or could . . . And not in the same way you love me."

I'm blushing, and have no way to hide it—no way that won't make it more obvious, anyway. "I can't leave you and Bunny. I can't leave the jungle. And why should I, especially if I don't want to? You're my family."

I feel something brush my leg—it's Bunny reaching for me. I take his hand, and the weight of it settles in mine as he drifts back to sleep.

"You said you wouldn't fight me on this," says Samson. "You said you trusted me. So trust me, V. I was older than you were when I was kidnapped—thirteen, old enough to have seen and experienced all the goodness of this world. You've never had that, and Thorn will give it to you. You deserve . . . something good for a change." This time, when he reaches for me, his touch is gentle against my cheek. I swallow the urge to cry, lay my head on his broad chest in case he can see it on my face. He strokes my hair, softly, and I hear his words, deep and muted through his chest. "One of us should be free, don't you think?"

It feels like déjà vu, like something I've said and can't quite remember.

I lean up to look in his face, but he's closed his eyes. I run my fingers over his brow and he sighs. He's exhausted. How can I argue with him, when he needs rest . . . when all he's doing is thinking of me? In his usual bossy, overbearing way, but still.

Besides, maybe . . . maybe I could love Thorn, maybe I already do. I'm not entirely sure I actually know what real romantic love feels like. Is it supposed to hurt your stomach, make you light-headed, make you forget simple skills . . . make you *burn* deep inside?

Sounds more like a fever.

"It's all set for tomorrow," Thorn says, approaching. He

cringes apologetically, putting his finger to his lips, then adds, quietly, "Dean took the news better than I thought he would."

I narrow my eyes. "He did?"

"He had questions of course. And lots of concerns. But I didn't sense any animosity."

"He's a liar," I want to say, but already my anxiety of what he plans to do with that lie is tightening at my throat, silencing me.

"Okay, all, listen up!" Thorn shouts to the group, clapping his hands to get their attention. My blood suddenly feels like sludge in my veins, my body and mind stupid and heavy and unable to stop what I know is about to happen. "There's been a change to the pecking order. You will now direct all tour concerns to Victoria, who is our new tour leader. Any questions about the change, however, should come to me. Thank you for your attention. Carry on!"

My heart pounds, plotting to murder me. If I had known he was going to announce it, I would've—I don't know. I don't *know*. Shoved leaves in his mouth or something. Kissed him, even in front of everyone. Anything to shut him up. As it stands, I keep my eyes on the ground. The hateful, scrutinizing glares of my fellow Wildbloods bore into me without me needing to see them.

This promotion is exactly what I'd wanted. So why does it feel so toxic? So wrong?

"Give me a minute," Thorn says, before my lungs will function again. "I have to go help pitch the tents before it gets too dark, then we'll plan for tomorrow. Don't go away."

He winks at me and jogs off to assist his party.

I take a deep breath, take one more glance at my sleeping boys, and then go look for Dean. Some of my peers are still staring at me. Fear, hate, and whatever else they had felt for me before has just been amplified tenfold. I don't know how any group of people could hate me more.

"Whore," someone mutters as he pushes past me, and my stomach twists, tears burning the backs of my eyes.

To them, my science is dangerous. I'm too quiet. I've dethroned their prince.

And I've slept with the client for a promotion.

I want to disappear.

But it's important I locate Dean first. He's talking to someone, his back facing me. Exactly the conditions I need.

I slip into the thick trees, the foggy surroundings offering me a bit of cover, before everyone thinks up another reason to hate me.

The last thing I want is for Dean to confront me—not now, before I know exactly what Thorn said to him. Besides, now that he's gotten good at punishing me in public, it's not as if I'll be safer staying around camp. And he *will* punish me, despite no longer having the authority to do so.

I check the area before standing behind a tree and release a slow breath. There's no way he took the news as well as Thorn said. I know him too well for that. Being demoted has undoubtedly bruised his ego, and he never lets anyone get away with that—especially since, with me as leader, his inheritance is in jeopardy.

I'm scared of what this means for me. Not what Dean will do, but how the boss will react. Even if I make enough money to send Bunny away—which, after hearing the points Samson had to make about it, I'm not positive is the best thing for him anymore—the boss has never forgiven plans that don't go his way, even if they succeed in other ways. So what if Thorn is pleased by my performance, if he'll give me an excellent report? I was never in the boss's plan for his heir.

Never mind that he pitted Dean and me against each other our entire childhood—he was never going to pick me. I'm a girl. I'm too soft-spoken. I stutter when I'm nervous. I'm too naturally tan and my nose is too broad to pass as white, even with my hair covered.

A spider crawls down a strand of silk, her legs camouflaged as twigs, her back the color and texture of bark.

I grin. "Hello there, sweetie," I whisper. I reach up my hand, slowly, and she graces my finger. "Why aren't you hiding against a tree?"

Like I am . . . like a frightened child.

Like the one time I'd tried and failed to hide from the boss's punishment. I don't even remember why he was angry with me . . . not that it mattered. The boss didn't need a reason to hurt us.

It was one of the few times I'd managed to sneak out into the jungle, unseen by guards. But I was too valuable to the boss, and he'd brought the dogs to sniff me out. I didn't get very far before they caught me. He's as afraid of the jungle as everyone else, so he didn't punish me there. Instead he grabbed me by the hair and dragged me out kicking and begging, all the way around to the back of the office, under the window of his bedroom where no one could see. Not that there was anyone to see but the guards. It was a Sunday.

The boss forced me onto my stomach, pressing the side of my face to the ground, my tears wetting the dirt under my cheek to mud. An outside punishment meant he was going to make me bleed—he didn't like blood on his hardwood floors.

"Bring me the switch, boy," he'd said to Dean, who was trembling as much as I was. And, despite my eyes begging him not to, he did. I suppose he figured there was no sense in us both being beaten over nothing. That should've been an early sign of his eventual betrayal, but in the moment I didn't blame him. We were both young and scared.

Dean held the wooden weapon out to him at arm's length.

I heard the boss chuckle. "Now beat her with it."

"But, Boss, she's a Rare Beauty," Dean said, and I could hear that he was crying. "The clients can't see her injured."

"So beat her somewhere they can't see."

Dean didn't say anything. I braced myself for a strike, my entire body shaking, but it never came.

"It's bad for business," Dean said, backing into my view, and his words gave me hope that this would be over soon.

It made little difference—the boss beat me himself anyway. *And* Dean, for disobeying.

Nothing good ever comes of hiding.

Enough of this.

I take a deep breath and inhale incense, and turn quickly to see Dean stopping only ten feet from me.

"Victoria," he says, his voice less a greeting than a dark confirmation.

I touch my thurible. I haven't lit it since that first stick of incense ran out, and no one has noticed. So he didn't find me based on smell. But it doesn't help that I'm wearing a white shirt. Maybe I should've climbed the tree, instead.

No, Victoria. No more hiding.

"Dean." I do my best to keep my voice even as I allow my little friend to leave my finger for the tree. She doesn't want to leave, instead crawling up my arm. "I was going to head back in a minute."

"You were hiding from me," he confirms, his voice constricting my lungs. His expression is like a worn-out leash tethering a violent dog. "Did you think I wouldn't know to look for you among your kinfolk?"

Something crawls down the back of my neck, and I hope to God it's the spider. "My kinfolk?"

He shakes his head and kisses his teeth, as if I should understand. "*Insect.* You know what you did."

Spiders are arachnids, but that's not his point, and I'd rather not make him angrier than he already is.

I step away from the tree and start heading toward camp. "I don't know why you're angry with me. Thorn told you, I'm sure. This was all his idea. I didn't do anything to encourage it."

"You didn't do *anything?*" He snatches my wrist and drags me through the trees, my skin burning at his touch like he's made of coals.

I should purposely make my steps louder. I should scream. I shouldn't be anywhere alone with him. Instead I let him lead me through the trees and into a narrow, camouflaged gully, deep enough that there's an extra foot of earthen wall above Dean's head.

Deep enough that no one will easily find us in the dark.

Samson was overbearing in his delivery, but he was right—I never cause a scene when I should.

"This is serious, Victoria," Dean says. "You have to tell him you don't want to be the tour leader."

"I tried." I tug away from him, rub my wrist. "He's too bullheaded."

"He's clearly attracted to you." Dean leans against the wall of the gully, folding his arms. "Maybe you can convince him otherwise. Use your feminine wiles."

"I don't have *wiles*," I say, holding back the urge to gag. "I don't manipulate people who are supposed to be on my side."

"Don't play high and mighty. Both of us have been lying to the boss since we were children."

"He's never been on our side."

"And Thorn is?" he says, scoffing. "That what you think? That a man famous for gold digging is on anyone's side but the ones who can help him reach his treasure?"

I falter. I'd never considered it, but it could be true. It could be true of someone like him. But not him. *Never* Thorn. "He's not like that. He would never do that to me—"

I stop myself, seeing the look of understanding on Dean's face. Dean betrayed me, and I've known him my whole life. I don't even know Thorn. What's stopping him from doing the same?

But I have to believe he's good. I need something to cling to.

"Relationships are nothing but transactions," Dean says. "We lie to the boss to keep him happy, we do as he says to gain leverage so we can one day get what *we* want." He steps closer as I try to make sense of my thoughts, his words. "If Thorn is kind to you, you need to ask yourself what he wants. How you can use it to your advantage."

"It's his nature," I insist. "I've spoken with him enough to know. Just because we aren't used to kindness doesn't make it false."

"You're so childish sometimes," Dean scoffs. "My God. The man has got you simpering."

My insides feel like a simmering pot of curry. "If you had

turned around when I told you to, maybe you would still be leader."

"And if you don't fix this, we'll both be dead when we get home."

I roll my eyes, secretly looking for a spot on the gully that's easiest to climb. No one has come looking for us. Why has no one come looking for us . . . ? "Weren't you just bragging about your expertise in lying? How about that option—?"

"He sends spies, that's why."

We both freeze. Dean blows air through his nose while I try to understand what I missed in my twelve years of working for the boss. "Spies?"

"This is what you learn when you become the boss's *heir*," he says bitterly, the final word like a curse. "At least one Wildblood per mission is a mole. A rat with a pay bump. Sent to report back to make sure the tour leader and client's reports can be trusted. With a party our size there's probably two."

"Any ideas who?"

"Nathan was one—he made it obvious, too, the little kiss-up. Luckily I didn't have to wait long for an opportunity to send him home after that duppy attack."

"And the other?"

He pauses just long enough to make my stomach hurt. "You don't need to concern yourself with that. The point is, neither of us are going to get what we want unless you make Thorn change his mind."

"There's nothing I can say to him that will make the decision seem logical. I saved everyone's lives. And you don't know anything about the jungle. You barely know anything about being a Wildblood anymore."

"What I do know," he says with a heavy sigh, "is that if you don't help me convince Thorn I should be the leader, no Wildblood will ever be safe."

"We're already not safe. You saw what happened to Bunny."

"Bunny's on his way out, and you know it."

I feel my science stir. "Don't you dare."

"I'm talking about Wildbloods with hope and years left in them. You don't get it. I was going to change the system. I was going to make sure everyone is paid a good wage, that no children were ever stolen again. I was going to turn it into a legitimate business. This is my last test. He's never going to let me take over the company if this report gets back to him."

"Why should I believe you when you barely care for the lives on your own team?"

"If the boss ever found out my plan . . ." He sighs, shakes his head. "I had to make it look like I shared his ideals. I couldn't risk—"

"So when you let the boss *rape* me, you were just proving you shared his ideals?" Dean is quiet for far too long, and my stomach twists with pent-up lightning. "Well?" I demand.

"Yes," he says. But nothing else. No apology. No further explanation.

I shake my head, taking a few steps back. "I didn't hate you before that, you know. Before then, we were both just victims of his cruelty. But we never hurt *each other*. And you—" It's hard to swallow now, my throat burning with a stupid sob. I can't cry over this. I've been living this life long enough that I should've seen his betrayal coming. Still, my voice is hushed, trembling when I finally say, "How could you stand by and watch? How could you let him hurt me like that?"

Dean doesn't look at me. "I did what I had to do for the betterment of everyone."

"The betterment of everyone?" I rush up and shove him in the chest. He's not looking, so he stumbles over a root, the dirt wall behind him knocking the wind out of him. "Thorn told me he never requested personal guides for his party. That was your idea, wasn't it? If you cared about any of us, you would've never endangered your own like that."

"There's safety in numbers."

"Not in the jungle there isn't, and you're foolish if you believe that. I'm not helping you anymore, Dean. If you want your position back, take it up with Thorn yourself."

"The boss isn't going to make you a tour leader," he calls after me as I storm away. "He never was. Burned the contract as soon as you were down the hall."

I halt, my heart throbbing.

"But *I* will." Dean has the stealthy steps of a Wildblood, despite having been on far fewer missions than I have, and my anger feels irrational but real at hearing his voice so close behind me. "Help me secure this position and I guarantee yours."

I turn around, backing up a few steps. "What makes you think I'll trust what you say ever again? How *can* I, when our relationship has been nothing but a *transaction* to you?"

He sighs, heavily. "I'm not using you. I *need* you. We need each other, if we're both going to get what we want. When I'm the new boss, you'll see that."

"He's not *that* old, you know. I don't see him keeling over anytime soon."

"Well . . ." His grin makes my stomach hurt in the worst way. "Not without help."

I freeze. "You'll never get away with it."

"Haven't you noticed he's developed a bit of a cough over the past few months?" He grins, satisfied with himself. "Poison is a gradual thing . . . hard to detect sometimes."

I feel too many things at once. If getting rid of the boss was his goal, I would've helped him with that a long time ago. I would've . . . if he'd never told me the boss wanted to see us that night, then claimed ignorance when I asked why. If he'd never kissed me like he loved me before we went into the boss's room. If the boss . . . hadn't been waiting on the bed naked and terrifying, hadn't shoved me down onto it, hadn't pinned my hands to my chest, hadn't—

I close my eyes, every inch of my body screaming, uncomfortable, repulsed by the feeling of my own skin and flesh, the awful sensation of needles tearing into everywhere he'd touched me that night.

I glare at Dean, now, rage wanting to take over my disgust. Dean, who had been my best friend, who had claimed to love me . . . who had stood there, watching it all, without lifting a finger to help me.

He sighs. Again, it suggests my apparent stupidity. "Don't you want to be free, Victoria?"

"Free of what?" I snap. "You're replacing one overseer with another."

"I don't like being beaten down any more than you do. I plan on being a fair employer."

"Then you'll let everyone leave of their own free will if they don't want to serve the company anymore?"

He tightens his lips, letting out an impatient huff. "It won't be much of a business that way."

"Even with our ability, not everyone is suited to this life. Some people have other passions. They want families, simple lives. Or something other than borderline enslavement. Why do you think we had deserters? And we'd have more, if they knew they could get away with it."

He sighs and scratches his head. His sandy tan hair has gotten a little longer, but not quite enough to curl yet. "You seem to love it. You can't be the only one."

"Don't you care that you're lowering your own people's life expectancy? Every time we use our science we're at greater and greater risk."

Why am I even asking? He doesn't care.

"This is what Wildbloods were made for," he says.

"All except you, right? You get to sit behind a desk, never having to use your science ever again, having stepped on the backs of your own people to get there."

We glare at each other. It's what we're best at, honestly. Normally, Dean breaks—and he will, if I let my eyes burn red with warning. But this time he knows he's the only one with something to lose. This time, the boss's decision isn't looming over me to break our tie, giving me no earthly reason to compromise.

My enemy is in the palm of my hand, and I can choose to crush him whenever I wish.

For now, his humiliation is enough.

"I have a team to lead," I say, turning away. "Feel free to stay here and sulk."

"I didn't know he was going to do that." His voice scratches out, like a never-healing wound, odd enough for him to make me halt, to make my muscles tighten in anticipation of the worst. He paces, and I turn to him, halfway, so I can keep track of his movements. "That night, in his room. He said the next day I would begin training, start really learning about the company—"

"Oh please!" I throw up my hands, disgust rising up in me.

"He said he had something to show us first. You know as well as I do, he doesn't dole out violent punishments in his room, so I thought . . . and then . . . and then he told me not to move. I was just as scared as you were—"

"You passed his test. He made you his protégé the next morning. Admit it, you let him hurt me to earn his favor."

"In order to gain his name and succeed him."

"And I was just a casualty on your way to the top."

"If I killed him *before* being handed his position, people would suspect me. I can't help any of our people if I'm being hanged for killing a man, and a white man at that." He's quiet for a moment, as if waiting for me to respond. "You really are not even *trying* to understand what I'm telling you."

No, you don't understand that I've found a way to get exactly what I want without being indebted to you.

The promotion is off the table—apparently was never on it, but I've been adapting to worse situations than that since I was six years old. Thorn has promised me gold, and I'm going to use it to take me, Bunny, Samson, and as many as will come with us away from this island for good. I don't know how that's going to work, exactly, and I'm sure I'll have to deal with the boss in some way, but . . . one step at a time.

"If you call me stupid one more time I'll punch you in the throat."

Dean scoffs. "Hit me without using your science? By all means, I'd love to see it. It's always been a crutch for you."

"Every single one of you would've been trampled to death by a giant bull without my so-called crutch, so you'd better be grateful I'm only threatening you with my fist."

I turn on my heel and rush off down the gully to get away, to find a suitable spot to climb. Rush, because Lord have mercy, the last thing I need is for Dean to call my bluff. He's a despicable, loathsome being, but he was brutally trained by a former boxer. A hand-to-hand fight against him would be, at minimum, incredibly stupid.

"Arrogant, ungrateful bitch," he says, his voice traveling closer, an edge to it that makes my lungs constrict. "Get back here."

He suddenly rushes at me, slamming me against the wall, and knocking the wind from me. I'm barely able to gain that air back fully before his hand grips my throat. He's so much bigger than me, invading my space, and I feel suffocated by more than his hand.

"What are you going to do, hit me?" I say bitterly. "You've already done your worst."

He winces, like he always does when reminded. As if that night hurt him more than it hurt me. His eyes are glassy, like he might cry, and I wish he would. But he continues to glare. I see his eyes flash bloodred before he backs down, burning away any sign of tears.

No, he won't cry, because monsters don't. And he won't use his science, because he knows it would then be fair game for me to use mine—never mind that I may not have enough oxygen right now to summon it. He doesn't know that. He only knows I could kill him if I wanted to.

And, my God. I want to.

"You think that was my worst?" Dean says, his voice low

and dark, like some creature pent up and impatient to get out. His strong fingers tighten on my throat, and I do my best not to release all my air at once, to save some, to keep my wits. "Tell Thorn you're stepping down from the leadership role, or I will show you how much worse it can get."

You're not the boss, I want to say, *no matter how hard you try to be like him.* But I don't want to waste air, so I shake my head quickly.

I force my shriek of shock and pain into a closed-mouthed squeak as he grabs the flesh of my stomach with his other hand, like he might tear me open with his bare fingers. I've lived so many years conditioned not to scream for help, that I can't even make myself do it now when I should. The campsite isn't that far. Someone would hear me—

"This doesn't hurt, does it?" he mocks, and I whimper as he twists my flesh. "Last chance to do the right thing."

I glare at him. He doesn't wince this time, my pain emboldening him. But I've felt worse. We both know that, because so has he. He's going to have to do a lot more to break me. A *lot* more.

And, by the look in his eyes, it's obvious he's willing.

Dean swears suddenly, jerking his hand from my throat to brush off my big barky spider from his skin. I still can't take a deep enough breath and there's no time, but if I can just get away from this wall—

Dean's heavy hand grabs my shoulder, shoving me back into the wall again, as his fist slams into my stomach. I exhale everything in me, blind to the fist meeting my cheek.

I don't have time to do anything but hit the ground, hard. My instincts kick in, and I shield my face with my arm, my gut simmering with energy. The impact didn't feel like much—

almost numb. But the dull ache is rising gradually, an ache I've felt enough times to know it's going to leave a purple bruise. But no sharp pain. Nothing broken. Still, my eyes tear without my consent. Another one like that might take me out.

But it's Dean, so I don't beg for mercy. I hate him too much for him to see me beg.

Instead, I glare through the crook of my elbow. "A grasshopper could hit harder than you."

I gasp and grit my teeth as his foot collides with my side. And now he's on top of me, his knee digging right below my chest, right into the muscle I need to breathe. I can barely catch my breath—but it's enough, and my core heats with lightning, but not before he squeezes both my hands in one of his and presses them to my chest, rendering my science useless.

But still, I don't beg. I don't give him the satisfaction. Even with my short, panicked breaths. Even knowing what he's about to do with that fist in the air, I glare at him. I hate him harder.

Only . . . his fist is shaking. He shifts his eyes to glance at it. Uncurls his fingers then curls them back, as if that will fix anything. An irrationally pleased chuckle slips out of me before I can stop it.

"She bit you," I say, "didn't she?"

"I have my incense. I'll be fine."

"You know the smoke only suppresses the venom glands. It looks like some got through anyway. You'd better poke some moss in your bite wound, unless you want to go into spasms."

Dean hesitates just as I hear swiftly crunching brush, and an uncontrolled gasp of relief escapes me as Thorn comes into view.

"Get off her." Thorn's voice is razor-sharp, sure with

authority, unafraid. It threatens death as much as the rifle trained on Dean's chest, as he slides down the side of the gully to join us. "Don't test me, Spitz. Get up."

"You don't know what you're doing," Dean growls. "What you've done."

"I know your chest is a nice big target for my bullet." I hear the click of the slide action on his rifle. All he has to do now is pull the trigger, and it's done . . . "Up."

Dean releases my hands slowly. I don't try to get up. Instead, I close my eyes, feeling his weight lift away from me, praying he won't do anything rash.

"Victoria, are you hurt?"

Thorn's voice awakens my body, and I open my eyes to stare up at the dark canopy. I can't see Dean. I should've kept my eyes open, kept track of him.

"No," I say, but my voice comes out in an unconvincing squeak.

"She's fine," I hear Dean say, followed closely by Thorn commanding, "You shut up."

I clear my throat. "I'm fine," I say, and push myself to my feet quickly.

The sound of Thorn's booted feet approaching soothes my anxiety, but when I look at him, he gapes.

"My God," he murmurs, his brows knitted with concern as his fingers skim my temple, my eye, my cheek. There's a slight ache where he touches, but I have a feeling it might feel worse later. Bruises always do, even if I have learned mostly to ignore them.

"You're making a big mistake," Dean says. He's found some moss to stuff in his wound, unfortunately. "When the boss finds out about this—"

"You *and* your boss can go to hell." Thorn laces his fingers, holds his hands down to me. I don't know that I need it, but I step on the perch he's created and he boosts me up the side of the gully. I reach down, though he seems a bit surprised before taking my hand and allowing me to help him up.

"I should've seen that coming," Thorn says as we hurry back to camp. "His acceptance of being demoted was a bit too easy, now that I think on it."

"It's okay, Thorn," I say. "Believe it or not, most people trust him."

"And it almost cost you your life. That's not a mistake I'll make again."

We make it to camp, stopping by my cot. The boys are still sleeping, thank God. I would hate to explain this to Samson.

"Thank you," I say.

"Don't thank me. Protecting you is the bare minimum I can do." He hesitates. Chews on his lip. "You can say 'no,' of course, but I want to reissue my invitation to—"

"Yes," I blurt out.

The corner of Thorn's mouth twitches into a slight smile. "Yes?"

My heart races as I nod. "Yes." But the longer he looks at me, the more nerve I lose, so I direct my eyes to the ground as I grab his hand and lead him to his tent.

Once inside, Thorn tugs me to him, gently. I blush and drop my gaze, but he lifts my chin with his hand. But disappointment quickly follows my excitement when I find that he isn't trying to kiss me, but rather is looking at my face by the lantern light.

"I'll kill him," he mutters, studying my bruise.

"It doesn't really hurt."

"That's not the point. In no scenario on this planet does he get to strike you. I should've shot him in the head."

I pull away, turning the bruised side of my face from his view. "I've had much worse. Honest."

He falls silent for a moment. "That hurts. I hate hearing you say that."

"It hurts me more, I think."

A slow grin brightens his face. "Look at you, dropping well-timed jokes. You're putting me to shame, Victoria." He walks farther into the tent. "Please, make yourself comfortable."

I stay close to the entrance. I feel awkward, and hope to God I don't look it. "Which side do you prefer?"

"Well . . ." Thorn sits on his blanket to remove his boots. "I usually just sleep in the middle, so . . . lady's choice."

"That side is fine." I hesitate, then go to it. Why do I feel so painfully nervous all of a sudden?

"Blast," he says, tugging on the blanket, "it doesn't reach all the way across. Do you mind coming in a little closer?" He looks up at me and cringes. "I'm not trying to be a scoundrel, I promise."

"You could never be a scoundrel."

I say that, and yet . . . I can't hold his gaze.

"I'll put my pack between us." He lays his backpack in the middle of the blanket—the most ill-conceived barrier I've ever seen. "There. Practically separate suites."

I laugh a little, and his eyes sparkle with pleased mischief.

I sit down on my side of the pack. The ground underneath the thick blanket isn't exactly smooth, but I've slept on far worse.

"Thank you for letting me stay, Thorn," I say. "You really are too kind to me."

"Thirty percent kindness, seventy percent selfish desire to be near you." He smirks. "No, but seriously. Anything you need, I'm here for you. I mean that."

"Thank you."

"Of course." Thorn pulls his shirt off over his head, and I try not to stare at his naked chest as he rolls up his shirt. "Do you pray, Victoria?"

"Sometimes I forget," I say, shrugging with a squinch of my face instead of my shoulders. "Sometimes I'm too tired. Sometimes I'm . . . too angry with God to bother."

"Relatable." He sniffs his shirt and cringes, shooting me a quick apologetic look before unrolling it and hanging it from his rifle. "So not often, then."

"I try. I just think the jungle listens to me more than He does."

"You ever think maybe He's using the jungle to speak to you?"

I raise an eyebrow. "Unlikely."

He kneels on his blanket, then fishes out a travel-sized Bible from his pack. "Well, I'm going to pray, if you don't mind. I always have horrible dreams if I don't."

"What do you dream about?"

"My parents, mostly. Their . . . death."

"What happened?" I ask, then immediately bite my tongue. I never had parents—never knew them, anyway. If they died, I would never know or care. I'm alone, but it's always been that way.

I've never had anyone to mourn.

"You don't have to answer that," I amend, quickly. "That was rude."

"No, it's alright," says Thorn, a sad smile pulling at his lips. "It was three years ago, anyway, so I'm fine talking about it—I mean, not fine, but . . . I don't know, I don't panic anymore. Don't immediately start crying." He sticks his fingers into his tight cushion of curls to scratch his scalp. "I guess there's no gentle way to say it. They were lynched."

I don't know what that is—we're only ever shot within the walls of the company. But his expression tells me I shouldn't ask. "I'm sorry."

"Thank you." He doesn't seem to know what to say, and continues hesitantly. "But it wasn't all horrible. It was a fresh start for me. I got into mining—met Badger there. We started a business." He shrugs. "I was eighteen, so I considered it a kick in the pants to finally move out of my parents' house."

"Don't joke like that," I chastise, grabbing his arm. "That's not funny."

He laughs, and I feel myself scowl. I want to slap some sense into him. But his laugh collapses abruptly as he presses his lips together tightly before letting out a shaking breath. "I'm sorry. Sometimes I feel if I don't joke, I'll scream."

"I'd rather you scream." I should talk. When have I ever screamed? "You know, there's a waterfall a few miles from the orchard. We could scream there."

"It would be my pleasure to scream with you, Your Majesty."

I blush and glance down at my dirty nails. When I finally look at him, his eyes are closed, and he holds his Bible in his lap. I lie on my side and watch him, his lips speaking silent words. Minutes go by, it feels like . . . the longer I watch him, the more I can feel my throat tighten from a sob. Why do I want to cry?

But I don't want to make a sound. I don't want to interrupt

this moment. It's too important, a moment I need to feel, experience, understand.

But I don't understand. I don't understand love that can banish nightmares. I don't understand it, and I . . . I don't trust it. And maybe that's my problem.

"Great is Thy faithfulness, O God my Father . . ."

Thorn's voice breaks through my thoughts, and I hold my breath to listen.

"There is no shadow of turning with Thee
Thou changest not, Thy compassions, they fail not
As Thou hast been Thou forever wilt be . . ."

If peace were a melody, it would be this. Not quite melancholy, with just enough hope to soothe my soul. And not only soothe, but stir emotions up in me. I've heard this hymn many times, but when Thorn sings, I believe his words in a way I never have before.

"Great is Thy faithfulness, great is Thy faithfulness
Morning by morning new mercies I see
All I have needed Thy hand hath provided
Great is Thy faithfulness, Lord, unto me . . ."

I let the words wash over me, drown me in their beauty. They settle, and my heart pounds with their weight.

"He's faithful?" I whisper stupidly.

Thorn grins the slightest bit. "He is."

"And He takes away your nightmares?"

"He's never failed me yet."

I take a few seconds to gather my courage. "Can you ask Him to take away my memories?"

Thorn falls silent, his eyes still closed. Finally, "He says, 'I'm listening, daughter. You can tell me anything. Tell me your heart and find peace.'"

"S-stop joking. He didn't say that."

"And the jungle didn't tell you where to find firewood, but you found it anyway."

The jungle *did* tell me . . . only it didn't *tell* me. I could feel it. I just knew.

I sit up, understanding striking me, knotting my stomach with anxiety. "I can tell you anything?"

"Anything, beloved," Thorn says.

His words crush my will to keep from crying. I break, choking on a sob. *Beloved.* Whether the message is really from God or from Thorn, I want him to mean that more than anything. I push his pack out of the way to get to him, blowing out the lantern so our silhouettes don't reveal what I'm about to do.

"If I tell you," I say, quickly before my voice gives out, my knees touching his, my hand on his thigh as I lean forward, "don't tell him that I told you."

"He hears you."

"Not God. Dean."

Thorn finally opens his eyes, his brows furrowed as he looks at me, and I quickly cover his eyes with my hand before they can adjust to the dark.

"Don't look at me," I say. "Please. I don't think I can handle being . . . seen by you."

"Seen by me?"

"You see me like no one else does." I remove my hand—it's trembling far too much, and I don't want him to feel that, either. Instead I straddle his knees and lay my cheek against his so I can whisper in his ear. "I can't explain it. I feel like you . . . see me as an entire, independent person. But if I tell you what the boss . . . if I look at you when I tell you, what if I see that spark in your eyes vanish? W-what if you no longer see me as whole?"

"Oh, beloved . . ." Thorn rubs my arms gently. "You are no lesser a person because of what you've survived. Your faults, vices, trauma, pain . . . those make you as much wholly *you* as all the joy and talent and love and vibrancy in you."

Tears run freely down my cheeks. Thorn shifts one arm upward, cradling my head, his fingers massaging my scalp.

"Dean hurts you that way all the time, doesn't he?" he says.

I can't answer for a moment. "I haven't seen him much in the past year, so . . . no. I mean yes." I take a deep breath. "It's usually just threats, and I threaten him right back. B-but a year ago—"

I choke on a sob, fight to swallow it. And Thorn waits for me . . . so patiently it makes the knot in my throat all the worse.

"The boss raped me," I gasp, finally.

Thorn's muscles go rigid against me.

This is a mistake. I shouldn't be so abrupt. I— Before I can move away, Thorn's arms slip around my waist, and it gives me strength to continue. "And Dean let it happen. He was my best friend, and he . . . he just stood there and watched. He could've done something. He's stopped other things before. But he didn't." For a moment, I can't swallow, can't catch my breath.

"He betrayed me. And now I feel like everything I do is based on that memory. I can't speak right. And I do stupid things to spite him. I think about him before I do anything, and why? Why, when I hate him so much? I don't want to think of him. I just want to forg—" My voice breaks, and Thorn grips me tighter. "P-please, ask God to let me forget."

Thorn holds me with one arm, adjusting to sit flat instead of on his knees, and then hugs me tightly. I bury my face in his neck, unable to hold back my crying. Thorn holds me without talking, without telling me to buck up, without making me stop.

He lets me cry freely.

He lets me cry . . . at all.

"Sometimes we can't forget what hurts us," he says at last. "Sometimes all we can do is move forward and find joy in something else. Sometimes . . . the only answer God gives us is pure, encompassing peace."

"You don't have peace," I say bitterly. "You joke to deflect. You pray away nightmares."

"Peace comes in more forms than you'd think—what's something you like to do, where the world fades away and gives you a private moment with your own joy? For instance, not all my jokes are armor—I love making people laugh. I find peace in journeys, in discoveries. Sunsets. Seeing you at peace."

I blink at him. "Seeing . . . *me* at peace?"

"You find peace in simple things, Victoria. Your patience with Bunny. Your contentment in touching a tree as you pass by. Your ease in navigating the uneven terrain. Your unbridled joy at having an incredibly dangerous and—I'm sorry, I have to be honest—disgusting insect land on you. That's peace,

Victoria." He wipes my tears away gently. "And, I have to say, watching you experience the jungle is therapeutic. It's as if you were born here."

"I . . ." I sit up, drying my eyes on my sleeve. "I was."

We lie on our backs beside each other, not bothering with a barrier. Thorn laces his fingers with mine and, for a while, we do nothing but stare up at the ceiling of the tent.

"You know why I love camping?" Thorn asks suddenly.

"Why?" I reply.

"Because it's intense."

I look at him for clarification and he bursts into laughter.

I smile a little—not because I understand the joke, or even because I'm trying to make him feel better by joining in. It's because . . . well, how can I not smile when he has such a hearty, joyful laugh?

"Do you get it?" he asks.

"No."

For some reason that makes him laugh harder, and his joy catches me by the heart.

CHAPTER 14

I open my eyes to the sweet conversations of birdsong as I stare at the ceiling of Thorn's tent. It's dark but a different kind than last night—the peaceful darkness of early morning with just a hint of timid, ambient sunrise beginning to peek through. Bright enough to see things, even if not quite bright enough to distinguish.

Only when I shift do I feel Thorn's arm, warm and weighty, resting across my stomach. His other arm cradles my head, his elbow bent like his hand wants to shield my face. I turn my head to look at him, grinning without even thinking about it.

My bent arm is pinned against him, but I can just reach my fingers to touch his chin.

Thorn gives me a lazy grin, pulling me closer.

I smile. Despite everything that happened last night . . . Dean, our confessions . . . this feels too perfect to let go. Even so, I attempt to peel his fingers from my waist.

"Why?" he mumbles, refusing to give in.

God, he's cute.

My only solace is that we can do last night all over again tonight.

Well, maybe not *all* over again.

"As much as I love this," I say, "I'm the tour leader now. I want to show everyone I deserve it."

His sigh sounds like an agreement.

"Besides, if I'm seen leaving your tent, it'll look like I was promoted because of favoritism."

Thorn mutters something, but he doesn't try to keep me when I wriggle out of his embrace. I kiss his temple, then press my nose to him. It's so tempting to stay . . .

"Do that again," he says.

I laugh a little, humoring him with another kiss. "I'll see you out there."

When I exit the tent it's obvious I didn't wake up quite early enough—Badger and Madelyn are already awake, not to mention Dean, who is apparently still on tour leader time. I take a breath and ignore them, heading to my cot.

And freeze halfway there.

A dark stain has spread on Samson's pants and my blood trips over itself as my pulse races. I had stopped the bleeding last night, I was sure of it—and it hadn't been nearly deep enough to bleed that much. I'd checked on him before moving to Thorn's tent. He'd been fine.

I rush over and stumble to a stop. The blood has soaked through the bottom of the cot, and drips onto the grassy dirt beneath.

"Samson?" I gasp. My chest constricts. I drop to my knees beside him, slapping the front of his shoulders firmly. "Samson," I say louder.

He's sleeping so peacefully, but he's never been a heavy sleeper. Is . . . is he paler than normal? No, it's the light. Please, God. It has to be the light.

"Sam!" I call, shaking him, my voice a trill of panic. "Sam, wake up!"

Bunny jolts awake, falling off his cot.

"What's going on?" I hear Madelyn ask, but she remains at a safe distance, worriedly looking on.

"Victoria!" Thorn trips to my side, shirtless and bootless. "What hap—?"

He doesn't need to finish. Bunny is sitting up now, staring at Samson, his one good eye like a saucer. We both watch as Thorn presses two fingers to the side of Samson's throat. Pauses.

My name is all he has to say, with that gentle, sympathetic tone, and a sob breaks from me immediately.

"No . . ." I shake my head, slow and uncommitted. But when he reaches for me, I jerk away, falling to the ground. "He's not dead. Check again."

"He's gone," Thorn whispers.

"No!" I scamper to the other side of the cot to escape Thorn's comforting arms. I don't want to be comforted. I want my Samson to wake up.

I tear the fabric of his blood-soaked trousers to get a better look and freeze. The leaf I'd stuck over his wound is too waxy to be compromised by liquid, and yet, a thin cut in it oozes red, like its own wound. I peel off the leaf and moss, choking as I wipe some of the blood away. Samson's wound is much bigger, much redder on the surrounding skin, the edges weeping a yellow infection. And it's higher up the thigh than it was last night . . . right where the main artery runs.

Someone did this . . . I gasp, trembling, unable to catch my breath. *Someone killed him.*

I press my face to Samson and cry. Already he feels cold to me, through his clothes. Usually he's like a hearth, and now . . .

Someone deliberately did this . . .

Someone, Victoria?

Hate ticks at the backs of my eyes, grips my stomach.

You know who.

People are staring now. Staring and standing and doing nothing. The death of a Wildblood means nothing to these mercenaries. Nothing but a moment of morbid entertainment.

"What's going on?" Badger storms over, halting as he stares at the scene. He swears. "I didn't think he'd die like that."

I glare up at him. "Are you admitting to killing him?"

"What?" Badger recoils. "No. Why would I kill one of the only things keeping us from dying out here?"

"He's not a *thing*," I snap, and I have to force back my science. "Wildbloods are human beings."

"Hal didn't mean anything by it," Madelyn says. Her face turns sickly pale as soon as she sees the blood, and she turns away to her husband. He wraps a comforting arm around her. "But do we have to look at him like that? Let's hurry up and pack the tents so we can go."

"We're staying put," Thorn says firmly.

"What?" Badger exclaims. He looks ready to explode, and I couldn't care less.

"You heard me," Thorn says, standing to face him. Despite his bed head and lack of half his clothing, he's still every bit the authority figure he has been. "We're staying put for the day," he announces to everyone.

"Wait a minute," Madelyn says, suddenly over her sickness enough to spin back around. "That's one whole day of travel lost—one whole day more of being stuck here."

"I don't know what to tell you, Maddy," he says with a shrug. "Consider this a day to rest your sore muscles. Sometimes that happens during expeditions."

"No, it doesn't," Badger butts in. "Our men have been dropping left and right and you declare a day of mourning for this blood summoner?!"

"Are you finished? I think you are. Arthur," he says to one of the men—his skin is just as dark as Thorn's, with a thick mustache and beard growing in from travel, whose name I don't think I even knew before now. "This is the perfect day to replenish our food supply. Get a small group together for a hunting trip. Greyson, gather a few others to organize and clean the gear." He claps his hands, a loud echo through the trees. "Let's go, gentlemen! The sooner we knock out these tasks, the sooner we get a day to rest."

I look up and see Dean standing a few feet away from Samson's cot, his brows pulled low. Thorn steps between us without my having to say anything, not that I need his protection from this distance. I could slice off Dean's hand quicker than he could throw a punch.

"At least he died painlessly," Dean says.

"Painlessly?" I shoot to my feet, trembling with fierce loathing. "You put enough salve on his wound to numb a horse."

I look at my blood-covered hands. I can't use it as a weapon, since it's not from living arteries with energy, but I want to rub it all over his face. That would humiliate him enough to shut him up. A weapon in itself, even if a pathetic one. "You stabbed him and let him bleed to death. What's painless about that?"

He raises his eyebrows. "I guess you didn't figure out he was the spy."

I freeze, trembling, but my brain is still processing at a mile a minute. Samson . . . a spy? He never told me . . . why did he never . . . ?

And then it clicks. He'd washed his hair on Saturday. He always saved that for right before a tour. He must've known, even before assignments went out to our cubbies. But that didn't justify—"And so you *killed* him?"

"It looks like his wound bled out, to me," Dean says carelessly, peering around me to look at Samson. "Maybe you should've checked in on your patient instead of playing newlyweds in the client's tent."

I step toward him, fire in my gut, but a firm hand takes mine. Thorn steps up beside me, glaring at Dean.

"I'm sure you have something better to do," he says, "than terrorize a poor girl mourning her friend. And if you don't"—he shifts me behind him as he steps forward—"I can give you something to do. Like lick your *own* wounds."

Dean scoffs but steps back from Thorn. Nothing good would come of starting a fight, not for him at least. Right now, most of the group doesn't hate him like I do. If he throws a punch, they might just see that he's worthy of the hate.

Besides, he's already won this battle, and he knows it.

When he walks away, I finally exhale. I close my eyes, and feel someone catch my arms. When I open them, Thorn is holding me steady.

"Victoria, darling," he says, a little louder than necessary, "are you with me?"

"I'm with you," I murmur.

"You were fainting. Come, sit down."

"N-no." I try to push away but he doesn't release me, and I'm glad, because my legs feel weak enough to melt. "We can't leave him out here in the heat. It's been too long already."

"Okay, okay . . ." Thorn holds me close, kisses my forehead, and I feel some semblance of sanity at his touch. "Where would you like us to take him?"

The river isn't far off. I lead the way while Bunny and Thorn carry Samson's cot between them. I would've gladly carried it—I still want to—but Thorn insisted on helping, even though I'm not 100 percent sure he can navigate the jungle floor with both his hands full. Meanwhile, Bunny's hands need occupying, or he'll start to pick again.

The jungle's whispers caress my cheek, but right now I find no comfort in them.

Thorn's solemn voice cuts through the whispers, a tune as haunting without music as it is beautiful.

"Be still, my soul, though dearest friends depart
And all is darkened in the vale of tears;
Then shalt thou better know His love, His heart,
Who comes to soothe thy sorrows and thy fears . . ."

A sob catches in my throat. I want to be soothed. I don't want to feel constricted, as if my body is trying to kill me from grief, as if it knows Samson is gone and isn't used to surviving without him. But if the jungle can't soothe me, and Thorn's tender voice can't . . .

God help me, I pray. *Please take away this nightmare . . .*

The boys lay Samson's cot on the bank, parallel to the river. I can't manage words, so I press my hands to their stomachs, and they take the hint and back away. The River Mumma is no respecter of persons, and she may very well drag them under and drown them—well, Thorn, anyway. Bunny is still young enough that Mumma's merciful heart would spare him.

But I haven't seen her since I was six years old, and it's been so long . . . who knows if she's still taking requests from me?

I reach my hand over Sam's body to touch the water. "River Mumma . . . please. Someone I love has been taken from me wrongfully. I know you don't like to interfere, but will you do it for me? Your daughter? The one you raised from the river when you swore you wouldn't? Don't you love me as your own?" I swallow a sob, taking a few ragged breaths. "As you love me . . . save him."

I stare at the water for what seems like minutes. Minutes upon minutes of torture.

Ripples spread, like a constant dripping, and I let out a breath of relief.

A woman rises from the water until she's standing on the surface, and I suddenly, vaguely, remember measuring her when I was little. She towers above me at seven-foot-two, and her skin is dark and deep and exquisite, her tight black coils full and extending out and cascading down into the river as if unending. She wears a dress of gold, sleek as liquid, that reflects and shimmers like sunlight off water. Rivulets of water pour from her, displacing, but not wetting her—she *is* the river, and water cannot wet itself.

If she looked any certain age, it would be thirty, but at the same time, she is ageless. She is radiant. Beautiful. Beauty itself,

and beyond. Nostalgia overtakes me, memories of my childhood hugging me, as my adoration for her swells.

"Hello, Mumma," I whisper.

"Hello, daughter." Her voice is a splash, a flow, rapids and
calm. I close my eyes to bask in it. "Why have you not come to
see me?"

"I am bound by my job, ma'am."

"A daughter of the ancient jungle cannot be *bound* by mortal men."

"I—I am mortal, too, ma'am."

"What difference does that make?" She looks down at Samson, finally. Sinks into the river down to her waist and leans on
the bank to get a closer look. "Have you finally brought your
Mumma a present after all these years? My, he is beautiful. He
will make an excellent mate."

Tears well up without any effort. "So you'll take him for me?"

"I have not resurrected since you, and certainly I do *not*
resurrect humans who have passed the age of childhood. The
circle of life must be respected. Who am I to play God?" She
looks at me, her brown eyes searching. She lifts my chin with
the gentle brush of her long, elegant fingers. "He is your love."

"Not in that way."

"But you love him."

My tears take over, and for a moment, I can't speak. "Yes,"
I squeak.

"If I take him, he will never remember you. And I must orient him, lest he be driven mad, so you may not speak to him
now. Are you prepared for that?"

I swallow. "I am. I've already mourned him, and I don't an-
ticipate ever seeing him again."

The water of the river roughens as Mumma scowls at me. "Is that what you think? When the jungle calls to you daily? When I"—she takes my chin—"call to you daily? That you never need to see us again?"

I tremble at her very presence. "I have people to take care of," I manage. "I can't answer that call."

"You would break my heart, my sweet daughter?" She kisses my head. Lingers. "You have suffered so. Would you like to forget as well?"

I freeze. Forget. Yes. Weren't Thorn and I just talking about this last night? Forget the pain and suffering. Forget Dean.

I look back at Thorn, at him standing against the tree line, gaping as he looks on. I don't ever want to forget him. I don't want to forget the kindness he's shown me, even if it means wiping away everything else.

When I turn back to Mumma, she's staring at Thorn, an uncertain expression on her face. "Very well, then."

She lifts Samson up, his heavy body light as air to her. She lays him in the water to float on his back, and his black hair swirls around him gently. Lifting her hand to her chest, she pulls from herself a small bead of glowing gold and places it inside his mouth. Ever so carefully, she places her fingertips against his chest and pushes his head and chest beneath the surface.

With her hands occupied, Bunny kneels beside me and takes my hand, and I gratefully squeeze back with both of mine.

Mumma holds him there, submerged. Anxiety knots my insides.

It must've been only seconds, but it feels like minutes before she allows him to rise. He floats, unmoving in the water.

Again, seconds like minutes like hours. I grip Bunny harder as he murmurs, "Come on, Sam. Come on . . ."

Samson's chest moves. I gasp, tears stinging my eyes. Bunny makes an excited noise, but I hold him back from reaching out.

We watch, holding our breaths, as Samson slowly opens his eyes, blinking against the sun.

"Good morning, dear one," Mumma coos.

She shields his view of us with her hand as he attempts to glance around. "Where am I?" he asks.

"You are home."

He stares up at her in awe, as if woken from a dream only to enter another one. "Home?"

"What is your name?"

"Um . . ." His awe is familiar, and I suddenly remember the moment Mumma woke me from the river. Beautiful and terrifying, radiant like the sun. She was all I knew. I could've stared at her all day if she had let me. "Samson," he answers, finally.

"Very good, you know yourself."

"Samson!" Bunny calls, and I hold him back.

"Bun," I whisper. "No."

But it's too late. Samson gazes over at us, his eyes searching us like a page and finding nothing. No spark of remembrance. No love. Nothing familiar except that face I grew up with . . . the face I'm dying to kiss goodbye, even knowing I can't.

His eyes well with tears, still searching. Still finding nothing. A small, pained sound escapes his throat.

"Where am I?" he asks again, this time with an edge of panic that tears my heart into jagged strips.

Mumma hushes him gently, redirecting his gaze to her with a

single finger. Her velvet-brown eyes are full of the deepest sympathy as she looks at me. "He is overwhelmed. I must orient him."

She doesn't linger, leaves no time to say goodbye. She simply sinks into the depths, taking Samson with her, and they vanish from sight.

"Hey, bring him back!" Bunny screams at the river. "You can't keep our brother! Give him back! Give him back . . ."

He wraps his arms around my waist suddenly, nearly knocking me over with his size, and lays his head in my lap as he melts into tears.

"He doesn't remember us, Bun," I say gently, rubbing his back. "To him, we're strangers."

"His expression was so blank," he says through gasps and sniffles. "It was scary to see him like that."

"His memory is wiped of everything before the water. It's as if he's reborn."

Bunny sits up, wiping his eyes before quietly staring into the river. "I've heard so many stories of the River Mumma, but they all seem like lies compared to the real thing."

"She's beautiful, isn't she?"

"Yes, but . . . I don't know. She's scary, too." He chews on his thumb, and I lower his hand from his mouth, nervous he'll draw blood. "He's always wanted a wife."

I swallow back tears. There's no sense in crying, not when Sam is well and safe. "That's true."

"Thought it'd be you, though."

I blush and shove him in the shoulder. "It was never going to be me." I get up, holding my hand out to him. "Come on. Let's get away from these memories."

CHAPTER 15

When I was reborn, there was nothing to distract me from Mumma's gaze. I remember opening my eyes, blinking to adjust to the night and the bright glow of her presence all at once.

She's starlight, I thought. *My mum is made of starlight . . .*

To me, she was my mother before she ever said a word. In my heart, I knew it.

"Hello, sweet girl," she said, her voice rolling through me like a gentle wave.

I didn't ask where I was—it was too dark to see much, and I didn't care. I don't even know if I realized I was wet from the river, my heart was so warm.

"Mummy, I'm hungry."

And when she laughed, I felt myself ready to burst from happiness, like butterflies breaking free.

"What is your name?"

I didn't answer right away. I was too busy taking her in,

wondering if she was real, deciding I would look like her when I grew up.

Finally, I whispered. "Huh?"

"Your name, sweet girl."

"Victoria."

"Do you know where you are, Victoria?"

I reached my arms toward her, and she smiled and took me in her embrace, rubbing my back as I rested my wet head on her shoulder.

Do I know where I am?

"Home," I said.

And she took me beneath the surface to begin my new life.

For the rest of the day, Bunny doesn't talk much. If he's not holding my hand, he's walking just behind me or lying at my feet.

"Like a duckling," Thorn says with a fond grin.

"A what?" I ask.

He wraps an arm around my neck, pulling me closer to kiss my temple. "A very sweet, devoted child."

I'm anxious to get away from the river. I don't want to see Samson again. I'll break down into tears if I'm forced to introduce myself to him all over again. But Thorn is teaching Bunny to skip rocks across the river to the opposite bank, and seeing Bunny smile . . . I can't deny him this happiness just because I'm a coward.

Instead, I climb the closest tree, feeling warm life flow through it with every touch. Up, up, up . . . until there is nothing but leaves and branches and . . . peace. I climb to the very top, breaking to the surface. The sun is hot and the breeze is strong. Together, they are calming. From up here, the jungle stretches, an array of greens as far as the horizon, and I can't imagine anything else existing.

I squint as I look out into the distance. Something rises up from the trees, wispy and dark, and . . . moving? *That can't be . . . smoke?*

I freeze. It *is* smoke. Thick and black and fluid as a flame. Not from any lost traveler—not a human one, anyway. It can only be from one thing.

A shadow creature.

Lord, help me. The bull. A vengeful spirit looking for me is the last thing I need right now.

I wait to make sure it's going the opposite way from us before climbing down quickly.

As if today couldn't get any worse.

I watch my boys skip rocks for a minute, but there's no joy in it.

"Thorn," I say, and I'm surprised he hears me—my heart is pounding so loudly, I can't even hear myself.

His smile drops at seeing my expression. "Victoria?"

I shake my head over and over until I can make sense of my own emotions. "I can't be team leader, Thorn. I can't be responsible for leading anyone else to their death."

Thorn cradles my face in his hands, kisses my forehead. "You don't have to think about that right now."

I pull away, taking a few steps back. "How many more have to die before you understand?"

"What?" Bunny scowls at me. "If we go back now, then what was the point of Sam dying?"

There was no point. There's no point in any of this. But that doesn't mean it can't end here. It *has* to. "You don't belong out here, Bunny. None of these people do. It's too dangerous."

"We've got to be closer to the gold than headquarters by now, right?" says Bunny. "Let's at least get some and then we can get out of here. We can go somewhere safe."

My words fumble. "S-something bad has happened every day since we left. The jungle doesn't want us here. We have to turn back before it kills everyone."

"Hold on, love," Thorn says gently. "Hold on. Bunny has a point. Going back now will make every sacrifice we've made be in vain. Let's do what we came here to do."

"You wanted me to be the tour leader," I snap, emotions tightening my muscles to pain, "but you don't care about anything I have to say. I'm telling you, the jungle *will not spare us.*"

"Let's get out of here, V," Bunny says, and his voice is so full of anguish that it breaks down my resolve. "Let's take the gold and run. Maybe we'll never see Sam again, but we'll have each other."

He takes my hand and I squeeze it, at a loss. How do you convince people to listen to reason when certain death doesn't deter them?

Walking back into camp feels like scraping a jagged rock across my face. Thankfully, most everyone is heading to their cots and tents. Still, I hate every moment of being back here, of seeing all these people who care nothing for me, let alone their own or anyone else's safety. Who care nothing for Samson, who was wrongfully killed by his own leader. Our group has fed thousands of ants this weekend, and the very thought of it makes me cringe.

For once, my sweet giant Bunny can't sleep. We put our cots directly beside each other to form one bed, and I lie beside him for what feels like an hour before his hand goes slack in mine and I finally hear his breath level out, no longer trembling from crying. By then, Thorn has finished talking to his party, receiving updates of the tasks they'd been given. Instead of going to his tent, he snuggles down on the other side of me, and I squish closer to Bunny to give him room. I feel overly warm between my two boys, but I won't make them move. I have them, here and alive, and that's all that matters at the moment.

And that Samson is safe. It could be worse. I'll never see him again, and even if I do, he'll never know me the same way. But he's alive and safe and, hopefully, happy. Because the way he died . . . I know Dean did it, but it couldn't have been for the reason he gave. Samson was a spy? He's never kept big secrets like that from me, ever. And even if it was true, why kill him? Why not send him home like Nathan? Was Dean trying to sabotage the tour? Get back at me because Thorn made me leader instead?

My science is boiling in my gut just thinking about it all. Of course Dean would never send him home—I cared for Samson too much. Out of pure spite for me, murder was his only option. All that talk about the greater good, about doing what's best for everyone . . . after all we'd been through, when did *everyone* start to exclude me?

What am I saying? As if I care.

I hate him as much as he hates me.

A shadow flies overhead, landing silently on one of the posts of a nearby tent. An owl?

No. It's too big to be an owl.

I sit up slowly, watching it hop off the post and into a tent. Then I get up more quickly, rushing to the tent and throwing open the flap. The owl has its claws dug into the back of the man lying inside, and I catch the end of the distinctive swell of white smoke of a soul being stolen.

I gasp. It hears me and its head twists backward to glare with bright yellow eyes, its hooked beak dripping dark liquid. That glare dares me to make another sound, and in response, my eyes glow red with a challenge.

"Soul eater!" I cry. "There's a soul eater in the camp!"

Its feathers flare in agitation, wings expanding to fill the tent as it screams at me, twisted bloody teeth like spines in its cruel beak, spattering blood.

I back up, drawing blood from my own pores, just enough to throw up a shield as the spirit flies at me, skirting off it to go in a better direction—to find easier prey in the form of the other end of camp still asleep. Maybe I'm so used to being quiet that my yell isn't quite loud enough.

But people's lives depend on it being loud enough, so I try again, screaming, "Get up! Danger!" and throw a dagger at the beast with a flash of lightning that, for an instant, lights up the entire camp. But not before the monster owl finds another victim, perching on a cot and biting into the Wildblood lying there, sucking his blood and soul together.

It's not Dean, but I don't have time to be disappointed.

I run to my cot. Thorn is up and has snatched his rifle from the ground, but I have to dump Bunny's cot over to get him moving. But now the camp has awoken, shouts of distress and gunshots ringing through the air. I grab Thorn's arms desperately before he can aim his rifle.

"It will never truly die unless we destroy its disguise with salt," I say, keeping my eye on the creature. "Take Bunny with you, outside the salt circle, and find the shed skin of an old woman."

He gapes at me. "What?"

"A big pile of skin! Bunny, go with him!" I hear them run off, but I don't have time to look as I throw up another bloody shield against the dive-bombing owl. It crashes into it, screeching its annoyance at me, and flies away to seek new prey.

"Come on, come on . . ." I mutter, even though I feel like I only just heard them leave.

I see a small flash and panic. Bunny is using his science. Why, when the enemy is in here?

"Greyson, watch out!" I hear a shout and turn in time to see Madelyn fire a rifle, hitting the owl with little result.

I throw my science out like a whip, striking the soul eater and sending it retreating temporarily with a bitter scream of pain and anger, but not in time to save Thorn's friend Greyson, who topples to the ground without a soul to hold him upright.

More bullets bounce off the spirit, useless. Screaming. Running. *Chaos.*

The gall of humans is a toxic thing. We shouldn't be here. In the jungle, messing with creatures beyond our knowledge. Warning after warning, every one ignored.

I have a feeling the River Mumma will spare no more of us, not even for my sake.

"Victoria!" Thorn comes running back, something dark

hanging off the end of his rifle. The leathery skin is in one piece, the mouth stretched and gaping where the owl crawled out of it—a wrinkled old woman with pits for eyes and curling bones for fingers.

"Throw it here!" I shout, pointing to the ground, and Thorn drops it off the barrel of his gun.

The trap works. Sensing its skin, the owl screeches and circles back, preparing to dive-bomb her casing before her immortal form is compromised.

I throw a handful of salt on the skin sack, shouting, "Now!"

The bodiless eyes and mouth of the skin sack widen in a wretched scream before the skin shrivels like dried leather and crackles into ash. Thorn takes the shot, and the owl tumbles, its momentum so great it skids a few inches before it, too, crumbles.

Relief washes over me. And then my insides turn over as Bunny screams.

CHAPTER 16

Thorn, stay back!" Dean shouts, and for once I'm grateful for him, because all I can do is think of getting to Bunny as quickly as possible.

I dodge under Bunny's swinging arms and wrap my arms around his waist from behind. I kick the back of his knee to buckle it, closing my eyes briefly as his science flashes. But he's too heavy and we're falling backward and—why have his arms gone limp? Lord have mercy, something's not right.

I feel another set of arms with him, a body pressing against my back. "Whoa, watch out!" says Thorn, who clearly didn't listen to Dean. But Bunny is heavy, and I use Thorn's help to regain my footing, my legs nearly giving out on me as we both lower Bunny to the ground.

Bright red blood stains the collar of Bunny's shirt. No . . . not just his collar. His throat.

My knees shake, and I drop to them beside him. His eye

color has returned to brown, but it's wrong, so *wrong*, gazing at nothing. His throat is torn open like a gaping wet mouth—and I'm grateful that the sparse moonlight through the trees prevents me from seeing inside.

"My God . . ." Thorn murmurs.

I don't have to look at Dean for proof that he did this. No smug expression, no knife cut that says he drew energy from his own blood. I turn and look at him anyway, and find . . . well, the knife. His sliced arm. But his expression is shocked, slightly shaken. All an act, I'm sure. A show to put on for the clients, to make them believe he's innocent. Because I *know* nothing about what just happened is shocking for him.

He killed both of my boys in the span of two days . . . Was . . . was this his plan all along?

Dean utters a dark curse. It makes me sick that he would show so much remorse, when he knows good and well that he did this. "Bunny's science was out of control," he fumbles. "I was protecting Thorn. I didn't think it would deflect back—"

The malice in my eyes shuts him up, but his eyes attempt to reason with me.

Victoria. Please.

Murderer, mine reply.

I didn't mean to.

Sure, you didn't.

He presses his lips together, looking away from me now that he knows I'll never forgive him, and turns to the rest of the group.

"Don't panic," he dares to say to everyone, as if they haven't just witnessed a murder. "His science backed up on him. That can happen if you use it irresponsibly like he's been doing. I just wish it didn't have to happen to someone so young, poor kid."

"That's a lie," I gasp, but not loud enough to make a difference it seems, because no one reacts to my words.

He looks at me, his expression fully aware of what I'm thinking, what I know, as he walks closer.

My hate for him is a broken dam, a burning sun. Unstoppable.

Unforgiving.

When my blood begins to catch fire, I don't stop it. My science ignites in my gut, and I can feel the warmth of my eyes glowing red, hotter and hotter.

I stand and face him, just in time for him to be too close, in my space, as if his soul is trying to consume mine. He grips my wrists, nearly hard enough to crush them.

"Back down," he whispers, a desperation in his voice. "It was an accident."

"You're a liar," I gasp.

"He raged all the time, did you think there'd never be consequences? This was inevitable. Let it go, Victoria. He's better off."

Better off?

A broken dam, a burning sun.

An erupting volcano.

I scream a war cry up into Dean's face, drawing blood from his wound with a flash. He rushes backward and out of the way before I can slice his hand off, but I don't stop.

I draw again, swinging for his head, but he blocks with his own bloody weapon. He doesn't hold his, letting the weapon burn away with the lightning as soon as he's done, only leaving it long enough to dodge out of the way.

He's used to fighting tactics, used to blocking attacks. But he won't overuse his science—he has no interest in raging. If I can get him to the point where he's forced to stop, if I can keep him far enough away that he can't attack me, I can land the killing blow.

Lightning spirals as I form a bloody sphere, attacking in quick succession—first his head, which he blocks, then his stomach, which he fends off with his own attack, and last, his legs, where I hit my mark.

With every attack, my core burns hotter and brighter, like something molten and unstable.

Dean's panting now, wincing. Using his own blood has worn him out. I slam him between two sheets of blood on either side, then slash blood at him like a whip around his feet, tripping him to the ground. I can't see him anymore, my eyes glowing so brightly that even the moonlight looks drenched in crimson. Still, I know I have him where I want him.

I stretch my fingers toward him and he gags. Chokes. A gurgling and a whimper, and then I begin to pull the blood from his arteries, through the soft membranes of his mouth, and out. Very, very slowly.

I want him to suffer. For Samson. For Bunny.

For me.

But something heavy as a boulder slams into my side, knocking me off my feet, pressing my body to the ground. I should've been less self-indulgent, should've slashed him in the throat like he did to Bunny. If this stupid boulder doesn't get off me so I can kill Dean, I might have to destroy it, too.

"This isn't you, Victoria," someone says, the voice distant and warped as if I'm being held underwater. "Snap out of it."

Except this *is* me. I am a Wildblood. Rage is all I have.

But my words are stuck in a cage deep inside me that's been shoved down by my rage. All I can do is scream.

"I know you're hurting," I hear the voice say. "But you're not a murderer, Victoria. You don't—"

My blood burns within my arteries, the crackle of lightning blinding my vision for a moment.

Don't use your energy. Use Dean's. Tear him apart.

I reach my hand toward where I last saw Dean but a hand closes around my wrist, dragging it back to my side.

Let me kill him! I beg, but my words don't reach the surface, only violent screams to match. *Don't you know what he's done?*

I'm pressed into the dirt and held there in a steady grip, and I glare at the lightning of my rage swirling and crackling around me.

Death whispers in my ear but I scream and kick and fight against it. It whispers again and again, until I can finally understand.

"I'm here, Victoria."

No. Not Death.

Thorn.

And, all at once, I stop fighting.

The world is suddenly too dark without my lightning to illuminate it. I hear myself panting loudly, my heart racing through me. Firm but gentle hands roll me onto my back. I stare up into the darkness of Thorn's face. He's cast in shadows laced with the cracks of silver moonlight that peek through the jungle's canopy, and my tears begin to blur them into one.

His arms cradle my back, the backs of my thighs. How can he lift me? *Is* he lifting me? My limbs are so leaden, it seems impossible. All I feel is numbness and the last sparks of lightning in my blood.

I say his name, but my voice seems so far away that I don't think the sound left my throat. Maybe I'm dead. Maybe I took Bunny's place. Maybe my spirit is the one screaming, and that's why Thorn can't hear me. Maybe this is Hell.

Thorn puts me down, and I'm no longer numb because there's something hard digging like teeth at my back. "No!" I cry . . . I think I cry. Thorn's lips move but I can't hear him because I'm screaming, "No! Don't leave me! Please don't leave me alone. Please . . ."

His hand cups the back of my head as he leans in, making sure I can hear him when he says in my ear, "I'm not leaving you, beloved."

I hold onto those words like a lifeline, they're the only reason I'm able to let him go. I blink and tears run from my eyes, so I can see him as he kicks off his boots and gathers the blanket onto me. I kick it away with a strangled whine. My gut burns with lightning, I'm so hot . . .

"I might burn it," I protest. I might burn the entire tent down.

Thorn makes a shushing sound and sits behind me, taking my arms below the shoulders to pull me up against his chest.

"I'm too hot."

He shushes me again, tips a canteen to my lips.

I can't drink, my throat is so knotted.

This is not Hell, but it feels like it.

First Sam. Now my Bunny. I want to be dead instead of him. At the same time, I want to be able to breathe. I can't breathe. Thorn coaches me to, but I can't.

But I can scream, and I do. No longer from senseless rage, but grief. I scream until all I can do is lay limp against Thorn's chest . . . until there are no more sparks in my blood . . . until my mind has stolen the numbness from my body.

Bunny is dead.

This time I drink when Thorn holds the canteen to my lips, my throat raw as a jagged riverbed as the water runs down.

Samson doesn't know me anymore.

"Don't leave me," I whisper.

Thorn kisses my temple and holds me closer, his arms strong and stable and the good kind of warm. I'm no longer burning.

My boys are gone.

I lay quietly in Thorn's arms, catching my breath. He's the only one who matters now. He's the only one I can protect.

And I want to do more than protect him, I want to take care of him like he did me. My tears stir up again thinking about it, but there's no more sadness behind them . . .

Is there?

I have one boy left . . .

I push up from his chest to sit upright, and he lets me, holding me steady from behind.

"Beloved," he whispers, and I turn to face him like the very word from his lips is a siren's call.

I lean closer, but he moves away quickly, and even though he strokes my cheek lovingly, I feel the razor-sharp sting of rejection.

He shushes me gently. "You're mourning, Victoria."

"Then comfort me," I gasp and kiss him softly.

He returns my kiss, but only until I move his hand to rest between my thighs. He turns his head just enough to escape my lips. "It wouldn't be right," he says, but the tremor in his voice and the rigidness of his touch against my cheek tell me he's fighting what he really wants. "And after what ... what your boss did to you, I—"

"Please . . ." I close my eyes tight, pressing away the memory. *Make me forget,* I want to say, but he'll think I'm using him, and I love and need him too much to scare him away. "I—I want you to."

Thorn swears quietly, his lips stopping just short of mine, his fingers hot with anticipation against my neck. He rests his forehead against mine, silent. "You tell me to stop," he says finally, "and I stop."

I feel breathless as I nod, quickly.

Without any more hesitation, he kisses me.

I don't panic, don't run. I hold the back of his neck, crawling into his lap as he grips my waist and pulls me closer. My lips demand satisfaction, and he gives it to me, willingly. His tongue finds mine and a sound escapes me that I've never heard from myself before, not one of pain or terror or anything in between. I tug at his shirt, and he helps, dragging it over his head. My buttons open for him easily, and he prompts me to my back.

"Ow." Now that I'm in my right mind, the teeth from earlier are clearly roots beneath the blanket.

"Sorry, sorry," he says quickly, but I drag him down to me, my arms around his neck, making sure he isn't directly on top of me—I couldn't stomach that, but I force myself not to think of it now.

"You picked the bumpiest ground to pitch a tent."

I wasn't teasing but he laughs, rolling to lie beside me, pulling me into him so we're facing one another, my back no longer on uneven ground.

"That better?" he asks between kisses.

"Uh-huh," I gasp as he nips at my neck—it hurts but I want more. I want everything. "Stop talking."

Clothes fit for the dangers of the jungle annoy me now— too many straps, too restrictive, too hard to get off. We fumble with them longer than necessary, mostly because I don't stop kissing him, I can't. If I stop, that emptiness might make room for tears.

Stop. Don't think of your pain. Stay in this moment.

Finally, my trousers are loose enough, and he pushes them down my hips.

He moves down me to finish the job, kissing my body the whole way down, caressing my legs to coax them open.

Don't think of anyone but Thorn. He loves you. He loves—

He kisses me . . . kisses me and . . . oh *God*, his tongue . . . kisses me . . . everywhere I didn't know you could, and my body is burning from something so . . . good, so *good* it borders on unbearable. "I want you beside me," I whimper.

He obliges and I press my back to his firm chest.

"This way?" he asks, as if confirming whether or not I'm crazy, but his tone can't lie—he wants it as much as I do.

"Not gently." I help him tug down his trousers with the one hand I can reach behind me.

"I don't want to hurt you."

But I want to forget . . .

I grab the back of his neck, pulling his face close to mine. "You won't . . ."

What's wrong with me? I shouldn't want this. Not now. But

I don't want to think of Bun—*No!*—of Samson—*Please, no!* No one matters but Thorn, no one and nothing, because anything else but this hurts too much to live through.

No, I shouldn't want this, but I more than want it . . . God, I *need* it.

But I don't want it to be similar in any way to how the boss gave it. No consent. No remorse. Face-to-face so he could see my fear and loathing. On top of me like I was his property. Every muscle rejecting him—cramping, pain, revulsion—as he forced his way in.

No, I want to be side by side, equals, even if I'm in front. I want us to feel love surge through us rather than look for something in our expressions. I want to feel my beloved inside me, strong and confident because we love each other, not because he's punishing me.

And I do—and nearly lose my tongue as I bite off a cry, my fingers gripping his hair. Lord, part of it is overwhelming pleasure even if part of it hurts like hell, but I want it, I *want* it, I want Thorn and only Thorn for the rest of my existence—

He moans a swear word into my neck, wraps his arms around me. "I love you, Victoria . . ."

I'm trembling so badly I can barely gasp, "I love you, Thorn . . ."

But I can kiss him, and I turn my face to distract his lips before he starts talking again.

CHAPTER 17

I can tell I overslept without even peeking beyond the tent—the sun shines against the tarp in a muted gold, bathing us in a sheen that's as blinding as it is dim. Nothing stirs except the jungle. I jolt up, rubbing my eyes.

"Did they leave us?" I ask the air.

"Badger was anxious to get moving, so I told them to go on ahead." I turn to see Thorn stretching out like a lazy farm dog, a contented grin on his lips. "Good morning, beloved."

"Almost afternoon, beloved," I correct, but grin right back. "Are you sure it was smart to let Badger get to the gold first? He'll photograph himself, or something, and steal the glory."

"How do you feel today?" he asks instead of answering, and the thought of last night caves my insides in on me. I turn away so he won't see my eyes glisten with fresh tears.

I look down at my naked body. So last night . . . *all* of last night was real.

Tears break, running freely down my cheeks, dripping off my chin to wet the blanket on my lap.

All of last night.

I get up and quickly start to dress, and Thorn follows my lead wordlessly, grabbing his rifle as he follows me out. Our tent is the only thing left at the campsite. No cots. No bodies. No . . . no Bunny. Even . . . even the blood has been eaten away by kala ants.

"Was he buried?" I ask, my fear of my own words planting a tremor in my voice.

"All of the bodies were moved outside of the campgrounds. This morning they were completely covered in some sort of creeping plant. Greyson was . . ." Thorn takes a heavy breath. "Well, it was quick, at least. But I'm not sure what I'm going to tell his wife . . ."

Covered in a creeping plant? The only thing I can think of that would want dead bodies and works that quickly is flesh-eating ivy. Our travel companions—Bunny included—are probably nothing but bones now.

I don't think even Mumma can resurrect someone from nothing but bones.

I turn to Thorn and gasp. His face, his neck, his arms. Red marks, like lightning crawling and branching up a tree, cover his skin. My God, it *is* lightning. When I was raging and he held me down—oh my God . . .

I rush to him and grab his face, a horrified gasp escaping me as he winces. "I burned you."

"I'm okay."

"You're not okay." I trace the thin branches down his neck. "These should've been treated right away."

"I had more important things to worry about," he says, and kisses my nose.

I love it, but scowl anyway. "I wasn't injured. You are."

"They're not that bad."

"Thorn—"

He shushes me. Kisses me. I feel as overwhelmed by his touch as I did last night and can't help but wrap my arms around him. But feeling him spasm, I pull away. "Not that bad?"

He gives me a sheepish grin. "Well . . . maybe some aloe might be a good idea."

"I know of something better. Come with me."

The waterfall is only a couple miles off—a leisurely walk. Sun streams golden-bright through the leaves overhead, the gaps between them waxing and waning the closer we get to the water. The jungle hums with a life I wish I had, soothing me. The energy within the trees rolls against my hand, the closest thing they can do to a hug, and I want to cry. I want to stop and kiss them and cry, and let them comfort me like sex clearly can't . . . but Thorn needs me. He's the only one I have left.

Up ahead, the waterfall cascades down large rocks, crashing into the lake that leads into Mumma's river. I crouch and skim some of the algae from the surface, pushed toward the edge by the falls.

"Take off your shirt," I say.

"What would you like me to do after it's off?" he asks, pulling his shirt over his head slowly—partially, I'm sure, due to pain, and partially, I'm *positive*, to tease me.

My face burns looking at him. "J-just stand there." I dab the blue-green algae across a burn on his chest.

Thorn makes a sound of discomfort. "Slimy."

The burns don't go any lower than his chest, thank God. As I dab, the algae clings to his skin like a small suction, hugging the lightning-shaped burns.

"I hate this," Thorn murmurs.

I kiss my teeth. Part of me is annoyed, while part of me wants to laugh out loud. "They're helping you."

He closes his eyes and takes a deep breath, as if he can't stand the sensation anymore. "Feels like a horde of slugs trying to eat me."

"Nature is healing you, Thorn. You don't think that's incredible?"

"Incredible," he grumbles, cringing.

I treat the rest of his chest and shoulders, neck, and face the same way until he looks like he was born in the lake.

"And now we wait," I say. I set him up so he can put his feet in the lake while he waits, and put my sun hat on his head. As for me, I dive in fully clothed—the sun will dry my clothes later anyway. I swim for a few minutes, then find a smooth stone at the bottom and scrub myself.

"You swim really well," Thorn says.

I break into a smile, but a skeptical one. "Thank you?"

He holds out his hand to me and I swim to him, surfacing between his knees. I lean on his thighs to pull myself up and sit on his lap.

He beams, wrapping his arms around my waist to hold me closer. "This is cozy."

"That's because you've been sitting in the sun, poor thing." I peel back a bit of the algae on his chest—it's stuck together now, like one entity, surviving off each other's moisture in the heat. "I don't think these are going away, but it looks less pink. How do you feel?"

"Better, now that you're here."

"Thorn."

"Please take it off, it feels like the slugs have eaten so much that they need a nap."

I laugh and kiss him before obliging, peeling each algae bandage off carefully before dropping them back in the lake.

"Do you swim well," he asks, "because you were born in the water?"

I hesitate, pausing in my work. "Reborn . . . yes."

"Like Samson."

"Yes."

"So, you . . ." He looks uncomfortable, shifting on his seat and breaking eye contact. Upset. "You died, first, too?"

"Mumma told me that I had drowned and . . . she showed me mercy. I don't remember anything before the river. For me, my life began at five years old."

"I would think you're lying if I hadn't experienced this jungle. Everything here is so unreal. So . . . *awful.*"

"The awful part is I only spent a year here before wandering into the touring company's headquarters. Trees are very diligent babysitters, but they don't have hands. Once I left the jungle they couldn't do anything but call to me."

"You're joking, right?" Thorn raises his brows. "You were left in the care of *trees?*"

I raise my brows right back. "What's so unbelievable about that? They see everything through their network, always knew where I was." I smirk at the memory of running through the jungle, their warm energy following me through the ground with every step. "It was hard to get away with anything whenever Mumma left them in charge. God knows I tried my best at every opportunity."

Thorn grins. "Is that why you left the jungle? Just to see if you could?"

"I was such an idiot."

He holds me closer, presses his nose to my cheek. "Not an idiot. A child."

Yes, a child. Who has spent more than a decade paying for one silly act of defiance. "Everyone at headquarters thought I'd been abandoned, that they needed to help me find my parents. Until I defended myself and they found out I was a Wildblood . . . they didn't really care about finding my parents after that." I breathe out my regret and peel off the last strip of algae. "You say the jungle's awful? Humans are far worse."

He scowls, and I kiss his scrunched nose, dropping the last of the algae into the water.

"Save your anger for the right moment," I say. I reach down and scoop some water, wetting his sun-heated body with it.

"What's the right moment?" he asks, curiosity in his sweet eyes.

I grin. "I'll let you know when we get there."

I lead the way up the steep rocks along the side of the waterfall. About two dozen feet up, there's a small cave behind the falls.

We make it to the top, and I move a few leaves aside to reveal the entrance, leaning back to catch my footing.

"Careful, beloved."

My breath hitches and I jolt to a stop at the pressure of his hand flat against my lower back. It's impossible that this is a dream, but it doesn't feel real, either.

"You alright?" he asks, and as he steps uphill toward me, his hand slides from my back around to my stomach . . . He's holding me. Securing me.

I press my lips together so I won't make a sound to disturb this, focus on the greenery around me so I won't cry. Together we step up the last bit into the small cave, Thorn never letting go of me.

"I—I don't—" I swallow, attempting to collect my words. Our voices are louder inside the cave. "I don't know what to do with this, Thorn."

"Do with what?"

"This." I lay my hand over his, closing my eyes as he presses me closer. "You."

"You can do whatever you want with me," he whispers, resting his forehead against the back of my shoulder.

I step out of his embrace to face him, even though it felt *so* good, far too good to leave . . . and maybe that's why I have to.

I chew on my lip. "Last night was . . ." *Selfish. Avoidant. A mistake.* I cringe at all those answers. "Very impulsive."

"I'll admit," he says, looking a bit sheepish, "it wasn't the right thing to do." He pauses, a grin slowly growing. "It was pretty amazing, though."

"Even so, maybe we shouldn't get too attached."

Now Thorn's grin turns dangerous. "A little late for that, don't you think?"

I throw my hands up, allowing them to slap down against my legs uselessly. "We're never going to see each other again after this."

"Who says?"

"You're going back to America, aren't you? And I'm staying here."

"Why do you have to stay? You could come with me."

"I can't."

"What's stopping you?"

"I . . . I don't know anymore." I rub hard at my face. Thorn's arms slide around me and my heart races, and for some reason, it makes me want to cry more than anything else. "Maybe because I love you and what we have, a-and—" I hold his face in my hands, wishing I never had to let go. "As you've seen, I don't have very much luck holding onto the ones I love."

He shushes me gently. For a moment, I just stand in his embrace, quiet.

"Why didn't you let me kill him?" I ask finally.

"Because you're not a killer, Victoria. You're a protector. And if you had killed him, I think . . . I think you would regret it for the rest of your life."

I wriggle out of his arms and walk toward the sheet of water concealing us. "That wasn't your call to make."

"You weren't in your right mind, beloved. And it's what you did for Bunny, when it happened to him. I thought I was doing the right thing."

He was . . . he did well. But I'm too angry, too heartbroken, to say that. Dean stood by and watched while the boss hurt me beyond healing. He took my brothers from me. Who cares about regret? Who's to say I would've regretted at all? My betrayer, my abuser—my enemy—would be dead.

I pace for a bit before letting out a scream. The waterfall thunders, its roar consuming my sound, so I don't know how loud I am—I'm not used to being loud—but what does it matter? I pocket all my pain into my screams, challenging the falls to rage louder. Louder. *Louder*. Higher, louder, longer, until my throat gives way to sobs.

I thrust my hands into the falls and splash my face with water. It's cold and crisp, waking me from the urge to cry again.

When I turn to Thorn, he seems uncertain whether to be concerned or not.

"Your turn," I say.

He grins and runs up next to me and screams into the crashing water. He's better at it than me, but it encourages me to keep going. We scream together, side by side, at the falls. At the world. At our enemies.

Samson and Bunny are gone . . .

And Dean is the one who took them from me.

But why should he have anything else of mine? When he's the one who destroyed what we had in the first place. When we could've found some sort of happiness, if only we'd stuck together . . .

And suddenly, all I can think of is that night.

Dean and me, hand in hand, heading across the moonlit grounds toward the boss's office.

"Don't drag your feet," I'd said, pulling him along.

Dean tugged me back gently, and I'd laughed at the pleading puppy look on his face.

"We can't keep the boss waiting," I added.

"Why not?" he asked, slowly inching me into his arms. "What's he going to do?"

I raised my eyebrows at him. "Any number of unspeakable things?"

He winced at my words. Beneath one of his eyes the skin was still purple and healing from one of those unspeakable things. "Just a minute of this." He held me close, and I laid my head against his chest. "And then—I don't know—we'll run for it."

"Away?" I whispered.

He sighed then, gripped me closer. "You know what they do to people who try to run."

"I know . . ."

We were quiet, our minute of safety ticking by far too quickly, poisoned by uncertainty . . . by fear. And then Dean tilted my chin up, leaning down to kiss me. As soon as his lips were on mine, there was no more fear. It was just him. Just us. Maybe everything around us was messed up, wrong, but we didn't have to be.

I went up on my toes to get closer, to make sure his lips would never leave, even though I knew they had to far too soon. But the promises inside them wouldn't—we were in this together, and we would survive, one day at a time.

And through it all, he would love me.

"No matter what happens," he'd whispered, cradling my face so sweetly that my core burned like I might cry. "We have each other."

"Always," I'd whispered.

And then we ran to the office and he'd . . . he'd stood there . . . just *stood there* as the monster consumed me. No arms around me, no kisses, no sweet words to comfort me.

But that one moment. That kiss. I hate myself for remembering it so clearly, for wanting it so badly now. It hadn't felt like a manipulation. In that moment, I'd felt so perfectly, incandescently happy. In that moment, I'd felt . . . safe.

And we would've been safe, maybe even won, if we'd stuck together. But Dean destroyed any hope of that in a matter of seconds.

Thorn isn't Dean. I have to believe Thorn isn't like that. I don't *want* to believe that something that can make me feel so good, so brave, so loved is a lie.

Dean was.

I scream into the falls against the thought, until the lingering want for his kiss is shattered and buried. Until I come back to my senses. Until I feel nothing but hate for him.

The screaming was supposed to make me feel better, and in a way, I do. My emotions are clear.

I lean against the stone wall to catch my breath. Thorn waits before approaching. When he wraps his arms around me, I'm grateful for the comfort, desperate for his touch. I hold his face in my hands, and we stand that way for a few minutes, forehead to forehead, nose to nose.

"Come home with me," he says, and I feel his words through my body more than hear them.

My only reply is my grateful kiss.

CHAPTER 18

"Oh, Shenandoah, I long to see you.
Away, you rolling river!
Oh Shenandoah, I long to see you.
Away, I'm bound away, 'cross the wide Missouri . . ."

We stroll along the riverbank, Thorn's song containing all the joy and peace of a beautiful, clear day. All the love and hope of our future together. All the warmth of his hand in mine.

Our group is probably to the gold by now. I hope so. I hope ages go by before we come across another human being. I don't want to fight anymore, with Dean, or the jungle. And I have a feeling those man eaters aren't going to let their gold go without one.

With all that's happened, there was never any time to discuss what anyone would actually do when we reached the gold, and part of me wonders if they are eaten by now. It's a morbid thought, but it's not as if any of them know how to deal with man eaters—I don't even know how. I just hope they're the sort of creature that remembers me fondly from my childhood. But at the moment, I don't care what's going on in the orchard. Everyone could be dead, for all I care.

I do feel bad for the Wildbloods who had no choice in whether they walk into danger or not. Forget what anyone thinks of each other personally, no one deserves this life. But I don't know what I can do about it at this point. To really help them would require confronting the boss, and I . . . I don't know if I'm ready for that.

For now, I take strength in holding Thorn's hand.

"'Oh Shenandoah,'" he sings to me sweetly, and my entire face burns as he presses his nose to my cheek. "'I love your daughter . . .'"

"Thorn," I protest, covering my embarrassment with my free hand. Someday, I swear, my body will get used to being loved.

"'Away!'" he shouts to the sky, and I jolt at his volume. "'You rolling riv—'"

Suddenly, a burst of energy runs under my foot, like the hiss of a snake ready to attack, and I trip to a stop. I slap my free hand over Thorn's mouth.

"Too loud?" he asks through my hand.

Instead of answering, I look to the trees, not quite near enough to touch them from where I stand, but I don't need to. The angry energy shoots through the ground, harsh whispers with it. Something is . . . gravely wrong.

"Come on," I say, and press forward, quickly pulling Thorn along.

"What's the rush?"

The gold of the orchard has never been mined and the jungle is suffering, I think. But I don't know if that's the reason. Maybe it's something worse—

I hear the distinct crunch of brush and my heart drops into my feet.

They took off their thuribles. The bitter thought hits me faster than I can turn—

Something hard slams into my head and my vision goes dark for a second as I stumble forward.

Thorn cries my name, and it sends my heart into a panic. I can't see straight, and frantically grope for something to keep me from falling over. I grab something—fabric, not solid like I need—and tumble anyway, briefly losing my breath as I smack into the rushing river.

My head comes up from the water long enough to see Thorn, his head bleeding as if he's been struck, his arms held behind his back by one of his own men, while Dean stands over him, glaring in my direction. But the river is too fast, too powerful, and quickly drags me under.

I manage to grab a rock just as my River Mumma rushes past. Downriver, I see Badger desperately claw for something other than the muddy bank.

Having been reborn from the river, the rough water doesn't interfere with my thoughts. Badger's been awful. *More* than awful. And I would let the river have him, but I need Badger more than she does. I'll never be able to walk into camp to save Thorn without being killed, not without some assurance from one of their own.

Not without bait.

"Mumma, no!" I cry. "I need him!"

I drop beneath the surface and swim toward him with the current.

Mumma looks vexed as she allows me to catch up. "I will not spare you another mortal."

Don't spare him. Just look the other way.

This angers her even more, her golden glow brightening with fury, but she doesn't move any closer, allowing me to flow past her.

I resurface to get my eyes on him. "Take my hand!" I call, but I'm not sure if he hears me over the rapids.

Finally, he sees me. But the strength of the water is too much for mere mortals, and no matter how he tries to fight against the current, he keeps being dragged farther and farther away. The only thing I can do is swim as fast as I—

Something grabs my arm, swiftly lifting me up from the water. I gape, my breath lost. I stare at the large hand holding me, tracing my disbelieving gaze up his arm to the familiar, beautiful face.

I'm on my feet now—he'd pulled me up, obviously, but details like that are lost. Nothing else matters. Not when I'm standing so close to Samson, to the same boy whose blood had soaked my hands not long ago, now dressed in shimmering gold like the river spirit who had saved his life.

"Is this a dream?" I murmur.

"I've heard a lot about you, Victoria." Samson grins a little. "You seem to be a favorite around here."

He sounds the same, but doesn't—the razor's edge of his former life is gone. He looks the same too, but *different*—no stress lining his face, no deep-seated anger at life in his eyes.

A sob lodges in my throat—joy or sadness, I can't tell. All I know is Samson doesn't look at me the way he used to. He doesn't know me. He isn't the same, and never will be. So maybe it's both—joy and sadness. Relief and heartbreak.

My heart is broken to have lost someone I love so dearly . . . but, somehow, the thought of freedom from his old life mends it again.

And part of me is jealous of him for that reason.

He's free.

I snap back to the moment, turning to look downriver, my emotions in too many places at once. It feels so strange and wrong to let go of Samson, but Badger is the only bargaining chip I have. His life is precious, even if I'm only going to use it to get what I want.

"Will you help me with him?" I ask.

Sam removes his hands from me, keeping them close as if to be sure I'm not going to fall over before stepping back. "My better half wouldn't like me interfering with the circle of life—her daughter is the only exception." He leans closer, and I have the urge to hug him. "But I can keep her busy for a few minutes."

I grin as he backs up a few steps and winks at me—but I have no time to enjoy this significantly less overbearing, unburdened Samson. Instead, I immediately turn and race along the bank to catch up with my enemy.

Badger has traveled downriver farther than I anticipated. I search below the surface as well as above, in case he's unconscious, in case the rapids are too much and he's gone under. I feel like I've run at least half a mile before I spot him clinging to a rock. He hasn't drowned—that's all I care about.

I grab his arm with both hands, just as he loses his grip

on the slippery rock, and I stumble forward with the force of the movement, nearly falling in. I dig my heel into the dirt and lean back, tugging hard. He manages to grab the bank with his other hand.

With one last pull, I free him from the water, and we collapse on the riverbank.

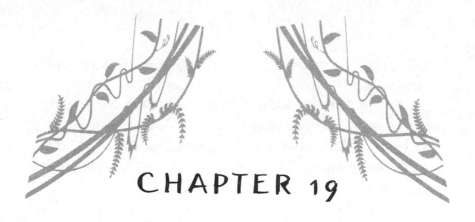

CHAPTER 19

sit there, panting. With the adrenaline gone, emotion overtakes me.

They've taken Thorn . . .

First Samson was murdered. Then Bunny. Now . . .

No. Thorn is all I have left. I won't let the same happen to him.

Tears are blossoming at the backs of my eyes, but I know better than to sit and cry with the enemy so close.

I shove myself up, stumbling to my feet, but Badger has the same idea, only he draws a knife.

My science flows, discovering a blood source that isn't mine before I even have to process that Badger's head is bleeding. With a flick of my fingers I pull blood from his wound, and a dagger flashes to life, bigger and longer than his and pointed directly at his throat.

"By now you know I can easily kill you," I say, backing him

into a tree. "And after what you did to Thorn, I might just be in the mood."

I won't, despite how I feel. I want to and can, but I won't. Still, I must sound convincing, because his back collides into the tree without a fight, chin tipped back away from my blade, as he glares down his nose at me with wide eyes and flared nostrils.

"Drop it," I say.

He lets the knife fall. It's clearly been sharpened for today, because it sticks upright in the root by his foot and stays there.

"I've been intimidated innumerable times in my life," I muse. "You corner someone . . . frighten them . . . take away their freedom. Then demand something that violates their free will." His eyes widen as I shift the blade closer. "Feels strange to be on the other side."

"Please don't kill me," he begs.

"I don't have to. You'll die quickly enough left in the jungle on your own." I pause. "Or we can make a deal. You want your gold and I want Thorn back, safe and sound. You'll get me what I want, and I might just lead you back to your precious gold in one piece."

I see Badger swallow carefully. "They'll shoot you on sight."

My blood dagger flashes as I shift it over his face, and he winces, a strangled sound stuck in his throat. I take a few steps forward. "I don't need you with both eyes, or ears—come to think of it, I don't even need you with every finger. Or *any* fingers for that matter. Which would you like to lose first? Name it quick, or I might choose for you."

"I'll do anything you say," he says with an edge of panic. "*Please.* My wife will be devastated."

I take a deep breath. It feels strange to abuse my power this way. Thankfully, the strangeness passes swiftly, and I'm left with only determined hatred.

"We work together to reach the orchard," I say. "Threaten me once, and you will be mutilated. Understood?"

Badger nods quickly.

I step away a safe distance before dissipating my weapon with a flash. Badger gasps for breath. He leans over, his hands resting on his knees. I use the interlude to check the pockets in the leg of my pants, pulling out the wax-covered envelope. I open it. Three sticks of incense left, all dry. That should be more than enough.

"Where's your thurible?" I ask.

Badger jolts back up, pats his waist, but when he grabs the little metal censer we both deflate. It's been crushed on one side, probably against a rock in all that thrashing water.

"Here," I say, unstrapping mine from my belt.

"Don't you need it?" he asks.

"I never did." I toss it to him—I know better than to get too close—and he catches it and attaches it to his belt. "Hold still."

I pinch the air with my fingers to take a little more of his blood, flicking it at the incense, the small flash of my science lighting it.

"I'm not igniting anything again," I say, "so we'll have to get there before nightfall. Unless you're fine walking in the dark with all the nocturnal predators." I have to save up my science as much as I can. I'll need it when we reach the gold. Even if no one else gives me trouble in retrieving Thorn, Dean certainly will. "And stay within the trees, away from the river. It's doubtful the River Mumma has it in her to spare you twice."

We have no salt, so duppies could be an issue still. But at this point I just have to hope that doesn't happen.

I turn and start walking away without him. Soon after, I hear his boots follow.

I underestimated how far the river had taken us. An hour later and there are still hours to go, despite our fast walking speed.

Badger is a less talkative travel companion than Thorn, but that suits me fine—the less breath we waste talking, the more we'll have to continue.

We pause sometime in the early evening, and I climb a banana tree to fetch us some substantial food. I drop a bunch from the height, and Badger catches them. The one thing we've done as a team today.

"You didn't run," I say, when I reach the bottom.

"What would be the point?" he says, handing me half the bunch. "You're the only one who knows what you're doing out here."

"Also, I could easily turn you into a bloodless corpse."

"Yes." He swallows, clears his throat. "That part, too."

"Let's rest a few minutes. Get off our feet." I sit and he follows my lead, slowly, at a bit of a distance.

He cradles his bunch in the crook of his arm, using his teeth to start peeling one banana to eat now.

"Careful of spiders," I say.

He freezes, then puts his bunch on the ground quickly. "You can't trust anything out here, can you?"

"I trust the jungle more than I trust humans."

"Humans." He looks over his banana carefully before continuing to peel. "You say that as if you aren't one of us."

"Maybe I'm not . . ." I stuff half a banana in my mouth.

"Dean was right about you. You're a force."

I nearly choke on my food. "Dean said that?"

"We were only going to capture you, like we did Thorn. But he said the only way to stop you was to kill you. And here we are . . ." He gestures to our surroundings, looking around cautiously. "Survived a raging river, don't even need incense, and halfway to the gold again. Maybe you *aren't* human."

For a few minutes, we fall silent, the only sound my chewing.

"Why are you business partners with Thorn?" I ask, curiosity getting the better of me. "You clearly hate each other."

"He always seems to know where to look for gold. He's a moneymaker, even if he is a tiresome glory hog."

"I don't think that's any more true than Madelyn calling him a libertine."

"Don't you have any sense, girl? Any self-preservation? I can't believe that didn't deter you."

I raise my brows. I hadn't thought about it much after Thorn had denied the allegations, but now it made sense. "Which was clearly your intention."

Badger bites the inside of his cheek. "This jungle is driving me insane. I'm talking too much."

"Madelyn was in on your plan to kill Thorn, then?"

"She just takes it upon herself to warn girls about the faults and cruelty of men."

By . . . lying about them?

"Strange she doesn't follow her own advice." With a sigh, I stand. "Let's keep moving. We have a long way to go."

I continue on without looking back to see if he follows. The frantic shuffle of boots clues me in.

We travel in silence for another hour. A sun shower comes and goes, drenching us. I don't focus on the time, only on how close we are to the orchard, and we're close—the sun is low now, but we're just a few miles off. Badger's pace has slowed. We may need to rest if he's going to make it.

Because I need him to make it. He's the only leverage I have.

"Not far now," I say. "Take a break, stretch your legs. A few more miles and we'll be—"

"Excuse us," a corrupted voice of death interrupts politely.

I grin, turning to see that same line of pickneys walking toward us.

"Excuse us," the little line leader repeats.

I move without her needing to ask again, then trip to a stop from my own shock.

There's a new addition to the line. A tall, dark-skinned boy at the very back, so much taller than the others he could be mistaken for a man. He holds hands with the little boy in front of him. Faceless, but with Bunny's narrow chin. Bunny's unkempt Afro. The travel clothes my Bunny died in.

I choke on a sob and rush toward him. I shouldn't touch him—I doubt he even knows me anymore, even if he could see me, hear me call his name.

"Bunny," I gasp anyway, and reach out, just shy of touching him. "My Bunny."

I let my fingers touch his free hand, and he turns his head in my direction . . . and doesn't turn away as he passes.

It's a natural reaction of pickneys, I remind myself. *The only sense they have is touch.*

Still, I can't help but think—

"Disgusting!" I hear Badger fuss, and look back in time to see him kick the little line leader. She topples over with a terrified cry and hits the ground hard, taking the two in line behind her with her.

My blood runs cold. "Badger, no!"

Like a hive of hornets, the pickneys swarm. They run at Badger, knocking him over with kicks and shoves, unable to heed his shouts and curses. I rush in his direction, but there are too many of them and they work too quickly. I hear a squishing, sick sound, and Badger lets out a desperate, sobbing scream before one of the children holds up a bloody eyeball.

Well . . . I *had* threatened mutilation.

Still, I have to do something quickly, but I refuse to hurt children, so I don't know what to do—

A long arm catches me and my heart trips. I look up to find Bunny's featureless face looking down at me. I don't move . . . and maybe that's why he takes my upper arms in his hands and shifts me himself, backward, away from the carnage.

"Bunny," I gasp.

Bunny's faceless soul holds me there, before releasing my arms and returning to his newfound family.

I stand there stupidly, until my wonder fades to uncover Badger's continued screaming, the sound of flesh tearing and blood being pattered—like children playing in a puddle.

It's too late for Badger, and if I linger too long when the pickneys are in a frenzy, I could be next, daughter of the River Mumma or no. So I run. Otherwise I'll vomit.

I might do that, anyway.

I run until I'm gasping, my throat dry, my legs burning from use, until I'm more damp from sweat than from the earlier rain. I collapse, barely catching myself with my hands, and pull myself to the riverbed. This is not my finest moment, but there's no one here to judge, so I proceed to cry and lap water up like a jungle creature, while my body makes multiple attempts to throw up every single thing in my stomach.

I roll onto my back, panting.

Bunny . . . my Bunny.

"He's dead, Victoria," I say aloud, so I'll believe it. "All you have is Thorn."

But is that even true? My only bargaining chip just had his face torn off. And if it's true what he said, that Dean told them to kill me . . . if I walk in there alone, that's the first thing they'll do.

I don't have a plan. I need one in the next two hours.

"God," I whisper, closing my eyes. "Is this enough like a nightmare for you to take it away? Please. *Please.* Help me."

The jungle is quiet, ominously so.

But I feel something hot and somehow also cold lingering over me like steam.

I open my eyes to the giant skull of a bull, horns curling upward to pierce the sky. Shadowy smoke drifts around the skeleton, licking the bones where flesh and organs should be.

The bull I'd murdered.

Now, a shadow creature.

"Please don't kill me," I gasp. "The love of my life needs my help."

He snorts at me, a massive, vibrating rumble, and black smoke puffs from his nostrils like a smokestack.

I close my eyes, steeling myself. *Get up, Victoria.*

I open my eyes again as the bull's snout presses into my chest and stomach.

"Hey, Biggs!" I shout, slamming my hands on his bony not-a-nose. "I'd rather you take my soul than crush me. You giant, heavy thing!"

The bull releases me, tilting his head like . . . like a confused puppy?

I escape from beneath him and run into the trees, skidding to a stop behind one. I shriek, holding my chest, the bull standing in front of me once again, as if I blinked and made him appear.

But of course spirits don't operate on the same physics I do.

"Stop that," I snap. "I don't have time for this."

I head back to the riverbank, back in the direction of the orchard where they've taken Thorn. But that steamy sensation remains.

"Don't follow me." I shoo with both hands. "Go on."

I walk a few more feet, then look over my shoulder, and the distance between us is no wider.

"If you're not going to take my soul, go away. I can't sneak up on the enemy with a giant skeleton following me. Just—I don't know—lie down or something."

The shadow creature makes a low rumble . . . and then folds his legs beneath himself and lies down.

I gape before a small smile slips to my lips. "You've got to be kidding me," I murmur. I hesitate, and then approach him slowly. I reach my hand out and stroke his snout. He sighs. "You're nothing but a giant sweetheart, aren't you, Biggs?"

Impulsively, I lay my cheek against him, shadows swirling around me. "I'm sorry I killed you. I had people to protect, but that's no excuse. You didn't deserve that."

He rubs his snout against me and I tumble backward, a laugh breaking out of me. "Hey!" I grin, shaking my head at him. "Are you the answer to my prayer, Biggsy?"

The shadow creature leaps to his hooves, smoke swelling around me.

I blink, and suddenly I can see the trees at a whole new angle—high off the ground, with the river below me. I look beside me at the long, curved horn and pat the skull I'm sitting on.

"Let's go save Thorn."

And Biggs takes off running as only a spirit can.

CHAPTER 20

I t's moonless, pitch black out other than the golden glow of the Gilded Orchard. A mile back I had left Biggs behind and taken to the trees—a tedious way to travel, crossing from tree to tree, but I don't want to have to kill anyone if they posted guards. Not that there are enough of them left to spare for a lookout.

From my perch, I can see everything. The Gilded Orchard is nothing but two dozen orange trees, but in the dark, the sap glows like molten treasure inside the cracks of their bark. The man eaters, which I only find hints of through the branches, must be asleep.

Why are they called man eaters? Did I make that name up, or did Mumma? And if no one has ever made it to the orchard, how many men could they have eaten?

These are the silly questions I use to ease my mind while I look for an entrance.

And, most importantly, look for Thorn.

"I am a poor wayfaring stranger
Trav'ling through this world with woe . . ."

Thorn's voice echoes up to me, through the trees. The sap creates a golden ambient light reminiscent of twilight. Enough light to work by. More than enough light to be spotted in if I try to slip down there.

The traitors are, unfortunately, not eaten by man eaters. They've pitched their tents, and are around a campfire a short distance from the end of the orchard. Where did they get the wood? In a disrespectful fashion, I'm sure. The jungle won't like that, but I'll let it deal with them as it likes.

I spot Thorn, arms tied behind his back, sitting under a tree in the middle of the orchard. I sigh heavily, relief washing over me, though I notice his head is down and he isn't very active at all.

"There is no sickness, toil, nor danger
In that fair land to which I go . . ."

The fewer trees—and man eaters—I have to disturb to defeat my enemies, the better. And conveniently, they're all in one place.

But even though I don't care about what happens to them, I don't want to be the one to end anyone's life. And a distraction will only hold them off for so long, perhaps not even enough time for me to climb down from the tree and get away with Thorn.

"I'm going home to see my mother
I'm going home, no more to roam . . ."

A pang of pain mixed with anger races through me. They . . . did they . . . ? Are his wounds so brutal that he would sing for his own coming death? First Samson, then Bunny, now—

No. *Don't think that way.* He's not going to die. I won't let him.

"I'm just going over Jordan
I'm just going over home . . ."

But I'm beyond the point of caring if these people die— these backstabbers and abusers who care for nothing but their own glory. Granted, I wouldn't feel right doing it with my own hands . . . but a less sympathetic adversary just might.

I take a deep breath. I'll only have moments to act. The flash of my science will alert them almost immediately to my pres- ence. The Wildbloods, in particular, will be able to pick out my glowing eyes in the darkness. Dean, most of all.

He knows my past. He'll know I survived the river, and to look for me in the trees.

I straddle the tree branch so I can use both hands, and take another deep breath. I test each person at the campfire until I find blood that draws easily—an open wound. I drag the blood upward above the trees, but the man I drew from sees it happen so already I've run out of time. Already the group is looking for me as I split the blood a few times and shape it into daggers. And then, with one more deep breath, I throw the daggers at a diagonal so they hit the tree closest to them with a bright flash, splattering half the people at the campfire in liquid gold.

Immediately, I start climbing down the tree—I only need to hear the frantic shouts, gunshots, and animalistic growls to know my plan had the desired effect. I run through the trees, looking over to make sure my enemies are well occupied. The man eaters growl like wolves and scream like wildcats, and I wince as I witness the beginning of one tearing off someone's arm.

But there's no time for me to be concerned. Most of the man eaters toward the center of the orchard are either still sleeping or only lazily curious, lifting their heads to see what the commotion is about. I'm careful to keep away from the trunks, to not linger under any trees in case sap drips from above, until I spot Thorn.

He's watching the commotion, too, terrified.

Poor thing.

I rush over to him and the movement of me kneeling at his side jerks his attention toward me. He gasps the beginnings of my name and I cover his mouth quickly with my hand, putting a finger to my lips. He nods. I glance up, finding three man eaters sleeping among the branches.

This is the first time I've ever seen the creatures up close. The nimble body of cats the size of wolves, with similarly long snouts. Razor-sharp teeth stick out of their snouts, numerous and jagged as a crocodile's—jaws that can snap bone with one bite, I guarantee it. I can't tell if they have shimmering scales or if it's just golden sap stuck in their short fur, but I don't want to get close enough to find out.

I don't even know if Thorn's seen them yet—with the way he's tied, I don't think he can look up very well. If he could, I don't think he would have sung his sadness quite so loudly.

I refuse to use Thorn's blood, even if he is bleeding, while he's in this weakened state, so I pull it from my own veins. Just a drop, too small to make anything but the barest spark. It cuts through the ropes easily enough, but we're far from safe.

Thorn isn't a silent mover like I am, and I'm sure his legs are cramped from sitting in the same place for hours, so I prompt him to crawl away from the tree. His wrists are raw from the rope, and it makes me angry looking at them. I look away. I need to keep a clear head.

I help him to his feet and guide him through the trees, making sure he doesn't touch any of them. My distraction seems to have died down—when I glance over, there are forms lying on the ground, and I can't tell if they're man or man eater.

When we make it to the trees, I push him behind one, out of view of the camp and the creatures. "Are you okay?" I whisper. "You look . . . okay."

"Nothing but some rope rash," he whispers back, looking at his wrists. "And a sore back."

I scowl and back away, but he grabs my waist and pulls me against him. "You were singing—I don't know—a dirge," I say. "I thought you were dying, you theatrical ninny."

Thorn stifles a laugh. "Aww, were you worried, beloved? I'm sure they thought the monsters would kill me. They were never going to get my blood on their hands, themselves—I mean, that's why they recruited you, right?"

I take a deep breath. There will be time to be annoyed with him for giving me heart palpitations later. "Let's just get away from here." I grab his hand to run, but he tugs me back.

"I have to get my rifle," he whispers.

"We don't have time—"

"My parents gave it to me." He kisses me quickly. "Wait for me here."

He runs off, around the perimeter of the orchard within the jungle's trees, and I mute my own frustrated yell before chasing

after him. Whether the traitors or the man eaters, there will
be no safe way to enter the camp, let alone find his gun in time.

In time?

I don't want to think about that. I can't. Thorn and I are
getting out of here alive, if I have to drag him.

I stumble to a stop at the mouth of the camp, the area destroying my night vision like golden hour ablaze. There are bodies strewn across the ground, unrecognizable from being toyed
with by the man eaters—chunks of faces gone, limbs torn clean
off, batted and scratched, bruised and bloody. I catch the sight
of Thorn, running into a tent, and breathe out a sigh of relief.
He's okay. Whether he'll stay that way is up to me.

My lungs compress as I spot Dean, kneeling before a slain
creature.

Of course Dean would survive.

The wicked always do.

He had watched Thorn enter the tent, but at my arrival,
he turns around quickly. His eyes lock with mine, and his expression would be so much less terrifying if I could make it out
better in the strange golden light. As it stands, it isn't exactly
sinister . . . but the way he rips the knife from the creature's
body as he stands, the blade dripping scarlet, has me on edge.

"Thorn!" I call, breaking my own rule about disturbing the
jungle. But it's well enough disturbed already, and we need to
go, *now.*

Thankfully, Thorn comes running out, with his rifle and a
small box of bullets. I join him in stride.

There's nothing we can do but run.

Thorn glances over his shoulder and swears. "If there was
one person who should've been eaten by those things . . ."

Dean is after us. I know without looking, without asking. I know *Dean*—and he isn't chasing us to join our journey back to headquarters. Everyone is dead but him. He has nothing left here.

No, he means to kill Thorn, just like he did my other two boys. I'd see Hell freeze over sooner than let him try.

My feet know this jungle, but Thorn's steps keep faltering. I slow to help, prompting him along with a hand on his arm. But, bless him, his footfalls in those boots are too loud—there's no way we'll lose Dean, even in the dark.

A small flash and a burning pain slices the side of my shoulder—Lord, he's attacking! Panic begins to overtake my breath. Next time he might not miss, and we have to make it to the riverbank. Or to where Biggs is waiting, at least a mile out still. But we can't outrun Dean, not at this pace . . .

Clarity.

I can't outrun Dean . . .

So I won't.

I skid to a quick stop and round back, fast enough to see Dean stumble to a sloppy stop, to throw him off—enough to launch an attack he can't dodge, lightning illuminating his shoulder as blood splatters from it. He blocks my next attack, and the one after. I can't overdo it like I did last time. It uses less energy to deflect than attack. Dean is smart enough—or scared enough of his own science—to know that.

"Don't make the same mistake twice," his voice grates out like a dying animal, despite there being far too much life in him for me to let down my guard. I must've torn his throat raw when I drew the blood from his mouth. "This time your lover can't protect you if you rage—"

A shriek sounds, but from something wilder than Dean as

a small form drops onto his shoulder and knocks him in the temple. Another bounds onto his head, and suddenly, I make out the outline of the small, fluffy rodents, their large ears veiny and translucent in the limited light. A half dozen fuzzies leap from the surrounding trees, scampering across the ground to climb his leg. Dean cries out as one bites him in the shoulder.

I don't wait. I charge at him head-on, tackling him to the ground, the fuzzies scattering to make room for me, screaming as if cheering me on.

"Thank you, my friends." I summon my science, my eyes glowing bright enough to see Dean's horror-stricken face, no matter how hard he'd had it punched into him by the boss to show no fear. "But this kill is mine."

Dean's on his back, while I sit on his stomach. Any other time, that would never hold him, but he knows better than to try to run from me. Lightning crackles around my open hand, my power deterrent enough.

But I don't strike.

This kill is mine . . .

That doesn't sound like me at all.

Thorn was right about me. I don't kill. I preserve. I protect. And even if I don't care about either of those things concerning Dean, I . . . I can't bring myself to do it.

I won't do it. I won't do things the way the boss does. The way he's trained Dean to. If Dean's going to die, it won't be by my hand.

But I'm not going to tell *him* that.

My friends have dispersed, and Thorn is smart enough to approach from the side, aiming his gun at Dean.

"Wait," I say, holding up my hand—and God, I love this man,

because he doesn't pull the trigger. Dean's eyes widen almost imperceptibly. Surprised, mistrustful, relieved . . . dangerous. Maybe I wouldn't have noticed if I didn't know those eyes so well. "We can't kill him here. It'll leave a remnant in the jungle."

"You mean his soul?" Thorn asks.

"Maybe. Or a few body parts, if the pickneys get ahold of him. I'd prefer to leave my jungle unstained by his presence."

Thorn nods. "What would you like to do with him, beloved?"

I chew on my lip, looking around quickly. I climb the closest tree, borrowing some healthy vines from its branches, and when I drop back to the floor, tug with both hands, testing the strength. Perfect. "We'll take him with us."

From the corner of my eye, I see a light, and as soon as I turn—

"Don't move!" Madelyn has a lit lantern strapped to her waist, casting dramatic shadows on everything surrounding us, but she stands only a small distance away—far enough to be a threat with her rifle without me being able to physically intervene. Her satchel is full of golden sap, tiny slivers glowing out beneath the mud she covered it in. Far more cunning than I gave her credit for. "I swear, I'll blow a hole right through your head if you move another inch."

"Maddy," Thorn warns.

"Keep your eye on Dean," I tell him.

"Yes, Laertes," she mocks, "watch Dean. I'm trying to speak to your all-powerful leader."

I take a deep breath. "You want to kill us, Madelyn? You'll never get out of this jungle alive without our help."

"Why do you think I'm here? I have no intention of dying in this dirty, monster-infested hell-hole."

"Then lower your gun."

She lets out a simple, amused laugh. "I don't think so. Not after all the antics you've pulled. No, you are going to answer my question and then you are going to die. I don't need two Wildbloods running loose—one is good enough."

I almost want to laugh at the absurdity of her demand, but I don't want to give her any ideas that would endanger Thorn. "I promise you, Dean will kill you quicker than I will just for calling him 'good enough.'"

The amusement drops away from her expression. "The jokes are cuter coming from Thorn. Now, answer my question so we can be done with it. What have you done with my husband?"

He got his idiot ass killed because he couldn't follow directions.

But I don't care about Badger, and, though in a different situation I would feel for her, I don't care to answer to her about anything.

Instead I say, "You don't want to know."

She pauses, but her expression doesn't waver. "I wish I had known you were this fiery sooner. We could've been friends." She smirks a little. "As it stands, I can definitely see why Dean insisted we kill you."

"Then shut the hell up and do it," Dean mutters.

"You were in on the plan all along," I confirm.

Madelyn rolls her eyes. "Of course I was, you stupid little cow. Did you *really* think I came on this dangerous expedition for a vacation? Now, on your knees. I'll at least allow a short prayer before you meet your maker."

"I'm not going to kneel," I say, my gut humming with energy. "If you think your fingers are faster than mine, go ahead and shoot."

She scowls impatiently. "I am a champion skeet shooter, and you're a much larger target than a skeet."

"And you have a wound in your left shoulder," I say, the red glow of my eyes casting an eerie light on my arm as I reach my hand forward.

I draw blood from her wound and simply allow it to hover near her face. Her eyes widen as they shift to look at it, but she shuts them as my science flashes.

"Witch," she spits.

Maybe she pulls the trigger, because with a flick of my finger I slice the barrel in half, setting off a small flash that makes Madelyn scream and stumble backward. Both halves of the gun drop to the ground while she stares at me, trembling all over.

"On your knees," I say.

Madelyn's face is a mask of terror as she obeys. I didn't have to do that, make her kneel like I'm some great authority.

But it sure does feel good.

"You can tag along if you want. I don't care either way." I snatch up the vine and head back over to Thorn and Dean.

"Am I supposed to thank you?" she bites out. "After you killed my husband and ruined all our plans? Well, I'm the only one of us here with gold, so if you think—"

A giant mass of bones pounces, enveloping Madelyn in black smoke. None of us—least of all her—have time to react before the smoke is sucked upward, dragging her soul along with it, into my giant bull's bony jaws. Her body collapses, lifeless.

"Biggs!" I chastise. I rush over and pat my big sweetheart around the opening which would've been a snout with both hands. "Hey, no more of that—look at me." My bull grunts but relaxes into my touch. "These two men here are off-limits. Do you understand? No eating."

He snorts and nuzzles his snout against me.

"Lie down."

He folds his legs beneath him and plops down with a clatter and a swell of smoke, like disturbing a bonfire.

I pat him hard so he'll feel it—if spirits made of reanimated bone can feel—and whisper, "Good boy."

I turn to Thorn and Dean to find them staring at me in awe and horror. Or, rather, at Biggs.

"Is that . . . ?" says Thorn. "That's not . . . *no*. That's not the same—and it's a demon now—?"

"This is Biggs. Don't worry, he doesn't *need* to consume souls to survive."

I look down at Madelyn's soulless body, her eyes staring up endlessly at the sky, the gold oozing from the top of her bag illuminating her.

I go to Thorn and touch his arm. "I've got Dean. You knew her longer. You can . . . do whatever you feel is right."

I don't wait for him to agree or move. I kneel beside a still-shocked Dean.

"You . . . you tamed a shadow creature?" he asks dumbly.

"What, like it's hard?" I grab his wrist, but he doesn't seem to notice as he stares at Biggs's gaping yawning mouth. "Now hold still. Just because my bull isn't hungry doesn't mean I won't let him eat your soul and drag your corpse out of my jungle."

CHAPTER 21

Tying a Wildblood's hands is tedious because you have to curl the fingers in to make sure their science can't be accessed. I had to pick open small slits in the vine and wedge Dean's bent fingers into them, then bind his wrists tightly. Everything in the jungle has been designed to defend itself if need be, including the vines, which have tiny barbs woven through the inner fibers—sharp enough to grip in place without really cutting him, unless he struggles.

But Dean has struggled on and off for hours. He's winded, but holding the ten-foot lead attached to his bound hands has worn me and Thorn out, too. We've certainly traveled farther than we would have with Thorn's entire group, but it hasn't even been a full day. In fact, the sun has barely risen, warm colors peeking through the trees. We've been walking for nearly half the night.

Biggs shuffles along behind us and, even without actual muscles to form expressions, I can tell he's getting agitated and is as fed up with Dean as I am—he shakes his head, grunts occasionally, stomps his hoof. And now he bows his head and digs his horns into the dirt, and I know I have to intervene before he eats—

I stumble as Dean tugs at the vine abruptly. "Okay, that's enough!" I shout, and I have to release the vine to catch my footing, regaining balance after a couple steps forward. "Stop it, now. *Stop it.*"

Dean looks shocked for an instant—probably more from my shouting than anything else—glancing down at the vine on the ground before snapping, "You want *me* to stop? I'm the one who's bound."

"Yes, and you deserve it. Not least for getting everyone in your party killed."

Dean laughs, a choking sound, before grimacing. "Blaming the wrong person, as usual. Not the man who abused us or the idiot whose idea it was to come out here in the first place."

"Shut up!" I move to shove him but stop myself. I will never be desperate enough to touch him again. *Never.* But Biggs aggresses him for me, bellowing like a horde from hell—a combination of a thousand lows and screeches that makes the trees shake and sends all of us covering our ears.

When I recover I demand, "When did you become a manipulator like him? Why—?"

I can't go on for a moment. I don't know why the words stuck in my throat hurt so badly. I hate him—and with good reason—so why . . . ?

I kiss my teeth at myself. I can't even ask myself the question. I can't even think it without wanting to cry. But whether sadness or anger is driving those tears, I can't quite tell.

Thorn takes my hand, and I squeeze it. Simply that, and after a moment I'm able to swallow the knot in my throat.

"We grew up together, Dean," I say finally. "I thought you understood me better than anyone. But you hate me, just like everyone else."

Dean's fair brows lower, but the mocking expression is gone from his eyes. "I hate a lot of things in this world, Victoria. Never you."

"Don't lie to me anymore." I swallow again. Take a deep breath. "How else can you explain all the horrible things you've done?"

He examines his bloody fingers. "I wish you understood how much I care about you. That I'm doing this *for you.*"

I feel my elevated heart in my temple, the fire in my core heating it. "Doing *what* for me?"

"Everything."

"Everything?" I snap, and I can feel my eyes grow red. "What, like kill my friends? Sabotage my promotion?"

"An unfortunate accident, a traitor, and he was never going to give it to you."

"What happened to you, Dean? We used to be close. When did you become so heartless?"

I don't know why I ask. I *know.* It was the day he stopped crying. His humanity dried up along with his tears.

Everyone knows monsters don't cry.

He doesn't answer. Coward. Traitor. I'm not leaving this spot until he does.

"There's nothing left for us, Dean," I say. "You might as well tell me everything." I grip my fists. "You're *going* to tell me, truly and honestly. We'll start with the most recent. Why did you work with Madelyn to . . ."

I pause. No. I don't care about that. Besides, money or gold is the most likely answer.

"Why did you kill Bunny?" I demand.

He clears his throat. Cringes at the very action. "An accident," he rasps. "Swear to God."

"I don't believe you."

He lets out a sound of frustration, and I feel like if he had his fists available he would use them. "Then why ask? If you're not going to listen to anything, why even ask? Is the possibility that I'm not the villain you think I am that outlandish to you?"

I scoff. "Oh please."

"You hate me because you *want* to hate me, Victoria."

I feel my science ignite in my core. But that would be too easy. Threatening him . . . killing him . . . I don't want any of it more than I want answers.

"I hate you," I say, my rage brewing, "because you led me to the boss, *knowing* what he had planned for me, and you just let it happen."

"I didn't know. Let's get that straight—I had no idea why he wanted to see us both. What kind of animal do you think I am?"

"The predatory kind," I hiss.

"And you know the boss as well as I do. You know there's no challenging him, not without severe punishme—"

"We were best friends, Dean, and you let him rape me!" I grip my hair with my fists and scream into my elbows, a strangled cry I don't even recognize as my voice echoing off the water, through the trees. I pant for a minute, catching my breath. I feel a hand on my back, and even though I know it's Thorn I yelp, "No!" and he removes it swiftly, giving me space.

I don't want to be comforted. I don't want to be silenced. Dean deserves to know how what he did affected me, even if it was a whole year ago.

Because a year feels far longer when you're the one living with it.

I stand upright and look at my former friend . . . my enemy. Who looks closer to tears than I've seen him in a long time . . . and maybe, just maybe, if those tears fall I might be able to feel differently.

Maybe I could see him as he was.

"I loved you, Dean," I say. "I think I . . . no, I did. I loved you as more than a friend. And you stabbed me in the back, let the monster we hated and feared hurt me worse than anything for a . . . for a stupid *promotion* that neither of us actually wanted."

Silence.

My heart stumbles, my breath caught.

"What do you have to say?" I demand.

Dean swallows. Grimaces from the action. "I told you why I did certain things. Back in the gully. My answer hasn't changed."

I kiss my teeth. "Oh yes. To play the boss's game."

"Yes."

"By stepping on me to get to the top."

He closes his eyes, as if against pain. "I loved you, too, Victoria."

"Please don't," I whimper.

"I did what I had to do to make life better for us."

"You disgust me. I mean, my God. Do you hear yourself?"

I huff out a heavy breath and pause to collect my words again. Dean doesn't say anything, so I go on. "The boss has always been horrible. I expect it from him. But you . . . I trusted you, Dean. I *loved* you." My stomach swims with the heat of my science, but something holds me back from igniting it . . . something raw and unhealthy, poisoned emotions I can't begin to understand. "I don't care what you do to him. Lie to him, beat him at his game, kill him . . . but why did you have to hurt me to do it?"

I wait for his answer, the silence stretching, broken only by Thorn's trembling breath behind me.

"I'm sorry," Dean murmurs, finally.

A bitter laugh escapes me. "No, you're not."

"You're determined to believe my intentions are cruel. That you mean nothing to me."

"Your behavior toward me for the past year proves it."

He shrugs. "Just part of the game."

"We could have this entire conversation through eye contact—that's how well we know each other—and you're telling me you couldn't find *any* way at all to let me in on your plan?"

"Of course you don't understand," he snaps. "You're his favorite, and a girl, and have never been punched in the face and told you were worthless for not having the strength to punch back."

"Is that supposed to make me feel sorry for you?" I snap back. I approach him quickly, my eyes burning red. "According to him, I'm as worthless as you are. You think his punches hurt any less just because they're aimed at places the clients can't see? You're not special."

Behind me, I hear Thorn curse, the sound of a cracking

heart, while Dean and I glare at each other, our eyes burning red. He's bound and can't do anything with his science . . . but, if I wanted to, I could burn him alive with my lightning. Tear him to pieces. Make him suffer like he has made me suffer.

But he must have read my eyes because he whispers, "If it makes you feel any better, I hate myself more for it than you ever could."

"I doubt that." Even so, my science is the first to back down.

His brows lower in confusion, his eyes searching me as they shift to gray. "You might as well kill me. Go ahead. I know you want to."

"You can die after we deal with the boss."

"And how do you plan on doing that?"

"I'm not telling you a thing until I know for sure that I can trust you." I turn away from him, unable to bear the sight of him anymore—why, I'm not sure. It just *hurts*. "And, right now, all I know for sure is that I can't."

"I hate him as much as you do."

I'm at a loss for words. Tired. Just so very tired of *everything*. I rub my forehead. "That I believe, at least," I mumble, and walk forward without bothering to pick up his lead. If Dean doesn't want Biggs to get too close he'll do the smart thing and follow.

We walk for a while, without talking. Not even Thorn. No stories, no songs . . . only the whispers of the jungle and the open air for me to think.

I look at Thorn. He's sweating so much, losing too much water too quickly. Thankfully we're following the river this time—which is the fastest way, even if it is the most dangerous.

Plenty of water, but that doesn't mean Thorn can just walk over and take what he needs. I don't really expect Mumma to be accommodating twice, even if I ask.

"Let's stop here to rest," I say.

"I won't argue with that," Thorn says, dropping his pack on the ground. He passes me Dean's lead and then points the rifle at him. "Where do you want him?"

"By that tree," I tell Dean, tipping my chin at the closest one.

"You heard your tour leader," Thorn tells Dean, barrel trained at his chest. "Move."

Dean doesn't move, hate radiating from his eyes. But he and I both know he's too tired and dehydrated to fight back, not to mention probably in a lot of pain from having his fingers bent in on themselves for hours. So he walks to the tree, ignoring the gun to glare at me. Thorn orders him to his knees, and then looks at me.

My beautiful Thorn. Love courses through me as we exchange a quick look. I've never met someone who's ever respected a request from me so fully. He's not going to kill Dean. Not unless I tell him to.

"Are you going to execute me or what?" Dean growls.

"Not today," I reply.

Thorn lets out a small laugh. Everything amuses him, but I hadn't meant my words as something impressive to intimidate, or as a joke.

They were simply the truth.

Dean's on his knees. He has no fists to threaten me with. It's far too humid on this island for blood to truly dry, so it's still smeared down his temple. The barbs in his binding's fibers must've really dug in, because blood stains the vine and the skin near it on his fingers and wrists. The crease in his brow is, I suspect, not solely due to his glare. Part of me wonders how much flesh the barbs have torn, if his hands will ever work the same after I take off the binding.

But he deserves it. Besides, this is mercy compared to what the boss has done to us.

"Are you going to stay put?" I ask.

"We should tie him to the tree," Thorn suggests, walking over to pick up Dean's lead.

"Come near me, tourist," Dean growls, "and I'll crush your idiotic skull."

Thorn scoffs, gesturing to Dean's unfortunate state. "Good luck."

"Are you going to keep hiding behind that rifle? Fight me like a man."

I wrap my arms around Thorn, using my entire body weight to push him away from Dean as he approaches. He yields to me, gripping my back, and I feel his adrenaline in the press of his fingers.

"Let me kick his ass," says Thorn, his voice tight. "Just once."

"We need him functioning well enough to walk," I say, taking his rifle from him. I don't say that I'm uncertain of his chances against Dean. When I'm sure Thorn won't charge, I let go and walk over to Dean, who hadn't bothered to get up.

I grip the rifle in both hands and slam the large butt of it into the side of Dean's face. Blood splatters from his nose onto the greenery, running down over his lips.

"That was for *this*," I say, pointing to the bruise on my face where he punched me. Bruises have been so common in my life I've barely noticed this one, but that's beside the point.

Thorn whoops in approval, rushing to take my face in his hands and kiss me.

"Did you just congratulate me for being horrible?" I gasp, when his lips release mine.

"Horrible? You're fierce." He takes back his rifle and trains it on Dean, a grin slowly growing on his lips. "But yes, I did."

Dean spits blood onto the ground, challenging me with his glare.

We should've been even. He punched me, I hit him back. And maybe I wouldn't have even been compelled to do that, if his answers today had been different. But the relentless glare has awakened the petty revenge in me.

Though, to be honest, with Dean it doesn't take much.

"You know, Thorn," I say, though I keep my eyes on Dean. "I like your idea of tying him up. One less thing to worry about."

I climb the tree Dean sits under, securing the vine holding his hands to a branch, keeping it taut above his head. I do a pretty good job—if the vine pulls Dean's arms upward any tighter, it will tug his shoulders out of joint. As it stands, he looks exceedingly uncomfortable.

He'll keep.

I help Thorn sit near the tree line, away from the water, and then fill both our canteens from the river, murmuring, "Thank you, River Mumma, for sharing with your daughter."

"Thank you, my love," Thorn says as I hand him his canteen.

"Of course," I reply warmly, and he beams at me.

I walk over to Dean with the other canteen and splash it in his face.

Dean coughs. "What the hell?"

"Your face is covered in blood. Do you want kala ants after you?"

"A little warning next time," he grumbles, and huffs water from his nose, more blood flowing with it. I think maybe I broke his nose. Ah, well. It's been broken so many times, I would've been more surprised if I hadn't.

I take a large leaf from a nearby plant, carefully filling it with water from my Mumma's river, and bring it over to Dean, holding it to his lips.

"What is it?" he asks.

"I wouldn't poison you. Drink."

"Why are you bothering? Am I a prisoner or not?"

"Right now you're a nuisance." I sigh. "*Drink.*"

I tip the leaf to his lips and he accepts. He drinks every drop, and then I go back and bring more. When I put the second leaf-full to his lips, his expression is so thoroughly his younger self—relieved, grateful, baffled, maybe on the verge of tears. Except I know the wetness in his eyes, this show of weakness, is fleeting, so I ignore him. After he's done, I drop the leaf and take some incense from his inner pocket, kneeling to relight his thurible.

"You've always been too softhearted for this life," I hear him say above me.

"If you get bitten by something venomous, you'll die, and I don't want you haunting my jungle. I gave you water because I'd rather you walk than me drag your dehydrated body back to headquarters. It's not complicated."

"That's the last place we should be going. You do realize our common enemy is still there waiting for us."

I click his thurible closed, then step back from him. "I'll deal with the boss when we get there."

"And then what? Where are we going to go? Where will we be accepted? People hate Wildbloods."

"Maybe they don't hate us everywhere. We've never left the walls of the company, so how would we know?"

"And that's a risk you're willing to take? You'd risk your own people?"

"The one who led *his* own people into an ancient, vengeful jungle to die is asking *me* that?" I scoff. "Anything's better than your plan to keep us in virtual slavery."

I turn, but Dean's voice stops me.

"They're going to shoot us without a second thought. You do know that, right? They don't care about us unless we're making them money."

Even tied to a tree, at my mercy and whim, he uses that insufferable tone that suggests I'm stupid.

I half turn to glance at him. "I don't plan on dying."

"Do you have *any* kind of plan?"

"To use you as a human shield for their bullets, if you don't shut up." I walk back to Thorn.

"You don't have to deal with him," Thorn says, tucking a loose curl behind my ear. "Let me do it. Just tell me what I'm not allowed to do."

"It's fine," I say, leaning against him. "Honestly." I look over at Dean, his head bowed, stewing in his own bitterness. I chew on my lip.

He's right about one thing. I definitely need a plan.

CHAPTER 22

Thorn insists on taking the first watch so I can sleep. There's not as much to watch out for during the day, but it's an endearing gesture if I thought I could actually sleep. I'm physically tired, yes, but my mind . . . my mind won't rest.

I pretend to sleep for Thorn's sake, mentally planning our arrival to headquarters. If we enter from the road, it will be less suspicious. The guards will know we've been on a tour, and so we probably won't get questioned like we would if we entered from the trees. Besides, I don't want a fight to break out. My quarrel is with the boss—no one else.

When it's my turn to keep watch, I make sure Dean is still secured, then I walk over to Biggs, who lifts his head in anticipation of my approach. I pat his bony face.

"What do we do?" I ask quietly, leaning against him.

Walking while dragging Dean along has been an exhausting way to travel. If I wasn't worried about him accidentally dying here and infesting my jungle with his traitorous soul,

I would've left him behind in the orchard. Or better yet, let Biggs eat him. But, as it stands, Dean can't die, and I can't handle another couple days of this.

A faster way would be to build a raft and take the river, but faster and easier usually equates to more dangerous—at least for the boys, if not for me. Maybe I can ask the River Mumma if she wouldn't mind. I grin. Maybe I can get Samson to distract her again.

"What do you think? Should we get Uncle Sammy to appease our vengeful Mumma?" I whisper. Biggs huffs out a breath, and I kiss his snout. "You think you can find some bamboo culms for me? Long ones, and mature. Not the bright green ones."

Biggs leaps to his feet, ready for action. Although, to be fair, he was never *not* ready—it's not as if shadow creatures need to sleep. He runs off. He seems to understand, but I don't know anything about bulls, least of all spirit bulls, so all I can do is *hope* he knows what I'm talking about.

I lie on the bank and lean my face close to the water, close enough to kiss it. "Mumma, I wish to travel by river. Please remember your daughter and allow for smooth sailing."

And now, well . . . all I can do is wait and keep watch.

I go check on Thorn. He prayed before falling asleep, and so far seems to be doing okay as far as nightmares.

I take a deep breath and turn to Dean next. He's barely sleeping, but trying. I'm surprised he's getting any rest, since I'm not sure how much blood is left in his arms—must feel like pins and needles all over.

I climb the tree and untie the vine holding Dean. There's no neat way to do it, and I hear Dean hit the ground and groan.

"What the hell was that?" he mutters, as soon as my feet touch earth.

"I'm giving you your blood back so you can get some real sleep."

Real sleep. When the numbness in his arms has worn off, he'll probably be in for a whole new dose of pain from the feeling coming back into his hands. I doubt he'll get any more sleep than I did.

He lies on his side in the fetal position, arms tucked into himself.

"Can't you take this off now?" he asks. His torn throat makes him sound terrifying and sad at once, but there's something else, too . . . something in the way he says it that makes me think of Little Dean. He's vulnerable and isn't hiding it, just like when we used to share a bed mat.

Unless . . . he's just trying to manipulate me again.

I err on the side of caution.

"It'll hurt worse if I take it off," I say.

He whimpers. I sigh. It's so much easier to hate him when I'm not behaving like . . . well, like him. Like the boss, who taught him far too well to be cruel. It takes a very sick person to actually *enjoy* kicking people when they're down.

I still hate him for everything he's done, but I can't stomach being cruel. I can't stomach it . . . but I don't know if I can trust him yet.

I bend down and peel some moss from the base of the tree, wrapping it around his bound hands. When I pour a bit of water on it from my canteen, the moss shrinks and gathers, molding to his hands like it would to a tree, clinging.

"Thank you," he whispers, barely audible.

"Don't talk anymore," I say. "Sleep."

"You're building a raft?"

That's not Dean.

I turn quickly and wrap my arms around Samson's neck before I can think better of it—although I should've, because I immediately feel stupid when he hesitates before patting me on the back.

He doesn't know you, Victoria. Don't be weird.

"U-um, yeah," I say, releasing him and taking a few steps back. My cheeks grow warm with embarrassment. But I'm so glad to see him that I couldn't help it. "Biggs went to get some bamboo."

"Biggs?"

"My shadow creature."

"You . . . *named* a shadow creature?"

I bite my lip. Samson stares at me so long I decide it might be better to change the subject. "I thought a raft would be easier than walking."

"For you, definitely. But my wife might not allow these two mortals safe passage."

"She will for me. I'm her favorite, after all." *She owes me for bringing her you,* I want to say, but I don't need to see his confusion. I don't want to cry.

He scratches his chin. "I mean, we could certainly try."

My heart beams. "You'll help me?"

He smiles. "Your mother would kill me if I didn't."

I laugh. It's strange to hear someone else talk about her. For so long I thought I was alone in everything.

"Samson?" Dean is sitting up, his eyes wide as if a soul eater was before him. I feel a smug satisfaction that the boy he tried to get rid of is back and more beautiful than ever.

"Yes," Samson says, with a puzzled raise of his eyebrow.

"Y-you're . . . alive."

"And who are you?" He sweeps Dean quickly with his eyes, his brows lowering. "A troublemaker, clearly."

The contrast of Dean's fear and Samson's disregard delights me to no end. "I have him under control," I say.

"You sure? I'll happily drown him for you."

"I didn't know you were a real river spirit."

"I'm not," he says, with a shrug, "But with this one, I honestly don't think she'd mind me taking her job, especially if I appease her afterward." He gives me a playful grin.

"Go back to sleep," I tell Dean, who still seems to desperately be deciding whether or not he's being haunted by the wrongful murder he committed. I take Samson's arm and escort him closer to the river. "You really love her, don't you?"

"Of course I do," he says. "She's my wife." He looks at me thoughtfully. "Don't you love her?"

Just thinking of Mumma fills my heart, warms me from the inside out. "I loved her from the moment I looked at her. I knew she was my mother, right then."

"Sometimes you just know."

"But she . . ." I chew on my lip, remembering when Samson was resurrected. "Mumma had . . . well, she had said you'd make a good mate for her, and now you are. Do you think she did that with me? Said I'd make a good daughter?"

"She could've. But what does that have to do with how you feel about her?"

"I . . ." I stare at the river. "I don't know."

"You know how I know there's no magic spell over us? Because sometimes I get angry with her. Sometimes I don't like the things she says about humans, and I tell her so, and we get into it. *Yes*," he emphasizes, and I realize I'm gaping, "the majestic, radiant river spirit, ruler of the jungle, sometimes starts arguments like a petulant child."

"She does seem to get angry at a moment's notice."

I hear water slosh against the rocky bank, and realize why too late, unable to dodge before a bunch of water slams into us. I stumble backward, a laugh breaking free from me. It's nice, laughing with Samson again. That, at least feels the same. Normal.

"I say it in love, my darling!" he calls to the river. He squeezes out his long hair and pats me on the back—I'll have to get used to these kind, yet distant, gestures of his. He barely knows me now. But I want a real hug. And I want Mumma to come to me. I wish I could wrap my arms around her, bury my face in her skirts. But Thorn and Dean are still here, so I understand why she's hesitant.

Biggs skids to a stop in front of us, dumping a pile of bamboo culms on the ground from his mouth. They're covered in tooth marks, and I'm now positive he didn't understand anything but the word "bamboo," but he's brought a variety we can sort through and find enough to use.

"Great job, Biggsy," I coo, and kiss him between the eyes.

Samson whistles. "I've never heard of a shadow creature without a constant taste for death." His comment makes me grin—he hasn't been reborn long enough to have heard of much of anything. He stares at me, with a look so significant I'm not sure what to make of it. "The jungle really loves you."

I feel myself blush, and push back any amount of guilt I feel for picking Thorn over the call of the jungle.

Thankfully, I have a good distraction now.

It's time to get to work.

We peel the skin from the bamboo culms with our knives, sand them smooth. After a little while, Thorn wakes up and comes to help. I don't blame him for not being able to sleep under these conditions. Some of the bamboo that are long enough are too young and green, and I wonder if I can use my lightning to dry them out a little. I need this raft to work—traveling by river will shave off at least two days of travel, and I'd prefer to not wrangle Dean for any longer than necessary. We can't afford to lose time tiring ourselves out from dragging Dean around.

Eventually, Dean comes and sits closer to us. I don't mind, since he can't cause any trouble bound the way he is. And for once, I don't think he wants to. It's odd that Samson, Dean, and I used to be something like a family. I know it can never, *will* never, be that way again, but . . . it's comforting. To have this sweet glimpse of peace. It's surprisingly nice.

It's a good thing there are three of us, because the raft requires five horizontal sticks bound across it—well, ten, because they need to be lined up evenly on top and underneath. And then we bind it together with strips of the extra bamboo. It's a couple hours before we've finished, and thank God for Samson, or it would've taken longer. Bamboo at this length isn't light, and I almost forgot how strong he is.

Shame on me for forgetting anything about my Sam.

"I'm wondering if this is going to be able to hold three people," Samson says, after we've finished, the bamboo lined up and bound nicely, directly next to the river. It's at least fifteen feet long, if not longer. If it doesn't hold us I'd be surprised.

"If not, we can always drown Dean," Thorn chimes in.

I raise my brows at him—I'm sure he was sleeping when Samson suggested it earlier, so this has to be a coincidence. "Not funny."

Dean lays a healthy glare at him. "Piss off, tourist, we're only here because of you."

Thorn scoffs. "Alternative—tie him to the back of the raft and let him swim."

Sam points to Thorn, wearing the slightest grin. "I'd like to see that."

"You can both piss off," Dean bites back.

"Everyone relax," I say, holding up my hands—specifically to keep Dean and Thorn away from each other. "It'll hold us. Now, stay here, and don't kill each other. I'm going to find us some food."

"Hurry back." Thorn wraps his arms around my waist and kisses me. "I miss you already."

"Kill me," Dean mutters.

"Don't tempt me, troll."

I roll my eyes. "Samson, could you—?"

Sam is already shaking his head before I can finish. "I don't interfere with mortals."

"Right." I take a deep breath. "Okay. Dean, you come with me."

"Are you sure?" Thorn asks, eyeing him in utter disapproval.

"One more hour of your time, Samson," I say, lacing my fingers in supplication and giving him the sweetest look I can drum up.

He sighs. Shakes his head. "Your mother said this is how it was with you. You bat your eyes, and she gives you whatever you want." A slow smile slips to his lips. "*Fine.* One more hour."

"Thank you!" I fight the urge to squeeze him around the waist, and instead grab Dean's lead. Biggs lifts his head and huffs out black smoke as we approach.

"I'm not getting on that thing," Dean protests, tugging his lead to move backward.

"You can walk, but you won't be able to keep pace with him." A blatant lie. Biggs trailed us this entire time, he can go as slow or as fast as he pleases. But Dean is afraid of heights, to the point where if the boss gave him an odd job involving climbing we would secretly trade. But that was back when I loved him and he loved me . . . and things were less muddled.

Haven't you tortured him enough, Victoria? Probably, if I were a better person . . . or if Dean were a better person, for that matter. But he made me miserable for a whole year, so him suffering for a day is the least I can do.

Vicious without cause, Victoria.

Dean seems to agree, by the way he's scowling at me. And, all of a sudden, I can't make sense of how his eyes—part hating me and part questioning *why*—are making me feel right now.

"It won't steal my soul?" he asks before I can think about it further.

"Like I said, I don't want your soul left behind in my jungle."

That seems to wake his petty arrogance, which has always been stronger than his fear, because he strides up to Biggs and steps up onto his snout with no further hesitation.

I grab his wrists to help pull him up, since he can't use his hands. He grimaces. I should apologize for grabbing right where he's raw, but I don't. I guess I have more of Mumma's pettiness in me than I thought.

The top of Biggs's skull is smooth, so I don't blame Dean for straddling a spot by the ridge where skull meets horn. With the raised area to keep him from falling off backward and the dimples and imperfections in the bone to cling to in front, he should be fine. And, sure enough, he handles it better than I thought as Biggs stands up without much warning, simply shuts his eyes and lies on his stomach to get closer to the surface, but otherwise I'm proud of him.

Proud of Dean? I shake my head at myself.

We travel in silence for a while. I stare out into the jungle, murmured words almost drifting away in my subconscious. But I know Dean's voice, even warped as it is by his injury, so I turn to him. "What?"

"I'm sorry, Victoria," he says.

"For what?"

"For . . . everything."

I pause. Stare at him. And then I pat my bull's skull. "Stop here a minute, Biggsy."

My sweet shadow creature obeys, and I sit cross-legged, arms folded. "You're 'sorry,'" I repeat. "For 'everything.'" I raise my eyebrows like a merciless shrug. "What's 'everything'?"

Dean glances down at the tremendous distance to the ground, then looks at me. He looks miserably sick, but I can't tell if it's from the height, from his hands—which have bled through the moss and onto the white of Biggsy's bones—or something else.

"For hurting you," he says.

"Be specific," I say, rather harshly.

"For letting the boss hurt you last year."

"All for a promotion. You forgot that part."

"No." His tone is final. "You really think I'm as heartless as all that? I was terrified, V. I should've protected you, but I didn't. It had nothing to do with the promotion and everything to do with me being a coward."

I pause. Dean's . . . calling himself a coward? I haven't heard him sound anything but arrogant for the past year. But then, I haven't spent much time with him.

But even though the honesty and crack in his ego are welcome, I feel like I can't allow him to speak this way. I take a moment to swallow the horrible taste in my mouth. "I would never call you a coward for fearing the boss."

"I was strong enough to stop him. I should've." He sounds angry now. Crushed, defeated. Humiliated. "That's all there is to it. I'm sorry, okay?"

We're quiet, my brain racing a mile a minute. Biggs must realize we're going to be here a while, because he lowers himself to the ground to lie down. Dean clings to the giant bones for dear life, letting out a heavy sigh when we've finally settled.

"Am I just supposed to say it's okay?" I say. "That I forgive you?"

"You don't have to say anything. I don't expect forgiveness. I just had to get it off my chest."

"To make yourself feel better?" I say harshly.

"I haven't slept in a year, Victoria," he snaps. He swears and presses his forearm into his eyes. "I think about that night all the time. I hate myself for it. Isn't that enough? That I hate myself as much as you hate me?" He drops his arm, stares at his bloody fists. "I mean, damn. Why does Thorn get a break?

He thought every single warning you gave about turning back was ridiculous, got every single person in our party killed for it, is not *nearly* as saintly as he makes himself out to be, and yet he's *still* on a pedestal."

"I do *not* put him on a pedestal." I bite the inside of my cheek and huff out a heavy breath. "Anyway, don't bring Thorn into this. Your answers keep changing, Dean, *that's* why I don't believe you. First relationships are 'transactions' and now you would've saved me if you hadn't been frozen by fear. How do you expect me to trust anything you say?"

"Look at me, then, if you won't trust my words."

It's the truest thing he could say. Because, even if I can't trust what he says, I trust his eyes . . . those beautiful, bright eyes, incapable of lies, incapable of hiding from me. They don't know how to lie anymore, I don't think, not since we developed our eye contact as a lifeline. At this point, they're the most Dean thing about him . . . all that's left of who I fell in love with.

So when I look at him, and his eyes tell me they're sorry, that he would do anything to take back what he did, that he would rather die than have to obey the boss ever again . . . I would have to be willfully vindictive to deny that it's true.

"Fear of the boss is something we both understand well," I say. "I want to say again, I don't blame you for that. At all. If it had stopped there, maybe we could've rebuilt us. If you had been there for me, maybe we would've been okay. But you accepted the promotion, Dean. The very next day. How else was I supposed to view that except for betrayal?"

"You don't say no to the boss." He closes his eyes briefly, looks away, as if he's ashamed of his words. "I thought I'd be more help to you by getting rid of him."

"But you treated me . . . so wretchedly. For a year."

"I'm sorry."

"Sorry isn't good enough. I can't forgive you. I can't." I swallow back tears, even though they're burning, hurting my head. "Your apology is genuine, I can tell that much. But you hurt me beyond healing, Dean. I don't trust you, and I don't think I ever will."

He nods, slowly. "Too little too late, then?"

I wince at his words, no matter how true they are. "Too little too late."

For forgiveness, maybe. But not too late for *me* to do the right thing.

We're quiet. I scoot forward and take out my knife, carefully cutting the vine from Dean's hands. His wrists are a little red and raw, but his fingers have the worst of it—cuts and tears all over, some blooming blood at the slightest movement. He takes a moment, and I give him that time, to figure out if his fingers work, but they don't seem to be able to curl out much on their own. He stares at them. They still shake, but now I'm not sure if it's from his earlier spider bite or from the trauma of the vines.

Wordlessly, he drops off Biggs onto the ground—not a horrible height, with my big sweetheart lying down—and walks over to the river. I slide down to follow, seeing as I can't have him dying here. I quickly lay the vine at the base of a tree, rubbing it into the moss. It will rejuvenate . . . unlike Dean's hands.

It serves him right for every time he used those hands against me, but part of me is still sorry. I don't know which is worse, constant stiff muscles from when I held in my hate and disgust . . . or the conflicted ache in my heart I feel now. At least the hate was sure, definite. I don't know what this is.

I don't know what I'm feeling. All I know is I don't like feeling this way. My feelings for him have melted down from pure hate to something different, but just as severe and painful.

And watching him submerge his hands slowly into the water, watching him wince, hearing him whimper . . . I can't trust him, true, but that doesn't mean I have to behave like he's some sort of monster. That doesn't mean I have to do what the boss would do. I don't need to be quite so vicious all the time.

I don't want to be.

He lifts his hands out of the water to stare at them. His eyes shift from gray to red, and I ignite my science in response, waiting. Nothing. Even while forcing his fingers straight with the back of his other hand.

"Just like your throat needs rest," I say, "so does your science. It's part of you, too."

He nods, reluctantly.

"Stay here," I say, and go gather some moss from the nearby trees.

"Why, if you don't trust me?" he asks as I sit beside him.

"I don't know." And I mean it. I don't. Or, if I do, I certainly don't understand. "Shut up before I change my mind."

This time I place the moss with more care, wrapping each finger. This must be cutting into the hour I promised Thorn and Sam, but it can't be helped—maneuvering around his fingers, taking extra care with the deeper gouges, is not something to be rushed.

"I wish I understood what you see in Thorn," Dean says.

"He's sweet, kind, generous, thoughtful. Not you."

"You barely know the man, Victoria."

"I thought I knew *you*," I say bitterly. For a moment I can't speak, my throat tight and burning. "So what does it matter, really?"

Dean winces as my vicious, petty hands press the moss against him too hard.

"Just be careful, that's all," he says, and I glance up to find he's watching my hands work on his. "The other night I . . . I panicked. Maybe it's irrational, but I pictured the boss all over again."

I picture the boss at his words, cringing, forcing my mind to my task. "The other night?" I ask absently.

"Yeah, the other night," he says, like I've lost it. "When you and Thorn had sex while surrounded by literal corpses like some cultish ritual."

I freeze. Finally look at him. I don't know if I feel my blush rise or see his mouth quirk into a sly grin first, but my heart is pounding, regardless.

"What makes you think we had sex?" I say, but the bite in my voice can hardly pass for innocent.

"What makes me—?" Dean chokes, biting his lip with the slightest grin as if holding in a laugh. "Victoria. The entire camp heard you."

"W-what?" My face feels like it's on fire. I cover it with my hands so quickly I accidently slap myself. But Dean is laughing now, so I drop them quickly to tell him off, but watching him, a laugh tumbles out of me instead.

He raises a teasing brow. "That's the loudest you've ever been in your entire life—"

"Shut up, Dean!" I shove his face aside, then drag his hand back to me by the forearm. But my hands are trembling as I handle the moss. I smile, unguarded. Uncontrollable. "It was nice . . ." But, just as quickly, I can't smile anymore, guilt over-taking me. "It wasn't right, though. In any way. We should never have done it."

"What about it wasn't right?" He sounds more serious, with an edge of apprehension, his gray eyes like a storm cloud. I miss his laughing, and the very fact shocks me. "He didn't force you, did he?"

"He didn't force me," I assure him. His words make me miss Samson. He always cared about my well-being. For me—not in service of my mother, his wife. Because he loved me. And, for a second, it feels like the old Samson is speaking through Dean.

But then, Dean used to care about me, too. The old Dean.

My Dean.

For an instant I miss him, too, but I push the emotions back.

He can never be the boy I loved again.

I finish covering his hands up to his wrists, then scoop wa-ter from the river and slowly, carefully pour it onto his hands. The moss tightens up around his fingers, sealing, creating damp velvety gloves.

A vast silence goes by, thick and heavy and full of too many memories and words—things I have no time or understand-ing to process. So I stand, holding my hands out to Dean. He reaches up, and I take him by the forearms instead of his wrists to pull him to his feet.

"I'm glad he didn't force you," Dean murmurs.

And I find myself grinning as I catch his blush of embar-rassment before he quickly turns and heads to Biggs without waiting for me.

CHAPTER 23

I put Dean's strong arms to use and fill them with mangos, pears, and callaloo before we resume our journey. Samson has left, which is disappointing, but I suppose I'd kept him from his love for long enough.

"Are you sure that was a good idea?" Thorn asks, frowning at Dean's unbound hands.

No. I'm unsure of everything right now. The whole point of entering the jungle was to free Bunny, but he's ... well, maybe "gone" isn't the right word. I've never actually spoken to a pickney, so I don't really know how they feel about their state. Mumma is the one who told me they enjoy their explorations, but to me it seems like they're stuck in an endless, senseless loop of wandering.

Except Bunny had protected me, like he knew me. And the others had defended their line leader. Nothing about either of those acts seemed senseless.

What *is* senseless was my cruelty to Dean.

"I think he got the point," I reply.

Thank you, Dean's eyes say. He won't say it out loud in front of Thorn, and I'm not feeling petty enough anymore to make him. We're both thinking more clearly now. Especially since our mutual enemy needs to be dealt with, and it's going to take us both to do it.

Besides, if Dean had the chance and the capability, I think he'd go for Thorn rather than me. Judging by the state of his hands, that isn't happening.

But then, I've seen Dean kick men's asses while barely having to throw a punch. Come to think of it, he'd choked out that guard back at headquarters with only his arms, no hands necessary. He's bigger than Thorn, and far less civil.

But I have to believe this is the right choice.

Still, I'm not stupid. I take the food from Dean and make him sit by a tree, hand Thorn three mangos—one for each of us—to keep him occupied with slicing. I handle the pears, cutting them in half through the rough skin to reveal the bright green insides. I wedge my knife into the giant pit to take it out. The pear is still a little firm, but I prefer it that way to mushing at the slightest pressure.

"I tried avocado on an expedition in Mexico once," says Thorn, and cringes. "Doesn't have much taste on its own."

"It's good for you," I reply. "Wrap it in the callaloo leaves with the mango."

He sighs, wistful. "I can't wait to get back to civilization and eat some meat."

"Eat your tongue," Dean mutters. "Then we'll both win."

"Rest your voice," I chastise. "I don't want you two talking to each other for the rest of the journey. I'm anxious enough as it is."

"Aww, beloved." Thorn kisses me on the nose. "Don't be anxious. We'll get through this together, okay?"

Dean scowls. "Don't tell her not to be anxious. You have no idea what we're walking into."

"Thought I told you to shut up, Dean." I hold the small leaf wrap I made up to him. "Open." He obeys, accepting the food from me.

"Excuse me, what the hell is this?" Thorn shifts his gaze from me to Dean, an edge in his voice that reminds me of how Samson used to fuss at me. "You two are cozy again after an hour alone?"

I sigh. "He can't use his hands, Thorn."

"You're too sweet. He doesn't deserve your generosity."

"I need him with enough energy to walk on his own." I kiss Thorn, and it seems to calm him a little. "Now stop talking for once and eat."

It's clear none of us can sleep, so after we finish dinner we gather our things to continue the journey.

We climb onto the raft—the boys near the back, with Dean ahead so Thorn can keep an eye out, and me up front. I let them sit while I stand, steering with a long piece of bamboo. The current does the rest. Mumma is merciful, as it isn't too rough, and just fast enough that I can keep control of the raft.

It's a peaceful way to travel. There's more sky here on the river, a break in the canopy with a foot or two of space to see all the way up to the stars. The moon caresses us in light, but I'm glad we still installed a small rack up front for a torch so I can see where I'm going.

"'Theeeeere . . .'" Thorn sings, holding the word out long

enough that I know he wants us to join in, but I wouldn't be able to identify the song if he paid me to.

"For the love of God," I hear Dean snap. "No more singing!"

"'... Once was a ship that put to sea, And the name of that ship was the *Billy o' Tea*—'"

"Shut up!"

I laugh and look over my shoulder at them. "Dean's uncomfortable, beloved. Keep singing."

Thorn bends over laughing, and I hear pure admiration in his voice when he says, "I love it when you're funny."

We travel downriver steadily, Thorn singing, Dean brooding, the jungle whispering. And I don't know why, but I love every minute of it.

My arms, shoulders, and back are sore from building the raft, not to mention steering all night. But it all feels worth it as the trees break and we float up to the jungle road bridge in the wee hours of the morning. We've shaved two days off our journey by taking the river.

I huff out a sigh of relief.

Thank you, God . . . thank you, Mumma.

I steer the raft to the bank, and Thorn leaps to dry land and pulls us closer. I think we all want sleep, but it'll only be a few hours now, by road. A few hours to freedom.

Biggs snorts at me from within the trees. Shadow creatures never travel so close to the edge of the trees, and his devotion warms my heart. I smile and hug his snout. "Good boy, Biggsy. I'll see you again soon."

He lets out a melancholy low and I suddenly realize "soon"

could mean years. Right. I'm going to America after this. Leaving him hurts, and I suddenly think of Bunny. My little Bunny . . .

"There's a very tall pickney," I whisper to his bones. "I want you to look out for him. Love him as you love me."

Biggs nudges me, as gently as a giant bull can, his version of a hug. And then he disappears into the trees, and I have to hold back the urge to cry.

Lord, I hope he understood that. I hope he and Bunny will be best friends. It's that one thought that gives me the strength to turn away from the trees and face the road before me.

Thorn wraps an arm around my shoulders, pulling me in close to kiss my temple. "I know that was hard for you. Everything's going to be okay."

His optimism is endearing. But it's a trick of the brain, just like any other manipulation. Everything isn't *going* to be okay.

Not unless we make it so.

As we walk, Dean peels off his moss gloves to test his hands. He attempts a fist, grimacing. His hands close, but not firmly enough to throw a proper punch. Then he moves onto his science. Sometimes he manages a shadow of a spark, but I don't bother remaining on my guard. His frustration with himself is obvious as he huffs out a heavy breath through his nose, his eyes burning red with barely a result. I don't know. It makes me sad.

And part of me feels protective of him—as a Wildblood, at least. And because we have a history. As much as I love Thorn, I don't want him to see Dean this way. He will never understand the pain of losing the ability to use something that is so deeply a part of you. Limbs, eyes, kidneys, injuries, those are part of the body. Take those away, and you're no less *you*. It's hard to describe to someone on the outside, but a Wildblood's science is more than just part of their body.

At least it is to me. Society has so long dubbed it a stigma that most Wildbloods don't get to experience being their true selves without fear.

It can kill us, yes. That's what makes it *wild*. But the jungle is wild, too. The most dangerous things are a gift if you can see the true beauty in them.

I touch Dean's wrist, lowering his arm so he won't focus on his hand anymore. There's no disgust in touching him, no adverse reaction, but . . . I still don't know if I should. I remove my hand, quickly sticking it in my pocket to meditate on what I just did. "You'll weaken yourself, using your own blood like that."

He utters a defeated scoff, wincing. "I suppose that'll make it easier for you to kill me."

I sigh. "I'm not going to kill you, Dean."

He looks at me, his voice quiet as he says, "I'd rather you kill me than the alternative."

My heart pounds, and for a few beats, it's hard to swallow. "He won't hurt us. We can't let him."

"We failed the mission, Victoria." He huffs out an uncharacteristically stressed breath, wiping his brow with his forearm. "He punishes us on a regular basis. What makes today different from any other time?"

"The difference is that he has more to lose than we do," I say. "And that I have a plan."

"What is it?"

"Well, for starters, the first thing we should do is negotiate better terms for all the Wildbloods."

Dean grabs his throat, his attempt to laugh stifled. "We're still talking about the boss, yes? He's never going to agree to that, not over his dead body."

"Then we make him agree."

"Oh yes, perfect plan," he says with a tone of sarcasm as he touches a bit of torn skin on his fingers, gingerly. "*Make* him agree. Why didn't we think of that twelve years ago?"

I walk backward in front of Dean, so I can face him.

"Listen to me, Dean," I say, hugging myself—if I don't, I may reach out and wipe the blood from his face, and I still don't know how I feel about touching him. "It doesn't matter what we do. From here on out, we remain a united front. I don't care what you think of me, or what we've done to each other. We have a common enemy. There are two of us—three, with Thorn—and one of him."

Dean scoffs. "I feel like I've been saying that since we left headquarters . . ."

I huff, annoyance rising. Good. A definite emotion toward Dean that I actually understand. "But your intentions were wrong. Working toward overthrowing the boss's work, even if it got rid of him in our lives, was wrong. This life he forced us into is *wrong*. He's a monster, and we'll never be free until he's destroyed."

"He's going to kill us, Victoria," Dean snaps, quickening his pace to confront me before tripping to a stop. "What the hell *don't* you understand about that?"

The tremble in his voice runs through me. We're connected in this steady emotion, this one true fear.

"No!" I squeak, holding out my hand to Thorn as he slides the action on his rifle. Dean's quick movement may look violent on the outside . . . but if Thorn could see Dean's expression, he would know. If he could read his eyes like I can, he would understand twelve years of fear and pain. Twelve years of hopelessness driving our lives.

"I'm scared, too, Dean," I whisper. "I'm terrified. I wish I could run without ever having to see that man again. But we have to do this. I can't live like this anymore—can you? We have to do *something*."

"My hands don't even work," he gasps, desperate. "I can't *do* anything."

"Then just stand with me. Please. I—I . . . I can't stomach facing him alone."

My own words strike me, bind me in memories of the boss's heavy, hateful hands, of pain my body will never forget . . .

"Okay, V," he murmurs. "*Okay*. I won't let you face him alone." His voice still holds fear, but his nod is certain.

I turn away from him quickly and continue down the road. The more I talk about it, the more my emotions bubble up, and I need to be able to function when we confront the boss.

We travel in silence. No songs, no arguments, nothing but the jungle's whispers and Thorn's booted footsteps. I take comfort in the colors of the morning beginning to rise—pink into coral, coral into blazing flame, all rimmed by a deep violet wanting to introduce the blue sky.

These are my ideal travel conditions, but today they feel poisoned. Because stalking behind them is the ever-present fear of what we're about to do.

Far too soon, the entryway to the company comes into view up ahead.

"Wait." I put my arms out to my sides, stopping Thorn and

Dean from going any farther. "I think . . . I need a minute to collect myself."

"No arguments here," Dean says quietly, fidgeting with his hands.

Thorn holds my face gently and kisses me. Temples, cheeks, nose . . . lips. I melt into his embrace, my arms wrapped around his waist. "Don't be nervous," he whispers. "I'll be there with you, Victoria. You can do this."

"Thank you," I whisper back. I press my face into his neck, inhaling his scent to calm my nerves.

And then I step away quickly. I need to be able to do this without clinging to someone. I need to be able to stand on my own two feet when I face the boss.

I need to show him I mean business.

"Okay," says Thorn, squeezing my shoulders, "you get your beautiful, powerful, brilliant self together, and I'm going to go relieve myself." He points to the trees and heads in that direction.

"He's too cheerful," Dean grumbles. "You actually *like* that?"

I smirk. "Are you jealous, Dean?"

He scowls and looks away, down the road toward our dreaded destination. "I just think he needs to learn how to read the room."

"A little positivity is helpful . . . in some cases."

"This is not that case. It's diminishing."

I nod in agreement. No amount of cheer can make what we're about to do feel better. "Where do you think you'll go when we get out of here?" I ask, to fill the silence.

"Go?" he asks, like he doesn't even know what the word means.

"Do you remember where your parents live? You should send them a telegram when we get back to headquarters."

"I couldn't even tell you what they look like anymore. I'm sure they think I'm dead by now." He shrugs. "Anyway, I wouldn't know what to do with a life like that. How do you know what isn't a trap?"

"There are good people outside these walls, Dean. Kind people, like Thorn, who don't devote their lives to hurting children."

"What's the cost of that, though? What's the trade-off?"

"There is none." I hesitate, his silence planting doubt in my gut. "I mean, there shouldn't be."

"Relationships are nothing but transactions . . ." Dean looks at me, like studying a picture. "What does Thorn want?"

I lower my brows slightly. "A life with me."

"And you don't see where there could be a cost for you in that?"

"U-um—" I snap my jaw shut as Thorn makes his way over to us.

"Ready?" he asks.

I nod, ready or not.

CHAPTER 24

The morning doesn't know there's about to be a mutiny. If it did, the bright blue sky wouldn't have such jolly fluffy clouds floating across it. The breeze wouldn't be so pleasantly cool to counter the hot sun.

Thorn, Dean, and I walk into headquarters by the main road. The guards at the entrance stare at our filthy, pathetic state, but don't stop us—everyone knows who Dean and I are, even if they don't recognize Thorn. We head directly to the office.

Louis gapes, standing from his desk so quickly that he nearly knocks his chair over.

"Mother of God," he exclaims dramatically. "No, no, no, that floor is freshly mopped! Get out!"

"We have to report on our tour," I say simply. I turn to Thorn as Louis continues to chastise us for not wiping our feet. "Do you mind waiting in here?"

"I'd wait forever for you," he says, and kisses me—I nearly laugh at Louis's huge gasp. "But I don't trust Dean."

"He's not going to hurt me. Don't fret, beloved."

We leave Thorn, ignoring Louis's shouts of, "You can't go in there," and Dean shoves the door wide enough to slam it against the inner wall.

The boss looks up from his desk, a cigar wedged in his teeth, predictably with his morning glass of rum and a stack of paperwork in front of him. His brows lower as he takes us in.

"You have an explanation for . . . this," he says, gesturing to our filthy, bloodstained clothing, "I assume."

"You're not going to ask why we're back sooner than expected?" I say, disgust climbing up my throat. "Or why your spies haven't reported back to you yet?"

"I'm not talking to you at all, girl," he growls, then turns to Dean. "Did you let her get away with that the entire tour? What kind of leader are you?"

Dean looks like he wants to both kill something and cry as he attempts to speak, his throat or his emotions not allowing it.

"What is this?" the boss scoffs. "Have you two switched places on me?"

"No," Dean manages, his voice like scraping iron.

"Then report, Dean."

Dean swallows. "You can tell by looking at us that it didn't go well. That's why the road was built, isn't it? The jungle wasn't designed for humans to survive."

His voice gives out at the end and he presses the back of his hand against his throat as if to soothe it, closing his eyes against a pain I can so clearly imagine. But his words shock me, though I try not to show it. All that arrogance while we were in the jungle and all along he had just as much awareness as I had.

The boss glares at him, laying his cigar in an ashtray. "You know, I had a feeling you weren't man enough to take over this company. What a waste of my time."

He goes back to his paperwork without another word.

Dean swipes the papers from the desk, and they scatter wildly onto the floor. "My entire life, I've done everything you asked," he says, desperate anger infecting his voice. "And you throw me away because I can't deliver the impossible?"

"You're still just a sentimental little boy, aren't you?" the boss says with a short laugh. "You're a Wildblood, boy. Scum of the earth. Did you really think you would ever amount to anything?"

Dean's hands tremble, from anger or pain, I don't know. All I know is we are not here to be insulted by this heartless monster.

Never again.

"Enough." I ignite my science, throw a bloody dart into the ashtray on the desk, slicing the boss's cigar in half. He jolts, escaping by leaning back in his chair. Dean steps to the side to give me space to stand beside him. We haven't stood side by side like this, genuinely working together, in a long time. As we stand in front of our common enemy, my mashed-up, uncertain emotions for Dean are suddenly replaced by an awareness of how tall and broken he is.

Maybe after we take care of the boss I'll go back to hating him, but for now . . . all I know is that I've missed this. That this is the only way confronting the boss could've been done.

Together.

The boss's eyes widen at me. "You're testing my limits, girl."

"It's my limits you have to worry about." I hover bloody daggers over the desk, between us and him. "You have been toying with us since we were six years old, and it stops today."

"Watch yourself, girl." The boss glares at me, but it's mixed with the fear of a cornered dog. Fear . . . of me. Violence will be his response if I'm not careful, and yet it emboldens me.

"Or you'll what? You have no power over me. Not anymore." To prove it, I shift my daggers forward, close enough for him to feel the sharp points against his chest. If nothing else, that shuts him up. "Take out your official stationery. You're going to write up an executive order."

The boss glares up at me but obeys, opening his drawer and pulling out a sheet. I let up on my daggers, just enough so he can reach to dip his quill.

"As of today," I say, "every Wildblood has been set free from their 'employment.'"

"You must think I'm out of my mind—"

"They are to be released and leave the walls unharmed and with five months' worth of pay, never to be bothered by anyone in your employment because of their abilities ever again."

"Without Wildbloods the company will cease to exist." He sounds sorry for himself. But that's not the same as sorry, so I ignore it. "You'd leave me with nothing. I'd be ruined."

"I don't care." I allow one of my daggers to cut his cheek—a surface wound, but his eyes widen. "Write the letter. Sign it."

It's a short letter, only a paragraph. But he hesitates. I let the dagger dig deeper, and with a pained sigh, he signs. Still, this feels too easy, so I watch him carefully. He finishes and I turn the sheet to myself.

"Good," I say, reading over the letter quickly. "I'll leave you to your ruin now—"

Something splashes in my face just as I'm looking up—I squeeze my eyes tight and whip my face away, smell the sweet and bitter spice of rum, taste the burning alcohol on my lips as I take a breath.

I swipe across my eyes quickly, and my defensive daggers drop away. A metallic click breaks through the silence.

My heart drops at the sound—I feel the moment completely, and yet it happens too quickly for me to respond, too quickly to come to terms with how there's no way I can stop him before he kills—

Something slams into me, and I trip to the side a step, looking up in time to close my eyes against a bone-shattering *bang*. It shakes my brain. My ears ring. My head swims sickly. My heart races in my temples.

When I open my eyes, Dean is standing nearly in front of me, trembling and hunched over the desk, only standing upright from leaning on it.

I instinctively rush to Dean's other side to press my hand to his wound. It was a small gun, but it was at such close range . . . Anger builds in my gut. And confusion.

And rage.

I knew it. I knew it was too easy. I should've kept my eye on him. I should've—

"You blood witches are a blemish to society," the boss hisses, aiming his gun at me again. "Yes, I'll let you filthy beasts walk out of here—tell them all to pack their things. And as soon as you step outside the gate, I'll have the authorities there waiting to gun down every single one of you disgusting—"

Dean, silent through everything, suddenly reaches forward and wraps his forearms around the boss's head, slamming his face into the desk.

There's an angry cry of pain and I gasp and scurry backward as Dean shoves the man's face into the solid wood desk again, over and over, until I hear the crunch of bone, until blood splatters across it.

He doesn't stop until the boss is no longer moving, no longer screaming . . . not even a whimper. Finally, he shoves the lifeless body off the chair and to the ground, slumping on top of the desk to catch his breath. He might've used the last of his strength for that, and my heart races at the thought.

Dean starts to slide down, and I help him, holding him steady to sit on the floor with his back against the desk. This is the first time I've looked toward the doorway since we entered, and Thorn is standing there, his rifle halfway raised for use. I don't know how much he saw of what just happened, but he must've seen everything right after the gunshot because his face looks struck with horror, like he might be sick.

"Victoria," he gasps. "What did I just . . . what did he—?"

"Can you lower your gun?" I ask. I sound angry, and I'm sorry for it, but I'm just so agitated by the situation. "You're making me nervous."

He does, but shakes his head the entire time. "What the hell was that, Victoria? I thought you were going to negotiate, not murder the man!"

"You threatened to shoot your business partner, so I think murdering our abuser is perfectly reasonable," I snap, turning back to Dean. I don't know if it is, and I don't know why I'm yelling. But I'm feeling too many things at once to think about it. "It's okay. Everything's okay."

Except . . . everything isn't okay.

The blood on Dean's filthy white shirt covers his left side. If he's lucky, it only hit flesh, but there's no real way to tell. I'm not a doctor, and I don't think any plant in the jungle is capable of healing internal wounds. "Dean?" I say, my voice cracking.

"That felt better than I thought it would," he rasps. He pauses, then laughs. A pained sound that crashes into sobs just as quickly.

I press my hand against his wound, and he winces and covers mine with his own trembling one. His sobs tumble into tears. He's crying. Real tears, without holding back. Relief floods over me, through me, to the point that I can't breathe. I lean against him and he rests his chin on my hair.

"He was never going to let me take over," he murmurs, through his tears. "Part of me knew it, but . . . the tests, the way he tortured us . . . none of it meant anything."

"He was clearly toying with us from the very beginning."

Dean sniffles. "Sick monster. Sick. I wish I'd had the guts to kill him years ago."

"We were used, Dean. We were children. How could we have known?"

He manages a nod, and I fall quiet. I just . . . What more can I say? I barely know what to think anymore. I should be happy for this newly born freedom, for never having to answer to that monster again. Except the boss being dead doesn't erase what Dean did to me. What he let happen.

But he was young. A child. Should he at least be forgiven for being used by a monster . . . that, if nothing else?

Or is my trust in him too damaged to ever be mended?

I sit up and look down at my blood-soaked hand pressing against him. "You need a doctor."

"I don't think it hit anything important." He grimaces, takes a wincing breath. "And the pain is nothing new."

I take my hand back, staring at the blood painting it, even deep into the lines of my palm. "Why did you take that bullet, Dean?"

"You couldn't have reacted in time." He shrugs. "And I can't use my science. It was all I could do."

"So you let yourself get shot?"

"What do you care?" he bites out. He glares at me, even if it's conflicted and half-hearted . . . but the longer we look at each other, the more his glare slips away to uncover pain and . . . and *longing*.

And all at once I don't know what to think. One gallant act can't possibly make up for what Dean did, the pain he put me through. But I realize his death is not what I want, as much as I thought I would find comfort in killing him.

"Don't die." I try to swallow, and it hurts. "Not like this."

Dean smirks the slightest bit. "I'll try not to."

"*Don't.*" I feel myself panic as he leans his weight on the desk, closing his eyes against the pain. I grab his shoulders and shake him. "I said 'don't.' Stay awake."

"*Ow*, Victoria," he says, shoving one of my hands away, his other palm pressing into his wound.

"Victoria," Thorn says, finally stepping into the room—and

I feel horrible, because I forgot he was even there, "what would you like to do? If you need a doctor, we have to go for one now."

"We don't need one," Dean says through gritted teeth.

I kiss my teeth. "Stubborn ass." I shift to kneel beside him, putting his arm across my shoulders so I can help him stand, but he doesn't move to assist me and he's too heavy to lift on my own.

"Would you help me," he says, "if you didn't think I was dying? We've done what we needed to do, Victoria. Don't feel guilty for hating me now. I deserve it."

I feel him try to take his arm back, but I cling to his wrist, freezing at his words. Because it's strange . . . I don't think "hate" is the right word to describe the emotions he drums up within me anymore. I release his wrist to face him. "Why did you take that bullet for me, Dean? Do you think that will atone for what you did? How you've treated me the past year?"

He sighs. "You should hurry and take the letter to Louis before he catches us."

"Louis is probably hiding under his desk from that gunshot. Answer me." I try to voice it as a demand, but the sound cracks at the end.

He takes a struggling breath. "You never believe a word I say, anyway."

"But now you have no more reason to lie." The silence stretches between us. I take his face in my hands. "If you won't tell me, your eyes will."

"You really have to read my eyes to know?" he murmurs. "It's for the same reason you don't want me to die . . ."

I release him, sit back on my heels. We look at each other. It's not in glares. No longer guided by hatred. I see him as he is—as he was, before a year ago . . . a broken boy looking at a damaged girl. Both frightened. Both searching in each other for some kind of solace against a cruel world. Only now, we aren't what the other needs.

But we were forced together from the age of six, so maybe we never were.

Even so, an emotion I finally understand seizes me, and I lean forward and kiss him.

Without being used as a weapon against me, the pull of his lips is just as I remember—beautiful as twilight through the trees, bird flight, and cricket song. I feel his hand at the back of my neck, his fingers in my hair, like the first time he ever kissed me in the darkness of our bedroom. There is desperation in his touch, but no malice.

No, he's not a monster like the boss was. He was manipulated, same as me. But some things are ingrained in him now, I think . . . anyone who can play games like the boss did—even just to beat him at his own—all while sacrificing the people he cared about along the way, can never be completely trustworthy.

And because of that, continuing a relationship with Dean— *any* kind of relationship—would be toxic.

So, even though all that's good in Dean, all that I love, hides in his kisses . . . they're kisses I shouldn't have again. They are a beautiful poison, a momentary perfection that I would be better off without.

I pull away abruptly, covering his mouth with my hand so temptation doesn't strike anew. "I never want to see you again," I gasp.

He makes a small sound of agreement, panting a little. "Sounds fair."

"Doesn't mean you should go and die."

"I won't." He smirks the smallest bit. "Not today. Not at the hands of that monster."

Tears break through, running down my cheeks. His fingers move to wipe them, but I move away from him quickly, stand and back up a few steps to give him space. Dean groans as he pushes himself up, using the desk to help himself to his feet. I don't help him. We shouldn't touch again.

He picks up the letter and holds it out to me. I take it. There's a little blood on it, but it'll still do the job.

"Sure you don't need a doctor?" I ask.

He nods. "Take care of yourself, V."

"You, too, Dean." I turn without lingering, halting when I see Thorn. He cradles his rifle, as if the souls of his parents live there, his sweet face filled with so much hurt and confusion I can't bear to look at him.

I should say something but I can't face it now—I don't know how, not while I'm feeling too many things, when I just want to get as far away from this place as I can. So instead, I rush out into the hall and to the waiting area.

"Louis," I call, and the nervous man pokes his head up from behind the desk—I knew he'd be hiding; too bad I hadn't bet money on it.

"What is going on?" exclaims Louis, not leaving the safety of his desk. "What is all the banging and shooting? This is a business—"

"Not anymore," I say, laying the letter on his desk. I grab the pitcher of water meant for tourists to drink, and Louis's expression turns hilariously horrified as I put my hand in and scoop out some water to clean the rum from my face before it gets sticky. "Executive order from the boss. You'd better tell the guards to find new jobs."

Most of my peers don't believe me when I tell them they're free to go. They've always been wary of me anyway, but even if they weren't . . . my God, I barely believe the news, and I'm the one delivering it.

The few who believe me cry, cheer, rush to collect what few possessions they own, to leave as quickly as possible. The rest will catch up—a copy of the letter will be posted on the cubbies, and then they'll have no other choice but to leave, whether or not they believe it.

I don't judge them. We've all spent many years of our lives here, even if none of them have been here as long as I have. Anything different—anything better—feels like a trap.

All I own is a boar's hair brush, a little conditioner, and a few items of clothing. Bunny's messy pile of clothes sits next to my neat one, and I nearly choke on a sob looking at it. I won't take his things with me . . . too painful, and I can't use any of them. For that reason, I don't even go looking for Sam's things.

For the first time in my life, I'm standing by the main gate when it opens. I don't know why I've never noticed how big it is, or how much it creaks when it opens. A covered carriage with two horses harnessed to the front is waiting there.

Thorn squeezes my hand, leading me out of the gate toward . . . no, not toward the carriage?

My heart races, and I pull him to a stop. "I can't ride in that," I protest.

"Are you carriage shy, beloved?" he asks with a joking grin.

"I trust the horses more than some . . . *thing* with wheels."

"Do you trust me?"

The edge of my panic smooths out, feathers, eases away as I look into Thorn's beautiful dark eyes. "Yes," I whisper.

He helps me into the carriage, and we make our way into the town I've only heard of.

It's bumpy, but not nearly as uncomfortable as most of what I've experienced my entire life. I stare out the window at the mass of water in the distance. *So that's the ocean . . .* It's big, I'll give it that. I still don't think it could ever compare to my river.

"Do you love him?" Thorn asks, breaking me out of my thoughts.

When I look at him, he looks serious. When Thorn looks serious, it means he's closer to devastated than anything.

"I love *you*," I say, snuggling closer.

"You . . ." His brows lower slightly. "You kissed him."

"I—I—" A flustered blush rises up my neck. "That was nothing. It didn't mean anything."

"I think it did."

I look out the window again, watching the world pass. "It was goodbye, maybe. I did love him at one point, you know." I fidget. I don't know why I can't sit still. Why am I so nervous? "But I can't see him again. I don't want him in my life. It would be like . . . destroying myself."

My hands rest in my lap, and Thorn covers them both with one of his, turning my chin so I'll look at him. "I just want to make sure this is what you want."

"It is. I just . . . so much has happened today. I need a little time."

Thorn seems to understand, giving me an encouraging smile. "Of course, beloved. I . . . can't even imagine."

I rest against him, the bumpy ride leading us toward our future.

I open my eyes and jolt upright. My heart races as I look around. I'm on a . . . a bed? But it's high off the ground, not like the bed mat I slept on in my hut or the cot I slept on during tours. It's big, with a wooden frame, and squishy, just like—

My throat closes in on itself, trapping a sob.

Don't panic, Victoria. This is not the boss's bed.

He's dead, I remind myself. He's dead, and can't hurt me anymore. And this is not his room—it's far too decorative for that. Although, other than the bed, it does have a dark-stained wardrobe with two doors, a desk. But I suppose all rooms with furniture have those.

I wouldn't know.

I look beside me and find Thorn sleeping. That's different, too. And a relief.

I must've fallen asleep in the carriage—I hadn't slept for at least a full day and night before then, so I'm not surprised— and he'd carried me here . . . wherever here is.

I get up carefully so I won't wake Thorn, and look around. It feels strange to be trapped inside, shut in by a window with glass in it and a door. The space feels small. Claustrophobic. There's no fresh air.

But there's a connecting room with a bathtub, and seeing that I'm still wearing the same filthy, blood-caked clothes, I start there. The water is cold, refreshing, and I scrub myself with the soap and brush until my skin almost feels sensitive to it. I've always relied on Samson to braid my hair, so after I wash it, I comb conditioner through with my fingers, opting to leave it out curly. The sun is hot enough to dry it quickly without leaving it frizzed.

"There you are." Thorn stumbles in, yawning and shirtless. He looks clean already, I notice—he must've bathed while I slept. His thin, lightning-shaped scars still trail from his chest, up his shoulders, neck, face, dark and slightly pink against his deep, beautiful skin. I feel warm all of a sudden, looking at him. I could heat my water with the power of my own blush.

I lean my arms on the edges of the bath as he kneels beside it.

"Good morning, beloved," I whisper.

"Almost evening, beloved," he whispers back and kisses me. "It's about five o'clock. We should get some dinner."

"Your kisses are all I want."

"Okay, then." He gives me a dangerous grin. "Kisses now, dinner later."

He scoops me out of the bath, and I scream and then burst into giggles. I slap my hand over my mouth in embarrassment as he carries me to the bed and drops me on top of the comforter, which I quickly wrap around my naked body.

"I love it when you get shy," he murmurs, and kisses my neck.

"I'm . . . usually shy, I think . . ." I close my eyes, give in to the comfort of his kisses.

"I guess I just love *you*, then."

I push his body aside so he isn't fully on top of me, until I feel like I have space enough not to panic. I should just tell him why, but I don't want to break this moment, and he shifts willingly without it. His lips are as gentle as a caress against my own. I shiver as he touches my hands gripping the comforter, the only thing keeping my body from his, and I let him take it from me as I pull his face closer. His touch is worshipful, so unbearably sweet I want to cry.

"Which way do you want me today?" he whispers.

I whimper, overcome by his presence.

And then my stomach rumbles. I press my hands against it to shut it up.

Thorn laughs. "Okay, that does it. Let's get you some real food."

As far as I know, I've always eaten real food. But his excitement is so palpable, I'm eager to taste what I've been missing.

"Wait, Thorn," I say, grabbing his arm. "What are we going to wear?"

"Oh, this is the hotel we'd been staying in before the expedition," he says. He pulls out a trunk from under the bed. "All our things from the ship journey from America are still here."

"We're almost the same height," I say, leaning over the edge to see inside his trunk. "I could probably get away with wearing something of yours just for today, if you don't mind."

Thorn gapes. Chews on his lip, looking at me sheepishly. "I don't think that's a good idea. Ladies don't generally walk around in men's clothing. Maybe in Europe, but not here."

I take out a top hat from the trunk and put it on my wet curls. "Oh."

"But Madelyn's clothes are still—" His enthusiastic expression dies with my cringe. "Yeah, you're right. That's a little morbid." He cringes, too. "Okay, I've got it. What if you wore one she had made especially for the trip? Something she's never worn? That way you won't feel like you're wearing a ghost's clothing. And then, I promise, as soon as we've had something to eat, I'll take you straight to the dress shop and buy you something that's all yours."

I don't know how I feel about wearing a dead woman's clothing, not to mention that Madelyn was a little shorter than me and a little more ample in the hips and bust. But I can't argue with the logic. In the jungle, I dress appropriately for the elements and dangers there. I've never been outside the walls of the company, so following Thorn's lead is probably best.

I nod, and he retrieves the trunk from another room.

I pull out one of the dresses and hold it at arm's length. I can barely keep it level; it's heavy from so much fabric. I deliberately control my expression, hoping my distaste doesn't read through. It's big and frilly and a ridiculous lavender color that makes me want to roll it in dirt.

"Do I have to?"

Thorn chuckles. "That's a party dress. Here." He takes out a cream-colored dress with a more sensible-width skirt and simple narrow sleeves, but still more lace and frills on the bodice than I'm used to. It's better, and I suppose if I only have to wear it for the evening I'll survive.

Although, if I'm honest with myself, I'd be much more comfortable in trousers, even if they were Madelyn's impractical puffy ones.

One evening, Victoria. It's not a big deal.

Thorn helps me dress, and something about the way he understands how all of these layers of clothing work makes me think that . . .

"Madelyn wasn't lying, was she?" I say. "About you having a lot of women."

Thorn hesitates at a button. "I wasn't lying when I said I've never fallen for someone in two days."

"How many of the ones you didn't fall for did you help into dresses?"

"Not . . . many." I turn to see his expression, and he looks deeply mortified. "I'm really sorry, Victoria. It was before I found Jesus, I swear . . . Wait, your buttons," he says as I try to step away.

I grin, despite myself. He's still very cute, even if he was deceitful.

"I love you more than anything," he finishes. "I just . . . I didn't want you to judge me on my past without giving me a chance. I didn't want to lose the chance to get to know you."

"For the record, I don't care about those other women," I say. "I just wish you had been up-front with me."

"I'm really sorry. I thought you might be, I don't know, scandalized."

I raise an eyebrow. "'Scandalized'?"

Thorn laughs. "I didn't know who I was dealing with yet, clearly."

I take a deep breath. Well, Samson did say real love isn't perfect. No love can be perfect . . . can it? Maybe Dean was right, too, then. Maybe I had put Thorn up on a pedestal.

Love the person, Victoria. Not the ideal.

"I forgive you if you promise there's nothing else."

"There's nothing else. Nothing." I hear Thorn exhale, and he wraps his arms around me, burying his face in my neck. "Thank you," he murmurs. "Thank you . . . I love you. You are a goddess among women. I'll behave, I swear."

I roll my eyes. Smirk. "Good. Now feed me before I have another reason to be mad at you."

We step outside and I immediately tuck myself against Thorn. I don't know why seeing so many people in one place makes me want to hide. More than twenty. More than fifty. *Hundreds* of people, all in one place.

I close my eyes. Think of everyone as insects, leaves, trees. Think of the smoke and dirt as incense. Think of the loud and chaotic mesh of voices, banging, wheels against stone as the jungle in all its activity and whispers.

But all I can think about is how everything out here seems specifically designed to give me a panic attack.

I feel horrible saying this, but as bitter and misguided as Dean was, he was also right about another thing. There's a cost to everything—a sacrifice of some freedom, the burning of something true to you in order to have something else you really want. I want Thorn more than anything. The cost? Living in a society that is noisy in a way that unsettles me. Walking down streets that frighten me, crowded by people who would judge me if they knew what I was. Unnatural smells of smoke and meats and filth that repel me to seek fresher air. Food that is so rich, full of fats and sugars, enough to give me a stomachache. It's fast-paced, and I'm nervous I can't keep up.

I don't know what I thought I was getting, stepping out into freedom. Nothing is as I thought it would be . . . not even Thorn. And something about it all is terrifying.

It's new territory. New things can be scary.

Maybe this is only the one town. Or maybe that's just

how things are on the island. Maybe when we finally arrive in America, things will be different. Maybe there are rivers and I can have a river spirit auntie at the very least.

But Thorn seems far too comfortable with all the aspects I hate about society for my hopes and prayers to be true.

Maybe I'll get used to it.

Or maybe the sad truth is it costs too much.

Instead of the dress shop, I ask Thorn to take me to see the ocean.

It's massive, stretching far into the distance. The sun reflects off it, shimmering like diamonds against the constant movement of the waves. I've heard stories of shipwrecks, but today the water is calm, gently rolling and flowing up onto the sand in a blanket of small splashes and foam before retreating back into itself.

I inhale the fresh salty air, huffing out the vile smells of town that I feel caked in my nostrils. I scoop some water in my hands and put it in my mouth, moving it around a little before spitting it out.

"It really is salty," I muse.

Thorn chuckles and crouches down beside me. "Don't swallow too much, it'll make you sick."

I should be awed by this, shouldn't I? I think that's what is expected when someone witnesses something as majestic and vast as the ocean.

But, honestly, feeling the water lap at my feet just makes me miss the river. Makes me miss Mumma.

Makes me miss home.

"Thorn, would you mind if we go see the jungle?"

"The ocean doesn't do it for you, huh?" he says with a small laugh.

"It's . . . nice."

Thorn scoops up some wet sand, then allows the water to wash it away through his fingers. "I don't blame you. If I grew up with spirit beasts and sentient rivers, I'm sure nothing much out here would impress me, either."

I grin and kiss his cheek. "I'm sure there's plenty to impress in America. I just want to see the jungle from outside the walls of the touring company, for once."

"You don't have to justify asking, beloved." He stands, wiping his hands on his trousers before holding his hand out to me. "Anything you want."

For the first time in my life, I walk beside the jungle outside the walls of the company.

The grass is overgrown here, tickling my legs, and I love it. No hard, cleared land. Nothing tamed.

I stroll, hand in hand with Thorn on one side, skimming the trees with my fingers on the other. Their life-pulse greets me warmly. *Welcome back, daughter of the jungle,* they seem to say.

"The ship doesn't leave for a few days," Thorn says. "What do you say we explore as much as we can of the rest of the island until then?"

"What ship?" I ask.

"For home."

Home.

I feel tears burning my eyes just thinking the word, and wrap my hand around the nearest skinny tree without a thought.

Holding my beloved's hand with one and touching the jungle—my very heart—with the other.

"Thorn, I . . . I don't think I can go."

"I know you're nervous," he says. "Society will seem a little strange compared to how you're used to living, but—"

"I don't want to go," I say, biting my lip against my unsympathetic tone. Thorn blinks at me, and I wrap my arms around him. "I love you, Thorn. But I don't belong in your world. The jungle is my home."

Thorn hesitates, as if taking in my words. "That's not a problem. I love the outdoors."

"Thorn." I take a deep breath. "You can't survive long term in the jungle. There's no salt or incense or—"

"Victoria, stop." His voice is tight. Pained. And now it's his turn to take a breath. "Let's take a day or two, to heal and rest. I'll just need to purchase a few things and—"

"The jungle has been calling for me ever since I wandered out of it at six years old. I don't want to ignore it any longer."

He shakes his head, his eyes glisten with the edge of tears. "Not without me."

"I have to."

"Why?"

"Don't think me awful for it."

He lets out a sad laugh, cradles my face. "Beloved. Try your hardest, you could never be awful."

"But I am a hypocrite." I look away, collecting my words. "All my life I've done things for the benefit of others. Because my science has always been more powerful, I felt—I don't know—a duty to protect people who I thought needed me. But now that those people are gone I just . . . I want to do something that makes me happy." I step back from his warm body, from his hurt and confused expression. "I said you were selfish for going after what you want, without a thought for anything or anyone. Well, now I want to be selfish. I want to have what I want, what I've been longing for for twelve years . . . my home."

Tears break the rim of Thorn's eyes with a single blink, running down his face.

I rush up to him and kiss his wet cheek. "You couldn't survive in there forever. I certainly couldn't keep you alive forever. And if, God forbid, you died, and Mumma agreed to resurrect you, you wouldn't remember me. That would be more painful than leaving you here, alive and well, loving me as I love you."

"I loved you from the moment I first saw you," he says, and if anything could've made this harder, it was those specific words.

"So did I, I just didn't know what it was."

"That has to mean something, doesn't it?"

"Of course it does. Thorn. Of *course* it does. But you love your job, you have a fortune, you have a soul that finds peace and happiness in new adventures. If I stayed with you, my only happiness would be you. I would be incomplete."

"I understand, I just . . . I don't want to let you go."

Thorn looks up and takes a step back, and when I turn, Biggs is sticking his giant, smoky head from the jungle.

"Your coach awaits?" he says with a sad smile.

I wrap my arms around his neck and he presses me close, desperately.

"I love you, Thorn," I whisper.

Thorn chokes on a sob, presses me even closer. "I love *you*, Victoria."

I kiss him for what may be the last time, every part of me wanting him, propelling me to him.

But I can't deny my heart any longer.

I force myself away, but Thorn doesn't let go of my hand, and I laugh and cry at his insistence of holding me till the very end. He pulls me into another kiss, and Biggs snorts his annoyance.

"You have the rest of her life, Biggs," Thorn says between kisses. "Wait your turn."

And I laugh, which makes Thorn laugh, but now we're crying again, and I don't want these emotions to get in the way of the decision I've made.

So I turn away and step up onto the bony opening where a flesh nose would be, thrilling at Thorn's hands on my waist helping me up.

"I'll wait for you," Thorn says as Biggs raises me up. "Here on the island. I'll wait for you for as long as it takes."

I can't tell him not to wait. He's going to anyway, I know. So all I say is, "Please be happy, Thorn."

And then Biggs carries me back into the trees as Thorn calls, "I love you, Victoria," over and over, until I'm too deep in the jungle to hear it.

I climb up onto the top of his skull so I can lie down and cry . . . cry until I can hear something other than my gasping breaths.

Branches sway. Birds squawk and sing. Small footsteps disturb the brush below. Insects buzz and chirp.

I sigh and close my eyes, a peace overtaking me.

The jungle whispers. Calls my name.

And, finally, I have the courage to answer.

Finally . . . I'm home.

ACKNOWLEDGMENTS

I can't believe my second novel is out in the world! Writing *Wildblood* was super cathartic, and I'm so grateful for every moment of the process (even the ones that felt like a private room in Hell, ha ha!). God is good, and I feel so blessed to be able to publish a book with a team I adore about characters of my own heritage.

Thank you to my family for (once again) tolerating my missed movie nights and dinners while I was on deadline, and for being the best support system I could've asked for.

Thank you to my agent, Lauren Spieller, for reining my crazy ideas into something marketable. My editor, Vicki Lame, who gave me the freedom to write the book I wanted to write and was chill through the chaos of revision. The Legend, Kerri Resnick—your covers . . . YOUR COVERS. No words. Scheduling goddess Meghan Harrington, who is smarter and more organized than I could ever be. Tiffany Shelton, my Jamaican sister—this one's for us.

To my friends who beta read *Wildblood*, who were so helpful with details I was worried about—Laura, Lyssa, Kamilah, Hannah, and Rory. To the friends who didn't beta but helped hold me together—Meredith, Rosie, Meg, Maggie, and Ashley. To my ride-or-dies Laura, Maleeha, Ayana, and Emily.

To the rest of the Wednesday Books team: Alexis Neuville, Brant Janeway, Vanessa Aguirre, Steve Wagner, Amber Cortes, Devan Norman, Claire Beyette, Lena Shekhter, NaNá Stoelzle, Melanie Sanders, and Eric Meyer. Thank you all from the bottom of my heart for all your incredible work!

And to all the readers out there who have connected with and loved my books—thank you so much for sharing these words with me.

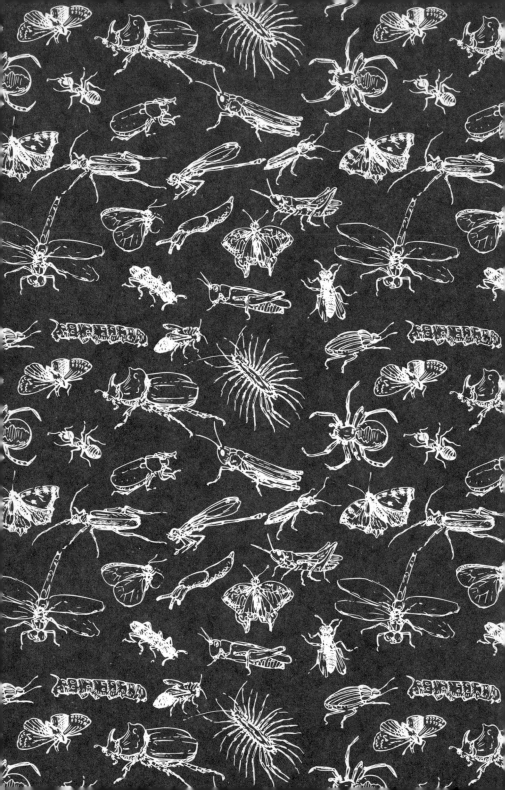